DISTURBIA 2

Table of Contents

1

The Getaway

Kali

I have to admit; this plane ride has probably been the worst part of the last twenty-four hours for me—which is shocking considering all the insanity that's transpired. This bastard flight was last minute, and has managed to run my credit card balance through the roof. Having never left Nebraska, I had no clue how costly traveling could be. Seven hundred dollars for a one way ticket? Jesus fuck that's high! Vacations are out of the question for a while and not only because of the turbulent plane ride. I'm entirely too poor to splurge on anything—much less a spur of the moment getaway.

The ride was exactly as I had anticipated in my worse nightmares. I've never flown, nor have I ever had the desire to do so. Between the movie Final Destination, and September 11TH, it was never on my list of to-dos—ever. The turbulence, which is the term the stewardess used as I began my first round of hyperventilation, was so bad that the oxygen masks even plummeted at one point, swinging in front of my face like a waiting noose with my name written all over it. The fact that I really thought I was about to die was ironic in the moment, as I had already told myself that if I had to stay and face Cris and Brian I would have opted to kill myself instead. Either way, I was inevitably and undoubtedly fucked. That's why I had no choice but to flee Humboldt. It was a choice of a lesser evil; throw myself into debt and go head to head with my worst fear of flying, or face the two of them. I chose—still confident that I would have rather taken a nose dive in that plane than to be any where near my home right now. I only hope they haven't killed each other in my absence. Though, knowing both of their tempers, I'm not sure either of them would have even noticed my presence while they ripped each other to shreds. Cris is short and fast, but insanely strong. Brian isn't much bigger, but he doesn't need size when there are five guns, a badge, and a convicted felon—my kidnapper—standing in our home. Lord be with them. I have taken the look away method. See no evil.

As far as I know, neither Cris nor Brian has a clue of where I am. And at this point, they might not even care. They both could have assumed that I've walked out on them and washed their hands of me, along with the drama that persistently follows me around like a black cloud. That's one scenario. Who the fuck knows what they're thinking right now? I can't even process my own thoughts; much less make assumptions based on theirs. There is currently no vacancy in the mental disruption area of my brain; so anything other than getting the hell out of dodge can just sit and simmer on the back burner until I return—if ever. I gave no consideration to what my next move would be. In that moment when they were both so desperately looking to me for answers, the well went dry—and so did my mouth. Somewhere deep inside I'm sure the answers they're craving are somewhere in hiding; but if they are, my mind isn't ready to release them yet—even to myself.

When Cris proposed I ran—literally—without passing go or collecting two hundred fucking dollars. I was scared shitless and opted for selfishness and saving my own skin over doing the right thing. For so long I had never given any consideration to marriage, especially to Cris of all people. She and I'd had zero contact during her stay in the mental hospital. I had moved on—or so I told myself. Seeing her has brought back everything I worked so hard to bury from my past. It's as if nothing has changed and no time has gone by. She's still the same person, yet vastly different. She's still shy and reserved, well kept and pristinely manicured as far as her appearance is concerned, but mentally she was so different tonight. It was noticeable right off the bat. For her to come to me and be so open—it was the miracle I had prayed to receive for so long. She has finally become the person I had always hoped she wanted to be. It was like a miracle presented itself right before my eyes. But there, in my peripheral vision, standing on the other side of me, was Brian— my beloved boyfriend, the supportive and always loyal man of my life. For the first time in our entire relationship I couldn't even look him in the eye. I admitted that I still love Cris—I had to. I couldn't just stand there and bullshit them both. But even as the honest words came out, I couldn't stomach to witness the look of disappointment and betrayal on Brian's face. Unlike Cris, Brian has never shown me anything other than love and support. With open arms he accepted me; damaged as I was. Even with that lingering in my mind I still wasn't able to choose. I let them both down with my cowardly move of running. They have both proven to hold a loyalty that I clearly don't possess. I'm a selfish, horrible person. When I ran out that door I fucked them both over, and basically left them there to duke it out over my own self-created mess. I should have never gone any further with Brian if I had any doubts regarding how I still felt about Cris. Now I have to live with that, along with figuring out what the fuck I'm going to do to fix it.

One thing is certain; I will need peace and solitude to accomplish any amount of resolution. I certainly couldn't have done that in Humboldt. I'm sure the entire town knows what's going on by now. The rumors are probably flying like colors about the lesbian and her victim, and of course poor officer McDowell. That's what has brought me here, stepping off a plane at Destin Florida's International Airport. I have no idea where I'm staying, or for how long, but I have a credit card and no good sense right now. I'll figure something out. Fuck it.

"Where can I find a cab at this time of night?" I ask a young heavyset blonde desk attendant, who wears an uncomfortable looking white button-down shirt with a navy blue scarf tied around her neck. "I really don't want to stay here in the airport until morning."
"Oh, no worries. A cab won't be a problem, Ma'am. This is a tourist area. We go all night long around here," she smiles.
"Thank you. Where I come from everything shuts down at sundown, accept the McDonald's they just built last year."

8

"Wow, you're in for a treat then. If you walk over to that booth in the lobby area they will arrange a cab for you. Do you have a hotel yet?"

"Um—no. This was kind a of last minute escape, if you will," I admit.

"Oooh, you chose a bad weekend to visit without prior arrangements. Word is that there is no-vacancy anywhere," she runs her fingers through her shoulder length hair, pulling it away from her bronzed face.

"Well, like a fine wine that pairs just perfectly with my evening… Damn it," I sigh, fighting off the stress induced droplets forming in the corners of my eyes.

"Come on now, no tears. I'll tell you what; let me call Breakers East Condos on Hwy 98. It's ten minutes from here. All the condos have huge balconies with a gulf front view, and wonderful amenities. It's located on the strip with all the restaurants, bars and main attractions. They also have 24 hour check in. Plus, I can make sure you get in. My sister works there," she grins.

"Really? You would do that? Are they pricey?" I cringe, given the description. They must be expensive with all those wonderful amenities.

"Well—yes—it's no Days Inn; but unless you want to rent a car to sleep in…"

"You know what, that's perfectly okay. I'll just put it on my credit card with all the other shit I can't really afford. Thank you so much—um," I glimpse at her nametag. "Maggie."

"Preach it, sister. You're talking to the girl who has to put ramen noodles on layaway. No shame in the game. Credit cards are a godsend for people like you and I. Just give me one moment," she picks up the phone. "What's your name?"

"Kalista Ness. You can call me Kali."

"Awesome. I'm calling my sister."

I take a seat and people watch for a moment while she goes back and forth playfully on the phone with her sister. It's nice to sit for a second and just relax on solid ground. To be a tourist area the airport is not as busy as I would expect—probably due to the fact that it's 2:00 a.m.

As much as I try I can't escape the thought of Cris's face tonight, with so much love and hope in her eyes; especially as I see a gay couple in their early thirties stroll past me, holding hands and showing off their love—publicly. I watch the other passersby lingering around, waiting for them to gawk or say something derogatory to the couple; but to my surprise nobody so much as takes a second glance—aside from myself. Back home they would have been harassed instantly. If I were to accept Cris's proposal, we would have no choice but to relocate. This is something that will have to be taken into great consideration. Leaving home would mean leaving school, as well as my family. It's a huge consideration.

"Hey Kali, I got you the room!" Maggie calls me over with an excited smile. "The only catch is that it's the honeymoon suite. It's the only room they had left."

Isn't this just the story of my life? Could this night get any fucking worse? The honeymoon suite… Fuck.

"But," she continues, "since it's a little pricier, I arranged for the hotel shuttle to pick you up and save you a few bucks on cab fare. It's one of the condo amenities anyway. Also, my sister is giving you the 'family' discount—Cousin Kali… You're welcome."

"You are amazing. I will definitely be sending a wonderful letter to your manager."

"Hey, that would be great. I am going for a promotion. At some point I want to get off the ramen noodle diet, you know?" She beams.

"Well, if I have anything to do with it you'll definitely get recognition," I promise faithfully.

***

After getting checked into my room I realize how incredibly tired I am. Not only physically, but also emotionally, I'm a train wreck. Throughout trying to arrange my travel plans and even something as simple as getting from the airport to my condo was flat out exhausting. Until now, where I sit quiet and alone, I haven't had much time to consider everything that's happening. Here I am, halfway across the country while my past, present and future have been left back in Humboldt to boil over like an overactive cauldron of insanity. I have no idea what the hell I'm going to do. I pray for answers but even they evade me like the plague. All I know right now is that if I don't catch a nap I will soon collapse. Brian and I have a tight schedule. He works such long shifts and my school schedule runs me ragged so we have to be in bed promptly at 9:00 p.m. in order to gain any real time together the next morning. He awakens me daily with hot coffee and a fruit salad…

I shake his handsome face from my mind. With his dark hair and nerdy glasses—he is too adorable for words. I hate myself for putting him through this. He is too good to me. This situation **should** be a no-brainer. If only I were more deserving… If nothing else, he deserves a call tomorrow. I owe him that at least.

As much as I want to explore, it will have to take place in the morning. Tomorrow I will begin freeing my mind of anything other than this beautiful place. I let the negativity slip from the sliding balcony door as I open it, welcoming the scent of salty air into my room. It's pungent in such a pleasing way, and out rates anything I've ever read about in books. The aroma makes me feel at ease, and the sound of the waves hitting the powdery white sand lull me into a deep sleep before I ever remember closing my eyes.

***

There is nothing worse than waking up from an emotional trauma. It's miles worse than any hangover I have ever had. The emptiness of rousing without Brian leaning in for a kiss with a cup of coffee in his hand is a reminder of what I left behind. I would be lying if I didn't admit that I am finding myself questioning what the fuck I was thinking when I took off last night. He is everything to me. How could I even question that? I miss that goofy smile of his. I miss his sweet hugs and cheesy come-on's. Shouldn't it mean something that I feel so incomplete without him here? But even with that said, there is the other part of me screaming, 'here's the chance you always wanted with Cris, take it before it disappears'. This getaway was supposed to be some sort of mental hiatus, yet I find that there is no way of escaping my own mind, no matter how far I am from Humboldt.

The strange outdated jingle of a landline phone is pounding at my ears. Wasn't I supposed to be escaping? Who would be calling me here? In any event, I answer so the damned thing will stop ringing.

"Yes?" I yawn.

"Good morning, Miss. Ness. We have a message for you in the lobby. Shall we have it delivered to your room or would you prefer to retrieve it after joining us for your complementary breakfast in the ballroom?"

"Um," I try to hide the sleep in my voice since it's already 9:00 a.m. and I should have stirred by now. I'm not typically a late sleeper, "I will come down to eat and then retrieve my message afterwards."

"Yes Ma'am. Breakfast will continue until 10:00 a.m."

"Thank you."

I throw on a pair of shorts and a tank top, eager to get a view of the beach first thing after breakfast. But the smell of eggs and breakfast meats do nothing for my appetite. I ditch the idea of breakfast for a moment, anxious to see who left the message with the desk. Part of me—a very large part—hopes to find a message from Brian, telling me he misses me as much as I miss him. The idea has me so excited I am smiling when I approach the counter, and greet a sweet little brunette no older than twenty.

"I have a message?" I ask eagerly.

"Kali?"

"Yes, Ma'am. That's me."

"I'm Tanya, Maggie's sister. You met her at the airport last night."

"Yes, sweet Maggie. She was so helpful. I can't even begin to thank you both enough for everything you've done. After the night I had, if I hadn't been able to find a hotel I would have literally had a meltdown. I owe you one."

"Ah, it's my pleasure. Here is your message," she hands me an envelope with my name written on it.

As much as I want it to be from Brian, he has no clue where I am. More than likely it's from Maggie, checking to see if everything panned out alright. But as I read the first few lines, I immediately know otherwise.

Attn: Kalista Ness, Honeymoon Suite, Room 234.

Received by Thomas Jacobs, Hotel Manager: May 30th @ 7:45 a.m.

Kali,

Please be careful down there all by yourself. There are some real creeps in this world. If you need me I can be there in a heartbeat. Also, I know funds are tight. I have sent you some money to the hotel for you. Please don't take this as odd; I was just worried.

Also, Brian and I are both okay. I can't speak for him, but I truly understand why you ran. He has opted to leave you alone, but you know me... I had to make sure you were alright. Be safe, honey.

I love you,

Cris.

"The message was taken by Tommy, my manager, I'm not sure what this is, but it was supposed to accompany the message," Tanya hands me a thick brown envelope just as I finish reading and stuff the message into my shorts pocket.

I'm surprised, but not shocked. Cris **would** be the first one to track me down. I should have known. I decide to take the envelope and walk out to the beach with it. But first, I turn back to Tanya, in desperate need of something to calm my nerves.

"I hate to ask, because I know it's early and people shouldn't drink in the morning, but…"

"Yes, we have an on-site bar. It's directly on the beach as you walk out, next to the pool and hot-tub area," she smiles. "And stop being so apologetic, most people are here on vacation and are at least two hours ahead of you on their first drink of the day. I suggest the 'Sex on the Beach'. It's delicious."

"I will definitely give that a shot. Thanks, Tanya."

"Yep. If you need any restaurant advice let me know. As you can see, I like to eat," she giggles, patting her slightly jiggly belly.

I'm feeling better already. The sun is shining and the people here are simply amazing. This kind of hospitality always comes with a price back home. I think I'm going to love it here.

***

"Jeeze, eight fucking dollars for a drink…" I sigh.

The Sex on the Beach is tropical and crisply refreshing in the scorching heat of Destin, Florida. It's perfect, just as Tanya promised. It's fruity, sweet, and tart at the same time. This easily could be the best drink I've ever had—and the most dangerous as well. I've managed to suck it down in only a couple of minutes, leaving the jingle of ice clinking against the empty glass. I could have ten of these and not realize how strong it was until I stood up. That's the sign of a really great drink. Plus, the little umbrella always makes it more fun. I'm no better than a kid with it comes to cute little embellishments. As delicious as this is I can't afford to splurge too much. By the time I leave Destin my credit card will be maxed out and I have student loans due on the first of the month—which is tomorrow. Brian usually handles the bills, but given the current situation it seems wrong to allow him to pay my student loans. Perhaps Daddy can spot me a little bit when I get home and I can try to squeeze in a part time job. Though, Brian would despise that. He was adamant that I focus on school while he took care of the household. So generous. I sure miss him right now. He would make

14

fun of me for drinking the girly drinks, while he would surely be guzzling down an ice-cold man brew. He's my All-American boy, and I love that about him. He would love it here. Maybe someday, once all this madness has subsided, we can return together.

I open the envelope, already knowing what's inside since Cris told me she had money sent for me. Enclosed is yet another note—a Cris trademark.

Splurge. Anything you want to do, do it. Let me know if you need more.

C.

"Five fucking thousand dollars!" I accidentally screech aloud. "Damn it, Cris!"

I came here to get away from everyone. Not to have them fund my runaway game. This is so like her. She hasn't even been out of the hospital for two days and she already knows exactly where I am, as well as sending money to try to take care of everything for me. I don't understand how she could have found me so quickly, but I do intend to ask. I'm not beating around the bush with her. I am going to have some time alone damn it. I'm calling her. Hopefully her number is still the same. That question is quickly confirmed when I hear that familiar voice answering on the very first ring.

"Kal, how are you, babe?"

"I'm alright, Cris. But listen, this is the exact reason you ended up in trouble to begin with. You can't just track me down like fucking Sherlock Holmes. I need some space. That's why I came here. And as generous as it was to send me the money, I am giving it back. I can't accept it. Brian will see to it that our bills are met. That's his job now, not yours," I firmly warn her.

"Kali, I know what it must look like, but I didn't 'track you down'. Brian went online and checked your credit card this morning to see where you were."

"And how the hell would you know that? I know he didn't tell you…"

"No, he didn't tell me. I overheard him telling your Dad at the coffee house. I got a call back from an application I put in yesterday. It's a pastry chef position, but it's work, right? I just happened to be there and overhear him talking to your father—as unbelievable as that sounds."

"Unbelievable indeed. Coincidences seem drawn to you like a moth to a flame."

"Are you saying I'm irresistible?" She jokes.

"No—maybe—ugh, just leave me alone so I can think. You're distracting me from my sunshine and Sex on the Beach."

"Mmmm, Sex on the Beach sounds good," she replies in a soft sexy voice.

"See that's exactly what I mean. I was talking about the drink," I shoot back, trying to shake away the tingles her voice causes within me.

"Yeah, so was I. Now whose mind is in the gutter?"

"Ugh! Just hang up."

"No. You hang up," she laughs.

"No you hang up. And you can expect your money back in the mail."

"And I'll send it back to you again, at twice the amount. You know money is not a problem for me. My parents still pay me to stay away. I have more money than any one person needs. Please, just use it to take some time away for yourself. I know you're in school right now and you don't really have an income. I don't want you getting into debt because you're running away from me. Plus, I won't miss a measly five-grand."

"I said no, Cris."

"It sounds to me like you need a few more Sex on the Beach's, and maybe even some real sex on the beach to get rid of that mood. I would gladly join you..."

I sigh, "No, I'm good. Just had sex two days ago. I'll stick with the alcohol."

"I could have gone without hearing that, thank you," Cris mumbles.

What I just did was rude. I really don't mean to be so snappy with her. My mind is just not functioning. And I don't like the way it makes me feel when she talks about sex with me. Because I like it—

too much—and that's bad. I have a boyfriend now—a wonderful caring boyfriend that I haven't even spoken to since last night.

"Sorry Cris, I'm just tired."

"It's all good."

"I know it's awkward talking about this with you, but before I go I want to ask you something."

"Hit me, cupcake," she replies, cheerfully.

"How is he? I mean, did he seem okay this morning when you saw him at the coffee house?"

A long silence and a sigh wash over the phone like the powerful waves of a tsunami. She's trying to be nice and cooperative, and I can feel the struggle.

"He seemed concerned. Sad. Scared. Angry with me, understandably so."

At least she's being honest and doesn't seem to be too terribly upset that I'm asking about Brian. Surely she knows what an awful predicament I'm in right now. I'm worried about him too. Thinking of him sad is torturous. He is usually so happy-go-lucky and cheerful. How can I do this to him? And Cris, she has worked so hard to try and change for me. They are both politely eating the shit I'm shoveling out, and I feel like a monster.

"And how are you, Cris? Are you okay?"

"I miss you. But yes, I'm okay."

"You miss me already?" I smirk a bit.

"Always."

I shake away the emotions coming on—whatever they are— and get back down to business. I decide that if Cris really wants me to have that money I won't reject it. She's right anyway, it's not even a sliver off her bank account, so why not? As long as she doesn't take it as some sign that we are together than I will accept it.

"Thanks for the money, Cris. I suppose it wouldn't hurt to splurge a little. I do really appreciate it. I have to ask though, what's the catch?"

"No catch, no strings. I just want you to relax, have a good time, and be able to think without worrying about every dime you spend. I promise, there are no expectations behind the money—only pure intentions."

"Well, thanks again. But I really should go now. I don't know when I'm coming back, and I don't know what I'm going to do about all of this mess when I do. I just need some time to think. Can you agree to just give me some space?"

"You have my word. I love you, Kal."

"I—I love you, too. Goodbye."

Saying those words to anyone aside from Brian is odd, but hearing the words come so easily from Cris is even more bizarre. It's like some Twilight Zone shit. I'm not complaining exactly. It's just so—different.

***

"Well, that call didn't sound good. Asking for some space is code word for 'fuck off'," a tall slender woman in her early forties lies stretched out on a pool chair beside mine, sipping on a Bloody Mary. "Men trouble?"

Is this what people are supposed to do here at the pool? Confide their troubles to strangers. Normally I would politely walk away, but I don't see the harm in chatting. It's not like I have anyone else to talk to. A stranger's perspective might be refreshing.

"Men trouble? Ha! If only it were that simple," I laugh, casually, taking a seat on the chair parallel to hers.

She snaps her fingers at the middle-aged pool server, which I find to be an incredibly rude gesture, grabbing his attention quickly with a smile. He all but stumbles over himself trying to get to her as fast as possible, barely missing the edge of the pool with his sandal. That would have been a laugh, but lucky for him, he rebalances before toppling in the sparkling aqua water. I'll bet five bucks this woman is loaded. Servers only run for money. And she sure as hell looks like money—if that makes any sense. You can almost smell it oozing from her pours.

"Bret, darling, you must be more careful."

"Of course Ms. Shay. What can I bring you, my lovely?"

"Bring this lady another one of whatever she's having, and make mine a double this time."

"Sex on the Beach?" he confirms politely.

"Yes. Thank you, sir," I reply.

"Call him Bret. He's my favorite," she winks, watching his firm bum as he walks back to the bar.

18

First name basis… She must be a local. Either that or she spends a lot of time here at Breakers East.

"So what's your name, tourist?" she asks in her fancy voice.

"Kali. And yours, local?" I smile.

"Please, darling, I'm no local, but I might as well be. I've been here for a few weeks celebrating. I'm Bridgette Shay," she shakes my hand, pleasantly.

"Thanks for the drink, Bridgette. I'll get the next round," I offer, fanning away the heat with the large envelope of money Cris sent.

"I wouldn't dream of it. I'm just buttering you up for some fresh gossip. I'm getting restless. This place is just so damned—peaceful," she replies, almost repulsed by the word.

"Isn't that the point of a vacation?"

"Perhaps to some. I'm used to a more—how would you say it—refined way of living. It's unlike me to co-exist with the likes of young spring breakers, but I was compelled to come here, for whatever reason. It's certainly no Maui…"

"I see," I find myself again smirking at her elegant and flawless speech. I'll bet this woman has a tale or two to tell. This conversation could be interesting—especially after a few more rounds.

"So what's your story young, Kali?" She swirls a long crisp stalk of celery around her glass, creating a red whirlpool of her spiked tomato juice.

"I'm here to think, is all. How about you? What are you celebrating?"

"Ahh, I'm here celebrating the sweet, divine, deliciousness of a three-yearlong divorce. I finally took out the trash on the ugliest, most flaccid, boring, and dull waste of space that ever walked on two legs. He fought, but he sank faster than the Titanic once the pre-nup was declared null and void. Word to the wise, **always** have your own lawyer draw up the pre-nup—works every time. You're welcome."

I should have pegged her for a gold-digger instantly. The giant framed Gucci sunglasses that would cost a month's salary to someone in my town could have been an indicator. Or even the typical floppy beach hat and Audrey Hepburn style retro swimwear that is most definitely worth more than my life's value, should have given it away. She has class, no doubt, but underneath she is a

19

sneaky black widow. Thank goodness I'm not a man. I wouldn't want to end up trapped in her web. Still, she is without a doubt alluring and entertaining to speak to. It's funny how opposites attract. I like her—kind of. But I can already tell that my friendly attraction to Bridgette the Black Widow will have to be moderated in small doses. Champagne and beer don't always mix so well in large portions.

"I think I'm going to stroll the beach. I've never seen it. This is my first time out of Nebraska. It's stunning here. I can see why they call it the Emerald Coast. It's the most brilliant aqua-green water I have ever seen. Pictures do nothing for how breathtaking it is here. You wanna come with?"

"Darling, we really must work on that vulgar usage of the beautiful English language. But later. I try not to stray too far from the bar. How would you feel about joining me for dinner tonight instead?"

Stranger danger doesn't really strike me in this situation, so I agree. It would be great to get out on the town with a girlfriend for once. I never do this at home. I have no time for friends.

"Actually that would be great. What time?" I agree, excitedly.

"Meet me in the lobby at 7:00 p.m. We can go to the Beachwalk Café. They serve dinner directly on the beach. Chairs in the sand and all. You'll love it."

"Is it affordable?"

"Oh child, money is irrelevant. First of all, you have all that money in your hand that this Cris person sent you here. Yes, I was eves dropping on your phone call—we all have our tacky moments. Secondly, I was planning on paying anyway. I have alimony to blow," she laughs.

"I am NOT spending Cris's money on junk. I will only spend it on responsible purchases."

"You will learn quick, dear. When a man wants you to have something—take it and ask no questions. The spoiling doesn't last long."

"It's not like that, there is a long back story here. And Cris is...well...a woman."

"Oh my, let's make it 6:00. I wouldn't dream of waiting a moment longer to hear this story," she perks up as I walk away chuckling at her excitement. She has no idea of the sorted past that drags painfully behind my cheap Wal-Mart flip-flops. At least she'll get her money's worth out of this gossip-session dinner.

***

The rest of my afternoon is spent nestled in the chalky sand staring into the vastness of the ocean. The powder blue sky meets the emerald water as far as the eye can see. It reminds me that there is a world out there that I've never known. There is so much more to life than pain and worry. Here, there is nothing but peace. There must be at least fifty people surrounding me on either side, sculpting sand castles, splashing in the water, bronzing in the sun—and yet my world remains silent and tranquil. There is no Brian, no Cris—only the sea and I. I could easily get used to this. If I remind myself of what I'm going back home to I might just never return. Brian weighs heavily on my mind. The guilt is beginning to catch up with me. He must feel so betrayed right now. And Cris, I still don't know how to feel about her. I mean, I know what I'm feeling right now—which is what I've always felt—I just don't want to admit it. Admitting it to myself confirms that I really am just as big of an asshole as I feel. I'm not cheating on Brian— technically; but if I admit fully to the feelings I have for Cris after all this time, I would also have to admit that these are feelings that have never subsided from the very beginning. Of course I never said it to Brian, and I hope I never showed it, but it's the sad truth. I have been emotionally cheating on Brian with Cris throughout our entire relationship. I always expected it to go away at some point, and I'm sure in time it would have. But now, it's as if I'm starting from scratch, and every time she enters my mind she is no longer a memory, she is real—here—and waiting for me. I'm in deep shit. No matter how much I tell myself that this is insane, and nothing more than a disaster waiting to happen, I can't seem to turn her off. She's just there. Always there.

Admittedly, the feelings I have for them are vastly different. I miss Brian terribly, and I can't wait to see his goofy grin and kiss is dimply sweet face, but Cris is different in a way. There is a need that creeps up on me when she's in my life. I adore Brian and I miss him, but not enough to take me home to him just yet. Yet the urge to run to Cris is strong. I **need** to be near her. I need to see her face again, before she disappears on me. Warm fuzzy feelings have never been something Cris has left me feeling—only fear. Our entire relationship was based on this intense need to have her with me always. She has used it against me time and time again because she feels the same way and she could just never admit it. She could never just tell me she needed me as much as I needed her. But now she is. Where would that even leave our relationship? Two people so passionately obsessed with the other that we would feel entirely broken when we're apart? Is that what real love is? Or is that infatuation?

I throw my head back in the sand, trying to make sense of it all and still end up coming to no conclusion at all. I would be lying if I didn't say I was considering jumping back on that plane right now and running straight to Cris before she changes her mind and fades to black again. But I can't, because I still don't know what I'm going to do. They will both expect answers and I don't have any. Brian is a safe bet, he'll wait like he always has. I only hope Cris's patience has improved over the last six years. Even after all this time, I don't think could handle losing her again.

"Fuck it," I sigh, irked that I'm letting my own mind ramblings ruin this beautiful sunset. I need a night off from the stressful wonderings of what will happen once I return home, and a night **on** with some stiff alcohol and some carefree fun. I hope the distraction works. If I can't drink them away, I may as well go home.

***

6:00 p.m. comes along way too fast. I literally had to force myself off the beach and back into my room. Leaving such beauty and returning to reality doesn't blend well for me tonight. But I did make plans with Bridgette so I don't have a choice. I arrive to a package lying on my bed, as well as another message envelope. I wasn't even aware that they were allowed to enter my room while I was out. Though, when I see the message I am no longer surprised. Bridgette was the sender this time, and I have no doubt that she has 'pull' with the staff here.

Kali,

I thought this would be the perfect dress for you to wear to the Beachwalk

Café. Enjoy. I went out on a limb and assumed you were a size eight. If not,

SUCK IT IN! See you in the lobby,

-Bridge

    I am immediately relieved to find that this was not another attempt from Cris to contact me. I had little faith that she could uphold her word to give me my space, but so far she seems to be playing along. Brian has made no attempt either—which is exactly what I would have expected of him, as he is always predictable. But strangely, it's somewhat insulting that he hasn't even called or left word to check on me. Either way I shrug it off and open the box.
    "Nordstrom? I have never shopped at Nordstrom in my life."
    The box is bright red and wrapped in a bow, just like in Pretty Woman when he surprises her with lavish gifts. I don't know why she is befriending me so easily, or why she would send me such a beautiful package after just meeting me, but I won't question it. I deserve a little happiness, right? No school, no partner, just a little something for me for a change.
    Coming from Bridgette, I half expect a skimpy little black cocktail frock as I pull the dress from the tissue paper, but what I find is entirely better. It's wispy and light—ivory in color, with a strapless bodice of stretchy form fitting nylon that spans from breast to thigh. Sheer ivory fabric has been sewn around the waist to give an airy flowing view to my newly tanned legs. The soft sheer train hits the top of my feet. She has also provided pearl white-jeweled sandals. This is beautiful—perfect for the beach. I use the sun's kisses to my advantage and just barely highlight my cheeks with a translucent dusting of shimmer powder and a sheer pink shiny wet

lip-gloss. I look natural and beautiful. My hair is pinned to one side and soft curls fall upon my shoulder. I pluck one of the red roses from the honeymoon vase on the side table next to my bed and nestle it behind my ear. It gives a perfect pop of color to my ensemble. I feel good as I walk out of the elevator to greet a smiling Bridgette.

"I knew it would be perfect for you when I saw it earlier. You look just stunning," she gushes, wearing the same black frock I was envisioning in my own gift box.

"That was so awesome of you. I can't even tell you how much I love this dress. Cris would go crazy over it…" I cut myself off, shaking the thought of her away. "I mean, Brian would love it too, but…"

It only takes a few words to wet her curious appetite. She is nearly shaking with anticipation for gossip. It's almost sad. She must be a very lonely woman.

"Oh dear me, you've got it worse than I thought," she snaps her fingers at the bellhop, grabbing his attention. "Has our transportation arrived yet?"

"Yes, Ms. Shay. Right this way," he leads us out to a black stretched limousine.

"Call me old-school, but I still love these big fancy cars," Bridgette boasts. "Reminds me of the red carpet days."

"Red carpet? Were you some kind of actress or something?"

"Fashion designer, dear. The big screen couldn't handle me if they tried. I have my nice moments, of course, but for the most part I'm worse than Shannon Dougherty with roid rage. I was born to make people as unhappy as possible and enjoy every moment of it. For the most part I am a raging success at being the most elegant and self-esteem destroying bitch in the room. Call it a natural attribute."

"Well you seem nice enough to me," I reply, hoping to never be on the other side of said personality. Though, I have no doubt of the truth behind her words. She looks like a raging bitch. But I keep that to myself.

"That's only because you intrigued me with your phone call earlier. It's interesting to see a young face look so old. It means you have a past—a story to tell. And I'm always dying for a good story."

I laugh slightly, knowing that even in her seasoned experience she will never see my story coming. My life is the shit soap operas are made of.

"You know, you remind me of Blanche Deveraux from the Golden Girls. You make me laugh; you're arrogant and feisty, and yet warm and inviting in the same. I've never met anyone quite like you, Bridgette."

"Oh, and you never will. Love me or hate me, I am **the** Blanche—I just have a better plastic surgeon. Not bad for fifty-one, aye?" she turns, showing off her modelesque figure.

"I should say not. I thought you were in your early forties. Great plastic surgeon, indeed."

"Yeah, too bad I just divorced him. I shall have to find another. He was the best in Houston, but there are others. He would probably carve me into a Gremlin if I went back to him now—even on a strictly professional level—especially since he would essentially be paying for his own services," she cackles loudly, sipping a glass of champagne poured by our driver prior to departure. "To alimony! Cheers!"

***

Beachwalk Café is even better than Bridgette had initially described. There was a table waiting for us upon our arrival, literally on the beach a few feet from the water. Warm soft candles top the pale white linens, and beautiful arrangements of teal orchids complete the tropical flair. A chilled bottle of white wine and some sort of weird looking appetizer complete the dinette. I try not to gasp as I attempt to figure out what it is. All I can say is that this is some kind of funky looking fancy shit that I have no interest in eating. I make a mental note for the next time I dine with a posh socialite to stuff a peanut butter and jelly in my pocket for when I visit the ladies room. This is only the appetizer and I'm already frightened. What's next on the menu, snails? Jesus, I should have gone to McDonalds.

"Um—what the hell is that? Certainly we aren't supposed to eat it, right? It looks like the Kraken," I whisper, as to not let the waiter hear me as he pours our wine.

She laughs heartily and plucks a piece from the platter, dipping it in a melted butter sauce.

"It's just grilled squid. Don't let the tentacles scare you. Try it."

Aside from imagining one of those tentacles gripping the inside of my throat on it's way down, I also think of Cris and wonder what she would think of all this fancy food fare—she would probably adore it. But definitely not Brian, he's your all-American meat and potatoes kind of guy. I'm more of an in-betweener, if you will. Still, this thing is a little much for me.

"No thank you. It's all yours."

"Oh, Kali. You have no manners. Rules of the house; you have to try everything—even if it's only a bite. How else are you supposed to experience all of life's little treasures? Come on down off your culinarily primitive horse."

She brings a valid point, worse case scenario I will spit it out. I cringe slightly and bring it to my mouth, pleasantly surprised by the flavor of subtly sweet meat and a slight char from the grill. It's really not bad at all, aside from the texture, which is somewhat rubbery. I still can't shake the feeling that it's going to latch to my esophagus as soon as I swallow it.

"Well? What do you think?" She asks, wrongly assuming I've had a change of heart after tasting it.

"Not bad. I wouldn't order it, but I'll eat it. The little suckers on its legs are throwing me off."

"Suckers?" she winces. "Kali, I normally try to encourage proper dining etiquette to my new friends, but you make me smile with your vile posture, your elbows on the table and your sloppy usage of the beautiful English language."

"I don't know whether to be flattered or insulted. Either way, I'm not a fancy girl. I'm from a small town in Nebraska. We don't eat Kraken's and sip champagne. We eat steak and baked taters. We drink beer and play drunken pool. That's me," I shrug.

"It's refreshing to see someone so true to themselves. I'm certainly not. That's why I like you. I admire the casual approach to all of your horrible imperfections. You're wearing barely any makeup at a fine dining establishment. No jewelry, no painted nails, and no frills—you're just so plain. No offense to be taken. I am complementing you. Not many people can pull off plain."

"Thanks—I think. I like you too, but that's subject to change the more you speak. Perhaps we should occupy your mouth with some grub?"

"Oh, dear. The chef would have a heart attack if he heard you call his masterpieces 'grub'. I might end up having to train you after all," she smirks.

We both end up ordering the Surf & Turf, which came with a filet mignon, grilled gulf shrimp, asparagus, and wild rice. It was fantastic. After dinner and a few glasses of wine I am feeling quite happy about my choice to come here. Aside from the Kraken everything has been superb, as Bridgette would call it.

"So what brings you to Destin? You know all about my divorce. What's the story with you and this crazy shenanigan you've worked yourself into?"

I laugh a bit, wondering what a perfect stranger would think of my current situation. I'm used to the folks of Humboldt knowing every microscopic detail of my history, but here, I'm not the victim, the purger, or the lesbian girl—I'm just me. Either way, I feel comfortable talking to Bridgette. And you never know, with her wiry past she might just have some good advice for me.

"The short version is that I am in love with two people, and two people are in love with me."

"That's the most pathetic version of telling a life story I have ever heard. Give me details. Nobody falls in love with two people without a story behind it."

This time I just unload everything, purging my conscience to her as if I've known her my entire life.

"Alright, I was abducted when I was twenty-four years old by a person who had been stalking me for nearly ten years. I was held there for close to six months. I fell in love with her—my stalker—captor—whatever you want to call her."

"Tell me it isn't this Cris person?"

"Yes, Cris. But before you make assumptions, she's really not like people think. She was very mentally disturbed, but deep down she is a good-hearted person. She took care of me—great care of me. She loved me in a way nobody could ever understand."

"Honey you don't have to preach it to me. I know better than anyone that good people can still make bad choices. Did she ever hurt you?"

"Mentally—yes. Though, I don't think it was ever intentional. She wanted the fantasy of having me, and I wanted all of her. She was just too mentally far-gone to live up to my unrealistic expectations, which in time, would fade. Honestly, I would have taken her as she was. Only, I never had the chance to tell her."

"What about mental help? A psychiatrist?"

"Well, that when the story gets even more bizarre," I gulp another sip of wine, as she signals the waiter for another bottle. "Cris had a psychiatrist named Valentina—which turned out to be a bit of a loon herself. She was the mastermind behind the murder of two unfortunate people who crossed paths with her; her ex husband was killed by a previous patient she'd had a love affair with—on her orders. And she did the deed herself on John, her fiancé. That's how I ended up being found in the end."

"The crazy psychiatrist turned Cris in? That's illegal," Bridge gasps.

"No, not really. She used it as blackmail against Cris. To make a long story short, my whereabouts were finally discovered by the police and Cris was arrested for my kidnapping—even though I adamantly denied it. Valentina figured it would be perfect timing to pin her fiancés murder on Cris since she was already in hot water for kidnapping."

"I must say, I certainly wasn't expecting to hear this kind of drama," Bridge says, appalled. "Please go on, you've wet my appetite for more. What happened after that?"

"I lied under oath and made sure the charges were dropped for the kidnapping, but Cris was under the spotlight of a murder investigation immediately following that. Valentina made up a bullshit story that Cris killed John and she was charged with no questions asked. But Valentina was sloppy and she reacted too hastily. She kidnapped me as a silencing chip against Cris. When Cris made bail she immediately came to try and save me, and Valentina tried to kill us both—she locked us in a basement, boarded it up and turned the gas on in the house. In the nick of time we were found and saved by an officer in training—Brian McDowell."

"Brian—your other lover?"

"Boyfriend," I correct her defensively, and then continue. "When we were found in the basement the murder charges against Cris were dropped, but they found evidence of my kidnapping that I couldn't dispute. She was sentenced to six years in a mental hospital for my abduction. After a few years I gave up on Cris. She wouldn't talk to me; she wouldn't let me visit the hospital. I was devastated. But Brian was my knight in shining armor. He saved me—in more ways than one."

"Brian sounds like good people. What became of Cris?"

"Well, that's what brought me here. Only two short days ago Cris was released from the hospital. I assumed she would go back to her house and I would never see her again. She had shut me out and abandoned me. I moved on and really had the perfect life with Brian. I honestly thought I was over her—at least—over her enough to move on. That is, until I saw her while Brian and I were out to dinner last night. She was looking for a job—she's a chef. Brian flipped out—which is very unlike him. He saw me, I saw her, and I instantly knew I was in deep trouble."

"So you mean to say that Cris came back and disrupted your entire life after six years of ignoring you? I think you have your answer, dear. Seek out the person who was loyal from the start. Brian." She downs another glass of wine, and picks an unnaturally long cigarette from a metal case.

"Give me one of those smokes," I help myself to one, taking my first drag in over seven years. The smooth familiarity is soothing. I exhale slowly, and continue, "That's what I told myself at first. But Brian wasn't making the situation any easier for me. He was furious that I was being so casual with Cris when we ran into each other. But I didn't see it that way. The truth is, no matter how much she hurt me there is no way I could ever treat her badly. Cris's problems were never her fault. She was damaged. Part of me needed to know why she would come back into my life after all these years of cutting me out of hers. I allowed her to explain herself, against Brian's wishes. And boy was I not expecting what happened next."

"Damn, there's more? I'm really getting my monies worth out of this dinner. Waiter, another bottle!" she calls.

"When I demanded to know why she abandoned me she turned around and asked me to recall the last thing I remember before we were rescued from that old Farmhouse where Valentina left us for dead."

"What was it? Don't keep me in suspense here!"

"I had asked her if we were ever able to escape from Valentina with our lives would she be willing to help herself, for me. And did she love me enough to fix herself—for us? Well, in that six years of 'ignoring' me, she was actually trying to get help so she could be the person I deserved."

"That is kind of—the most romantic thing I have ever heard. That is a huge sacrifice. How is Brian taking all of this?"

"Bad. He turned aggressive and mean—something so unlike him."

"He's threatened by her—rightfully so. As you said, there is a mental connection between yourself and Cris that nobody could ever understand," Bridge replies quickly.

"I know. He stormed off to work last night after we ran into Cris at the restaurant. He accused me of defending her and we ended up in a huge fight. But later on he realized he was being unfair to me and he came home with flowers after few hours of cooling off and apologized. Unfortunately, Cris had already beat him there and had stopped in to talk to me."

"Oh shit. He found her there in the house," she gasps.

"Yeah. It was fucking horrible. Here is Cris, whom I haven't seen in six years, only known to me as being mentally unstable and very fluent in martial arts; and then on the other side of me stands my boyfriend, a cop who carries and gun and is the most furious I have ever seen him. I was terrified for both of them. I thought for sure they would kill each other right then and there."

"Did you just take off? Is that how you ended up here?"

"Yes. Right after Cris proposed to me and asked me if I still loved her—all in front of Brian. I had no choice but to admit the truth. I love them both."

"Cris proposed? In front of Brian!"

"She sure did. I bolted. I didn't respond, I just grabbed my purse and headed straight for the airport. The cheapest flight with no advance purchase was to Destin. So here I am," I inhale another wonderful drag.

"Good choice. I'm personally thrilled that they pushed you over the edge. Otherwise, I wouldn't have met this divine woman who has been through more than I could ever imagine. You really are amazing Kali, for surviving all of this. Now for the real question, what are you going to do? Who will you choose? The forbidden lover who changed everything about herself for you, or the man who saved your life, and has been there for you through years of recovery?"

"I have no fucking idea. Maybe I should just stay here… Perhaps you and I both can just never go home again," I smirk.

"Don't twist my arm too much, I was already leaning towards purchasing the condo I've been in for the last three weeks. It just so happens to be on the market for a steal. There is nothing for me in Houston any more. I want a fresh start, somewhere fun—like here. New men—new victims," she smiles excitedly.

"Why the hell not? You should do it. Unfortunately for myself, I have to be back for school within the next couple of days. I'm stuck there for the next six months until I graduate."

"Graduate?"

"Law enforcement and Forensics. I have a psychotic psychiatrist to find and put behind bars. If it's the only thing I accomplish in my life—I will find Valentina and she will pay for what she did to us."

"Somehow, I have no doubt in you whatsoever. You're a lot stronger than the eye reveals."

"Yeah, but not so much when it comes to my own love life. I ran like a child."

"You needed thinking time."

"I still don't know what the fuck to do. I love them both, and in completely different ways. Still, they are connected, even to each other in a strange way. Brian saved Cris's life just as much as he saved mine. Without the other, none of us would be in each other's lives. We are all a part of each other—as much as Brian hates the idea. To me, there is no Brian without Cris's ghost, and no Cris without Brian's ghost. I'm fucked."

"I have an idea," she smirks. "You must develop separate relationships with them both. You need to establish whom they really are without the other person lingering in the past. Find out who Cris really is. And find out who Brian really was before Cris was a factor in his life. Start over."

"How can you just start over? There is way too much history there."

"Date them both. Establish rules and abide by them until you're ready to choose one."

Rules. That is something I can definitely understand.

"You are so fucking right. Date them. Get to know them on my own terms. That's perfect. Though, I don't know how either of them would feel about sharing. Nor do I even know that it's right for me to ask them to."

"YOUR rules, Kali. Be like me. Only, do it for your heart, and not for money like I do," she laughs.

"Do you think I'm crazy for loving a kidnapper and an opportunist?"

"The heart wants what it wants. I would never judge you for that. You have the right to choose what makes you happy. Fuck everyone else in that bumble-fuck town of yours. You have cared what others think for far too long. Do YOU. That. Is. All."

"Okay. I'll try. Thanks for the session, Doctor. What do I owe you?" I giggle.

"I won't charge you for the session, but Cris can buy the next round of wine with all that money she sent."

"I don't think she would mind." I raise my glass, "To dating again. May it be better than I remember as a teenager."

"Here, here!"

We toast, laughing the rest of the night away.

***

After a wonderful week in Destin I'm forced to go home. I did as Cris asked, spending every last dime she gave me to pay for my hotel stay, my shopping, as well as put aside the money to pay off my credit card. I am very grateful that she did that for me. Otherwise, I would have never afforded a second day here in my new favorite place, and I wouldn't have had a chance to get to know my new and dear friend, Bridgette, who seems deeply saddened that I'm leaving.

"Okay, I have arranged for the limo to take you to the airport. No shuttle this time for my new best friend," she hugs me.

"It's been so great. Thank you for everything. Let me know when you close on the condo, I'll come visit."

"You better. And don't forget to stay in touch."

"Of course."

I stop by to thank Tanya again for making this stay possible. I have met the most wonderful people here. I can't wait to return in the near future. But for now, it's back to Humboldt I go. Time to face the music, and time to set some rules. God help me.

2
Love Connection

<u>Kali</u>

A dark cloud is looming over me the moment the plane touches the warm Nebraska ground. Not only have I failed to figure out how I plan to approach the situation, but also I have resorted to blasting them both with some preposterous suggestion that they should share me and start dating all over again. I have to tell you, the idea sounded way better after having guzzled down several bottles of wine. Still, it's a week later and this is the only plan I've got.

I find my worn down black sedan right where I left it in the parking deck. Even as I approach it I can see flowers and a card in a pink envelope resting on the windshield. An odd cocktail of dread, excitement and dancing butterflies create a tingle in my stomach. Of course I assume it's Cris. Brian doesn't do the flowers on the window gig. Brian would have waited at my car and handed them to me himself—that's just him. As frightened as I am regarding the impending doom I've returned to, I'm still a girl and the sight of flowers is always a welcomed addition to my day. And not just the flowers, it's also the fact that Cris took the time out of her own day to choose a card for me. This is a great homecoming gift. It's romantic. I never knew she had it in her.

I slide my finger under the back flap of the sealed envelope, smiling at the card face that is covered in hearts. The print reads, 'Missing You'. I anxiously check the inner message, which is always the most exciting part. I recognize the handwriting, and I am shocked to realize instantly that this is definitely not Cris's writing. It's Brian's. I stand corrected. I suppose he is going out of his way to give me my space. This is one of the things I love so much about him. He has always connected with my emotional needs, pulling back when I needed room, and coming closer when I felt alone. You could never accuse Brian of being inattentive.

"What a little sneak," I shake my head and begin reading the card, grinning like a Cheshire cat. Oh, how I adore that man.

Babe,

I hope you enjoyed your trip. I know you needed to get away and I understand why. I just wanted to give you a little space. That said, I can't wait for your sweet sexy self to come home. I've missed you like mad. I was so lonely I even considered finding a replacement while you were gone, but nobody around here has as many tattoos as you—and you know how I feel about your tattoos (HOT!!) So I gave up. I figure there will never be another you. On the real though, it hasn't been the same here without you. I miss your fucking face off. COME HOME! I love you a milli!

Your charming and always adorable,

Brian

I don't even realize I'm still smiling until my jaw begins to strain. I've missed him terribly too. Waking up without him has been like training myself to breathe under water. He has been my lifeline for so long that I really don't know how to exist alone. I realize how desperate that sounds even thinking it, but it's the truth. Being back home and closer to him is comforting. I feel like I can relax again. Still, I'm not sure if going home is the best plan of action right now. As much as Brian has been on my mind, so has Cris. It wouldn't be fair going back into a situation when there is an additional person taking up space in my head and my heart. I owe Cris nothing, but I do owe it to Brian to be truthful and faithful—neither of which I feel confident in doing with Cris back in the mix. Going home would give Brian false hope, and it might just drive Cris away. It would be completely misleading to them. I need to stay neutral, as difficult as that is going to be.

I sit in the car and think for a moment, yet nothing is popping into my head. My brain somehow managed to shut off once I stepped back off that plane and back into the harsh reality that is my life. I don't really know what to do first—or where to go. I call the only person who can help, praying she is still awake and not in some kind of alcohol induced coma.

The phone rings several times and I nearly hang up, but I hear a chipper voice right as I pull the phone away from my ear.

"Hey Kali, I was just wondering how your flight was," Bridge chirps.

"Eh, the flight home was better than the flight down, but probably only because I am so fucking panicked right now that I almost wish the plane had taken a nose dive. That way I wouldn't have to do the honors of crashing and burning my own life into the ground, and taking two of the people I love down with me. Jesus. I'm freaking out, Bridge," I ramble, twisting a lock of my hair and clenching it between my lips as I finally face the reality of what I'm about to do.

After reading the card, as cherished as it is, I instantly became wary of how I am going to do this without crushing Brian. The reasonable part of me screams for me to go home and forget any of this ever happened. But unfortunately, it did happen—is happening—and I can't run away this time. I'm genuinely at a loss. And genuinely scared. One wrong word or one ill-plotted move could ruin my life. The pressure is growing with every second, filling my stomach with that feeling you get when a rollercoaster begins inching its way up that first steep incline of a massive hill. It's too late to get off, and you are too wound up with thrill, fear, exhilaration, and anticipation that you begin losing sight of whether you ever really wanted to get on that ride to begin with. I'm flipping out right now. I'm not built for this kind of pressure. I'm buckling already and it's only just begun.

"Oh, calm down, child," Bridge urges. "Remember what we talked about. It's time for you to take the reins on your own life. You can do this."

"How? What do I do now? I'm back. Brian left flowers on my car telling me how excited he is for me to come home. I can't go there—or should I? If I go home Cris will still be there in my mind. It would be like emotionally cheating on Brian. I'm not a cheater. And he was so sweet in the card. He is going to be crushed by all this. Cris is different. She knows how to handle pressure—her life IS pressure. Brian is a man's-man, but when it comes to me he is extremely sensitive. Jesus, I should have stayed gone. Shit, shit, fucking shit. Mother-cunt-whore-fucker, I think I'm hyperventilating…"

Bridge tries to disguise her chuckle, but it's impossible given the shriek in my voice.

"Shhhhhhh, darling. Take a breath and listen to me. First, you need to start by acting like a lady. Your usage of profanity is absolutely despicable. Even in your own vile interpretation of the English language I do not think the word 'mother-cunt-whore-fucker' exists. Ladies earn respect and status, sailor mouthed children do not."

"Oh save the fucking lecture. Tell me what to do!"

"As I was saying before you so rudely interrupted me, you're working yourself into a panic for no reason. You're not hyperventilating; otherwise you wouldn't be talking a mile a minute. Turn off the drama and focus."

"Okay."

"Now, here is what you're going to do. Drive to the nearest bar and have a couple of drinks—try to relax a bit. Send both Brian and Cris a text message telling them to meet you there."

"Together? That's out of the question. They will beat the mother-cunt-whore-fucker out of each other—trust me. No, no, and fuck no," I shake my head fiercely, as if she could actually see me, disregarding her extreme distaste for my choice of words.

"Listen, if they are going to share you than this is the perfect way to dip their toes in the water. Anyway, as I was saying, have yourself a few drinks and go over the dating rules with them. Be firm. Be direct, and play it cool. If you're too wound up they will sense it like a couple of dogs, and they will take advantage of you. Got it? You are the one in charge."

I sigh, trying to regain my sanity. I never would have thought it was possible to get this wound up, but here I am, flipping out like a crazed psycho. She's right though, and this little spaz attack is doing nothing for my psyche. I listen carefully, gearing myself up for this. I know have to do this—even if I don't want to. And if they don't want to be part of it, I will have to accept it, but I need to do what's right for me or I'll never be happy in the end. This is my life and I am in control. It's now or never.

"Okay, text them both to meet me. Then what? What about the rules?"

"I can't make the rules for you, but I strongly suggest that you do not go home. Get a hotel, or an apartment. Going home is not a good idea. Jot down a few rules while you're waiting for them to arrive. Once you start writing them down they will come easier. But one rule is not to be broken—NO SEX."

"Are you fucking crazy? No sex? Where will I find my sanity?"

"In an adult toy store. Sex will only complicate matters more."

"Ugh! Fine. No sex."

"Good girl."

"Well, I'm headed to the Blue Rose Lounge now. I should be there in about three minutes. Any other advice that I should know?"

"Yeah, they will both try to spoil the mother-cunt-whore-fucking hell out of you. Let them. This is what dating is all about. Have fun."

"Aww, honey, you cursed. It was beautiful," I joke, finally relaxing a little.

"Yes, it was quite liberating. I'll talk to you later, darling. I will expect details—soon."

"You'll be the first to know. I'll holler at you later, Bridge."

Against Bridgette's advice I choose **not** to drink tonight. After the week in Destin with her my liver needs to be wrung out and hung to dry for a while.

"Bartender, may I have a ginger ale, please?"

"Absolutely. How've 'ya been, Kali?"

I've seen this dude before. I think we went to school together, but I can't quite place a name to his face.

"It's me, Chubby Drew. Everyone remembers me," he smiles.

"Oh my god! Yes, I do remember you. Long time, no see," I reply.

Though, nobody would refer to him as chubby anything now. He has lost his baby fat, it seems; and possibly taken to steroids, as his arms are literally bulging from his blood red t-shirt sleeves. That cannot be natural. Veins should never look like snakes under a skin blanket. Perhaps Chubby Drew has a complex...

"Waiting for someone special?" He picks, perking my ears up. Everyone in this town knows I'm with Brian. My 'someone special' is always him, so the gossip must have already started to spread like wildfire, leaving people wondering whom Kali is going to choose. It's infuriating that I can have no privacy in this nosy ass town.

"Actually, yes. But I think I will go find a table so we can have some privacy," I reply snidely.

I walk to the back room, away from the bar, once again enjoying my peace and quiet. I miss Destin already. I kind of liked it when nobody knew or cared what the hell I was doing, or with whom. I will simply have to grow a thicker skin if I am going to deal with all this. Honestly, I wouldn't have to think twice about relocating if I weren't in school right now. But this is the way of it. I can consider other options later on down the road. If this situation plays out badly, I might have no other choice.

I text both Cris and Brian and hit send before I talk myself out of this insane idea. While I wait I work on the rules on a small bar napkin. Bridgette was right; it's not that difficult. Implementing them will prove to be much more difficult, however. I don't like the 'no sex' rule at all. I love sex. And while I have only ever been with

Cris twice, I have thought about it—a lot. Sex with Cris was like a dirty tornado of all things sexy and dark. And Brian—he is twenty-four years old; his drive is amazing, along with his performance. His oral has nothing on Cris's of course, but he knows how to work my body just the right way. They are both amazing in bed. Again, I am not going to like this rule.

Brian is the first one here. He is wearing his uniform; he must have come straight from work, which is literally right across the street.

"Baby," he grabs me in his strong arms, lifting my feet off the ground. "Baby, baby, baby."

I squeeze him back tightly; I've missed him more than I would like to admit. His delicious cologne fills my senses, almost knocking me off my feet. As I catch my breath I see Cris walk in. She's in her typical white t-shirt and jeans with those awesome red converse that I love so much. She takes a long deep breath, keeping a slight distance, visibly confused and wondering why I called her here. Her eyes lock with mine and I instinctively pull back from Brian and walk over to her, hugging her softly. Her grip firms up around me. She can't seem to let go.

"Hey baby," she smiles, kissing my forehead. It feels good, but she pulls back quickly, as I am obviously radiating nervousness. I like the physical contact with them both, but I don't think it's fair for the other to have to watch it. I know Brian spotted that kiss and I'm waiting for him to flip his lid. I place an adequate amount of space between us all and initiate the conversation, first acknowledging why they are both here.

"Okay, I know this is awkward, for all of us. But I did some thinking in Destin and worked out a sort of—compromise. This is something we all need to discuss together."

Brian comes to my side, scowling at Cris.

"You're kidding me, right?"

"Look, I know this is weird, but it's important that we are all on the same page," I repeat firmly.

The tension is thickening fast. Brian seems more bothered by her presence that Cris does by his. She just leans against the wall, doing her thing, watching the situation evolve in silence, though hearing every single word and soaking it in.

"Kali, when I got your text I took that as an indication that you were coming to your senses. I thought you had called me here to tell me you're coming home and you were going to tell Cris to fuck off," Brian says bluntly.

"That's not why I called you here at all."

"Babe, you are going through so much right now and I'm trying to be understanding, but this is an ambush and I don't like being cornered. I am going to forgive this little meet and greet you tricked me into and just let it go. But the only words I want to hear coming from your mouth is that you're going to let me take you home and we are going to work this out—like couples do," Brian says.

His tone isn't aggressive—exactly. More like extremely persuasive. He isn't yelling, but his volume has raised enough to pull Cris from her spot against the wall and into the conversation.

"Brian, we are all adults here. Why don't you let her talk?" Cris suggests as politely as possible.

"I have a better idea; why don't YOU shut the fuck up and get back against the wall where you were. I'm talking to MY girlfriend."

You can see the conflict in Cris's eyes. The awareness that she has absolutely no right to be in this conversation is written all over her face, but she has stepped in now, and she does have a place in this predicament—she came back for me and I accepted her advances, somewhat. I wouldn't want to be her right now, with Brian's hatred and my uncertainty. It took a lot of balls for Cris to have done what she's doing. It's commendable, but certainly no easy task for her.

"I'm going to be the bigger person here and keep it clean. I'm merely suggesting that you should let Kali speak for herself? I don't think she needs you to tell her what she has to do. If she wants to go home, she'll go home. If not, it's not your place to force her."

"Ha! That's rich coming from you," he laughs loudly.

Cris is struggling to keep her mouth shut. She knows what she did—so does the entire city of Humboldt. This is unnecessary, and adds nothing to the solution.

"Dude seriously, give your mouth a rest for a second. I didn't come here to listen to a toddler boss a grown woman around. I realize you are way younger than us, and clearly more immature, but

41

I'm only interested in hearing what Kali has to say. Your temper tantrums and stone throwing won't deter me from being here for Kali. Grow the fuck up." Cris shakes her head, trying to ward off the irritation.

"Toddler? I don't think so. This is all man right here," he sneers. "Kali doesn't seem to have a problem with my maturity level or my manly performance. In fact, I remind her of what a man SHOULD be every single night, and sometimes in the morning too. In the shower, on the hood of my truck, in the back of the theater... Right babe?" He looks to me with a grin.

It's obvious what he's implying and it has nothing to do with this situation, his maturity, or Cris. He is getting defensive and trying to show Cris who holds the macho card. Cris isn't buying into it and quickly bores of his antics. The last thing she wants to hear about is our sex life. The mere implication of it has her scowling with disgust. She tries to hide it with a snide grin, but I can see through it. She covers her anger with her other favorite tool—wit.

"Just remember who had her first," she winks. "I've never felt someone cum so hard in my life. Don't try to keep score with me, kid. Quality over quantity. End of discussion," she turns from Brian feeling victorious for the moment.

She looks at me, who has crawled into an invisible hole and pulled the dirt in over my head. They are acting like a couple of hungry dogs with a single steak dangling in front of their drooling mouths. The good girl within me feels degraded to be spoken of in such a way, as if I'm some sort of toy at the bottom of a cereal box. But the little devil on my shoulder takes me back to that day on the couch with Cris. I shouldn't be thinking about it, but damn...

Cris senses my discomfort and quickly shifts the subject away from sex, and just in the nick of time. I was becoming entirely too entangled in that wildly delicious memory—and that's bad. There is no sexual relief anywhere on the horizon for me. That subject is not on the list of 'okay' topics.

"Sooooo, Kali," Cris continues. "What's up, kitten? What do you need to talk to us about?"

I try to forget about the tension and project this a matter of business. I can already foresee Brian's reaction, which will not be good. Cris is a wildcard. All I know is that I don't want a scene so I try to handle this the way Bridgette would. She would never let a man tell her what she was going to do. She would be a lady, she would take charge, but with style and grace. She would demand the stage—take the lead on the red carpet. While I am NO Bridgette, I've got this—I think.

"Come on, Kali, spit it out and stop stalling." Brian says flatly.

"Alright, I'll tell you what's going to happen here. You and Cris will sit down and not speak to each other; in fact, don't even look in the other's direction. **I** am the person you came here for. If you aren't interested in what I have to say, you know your way out. My feelings will be heard and you will not interrupt me. I deserve to speak for myself. You will respect me or you can be gone. Now, sit down, please."

Cris takes a seat without hesitation, but Brian is uncomfortable with this new bold approach I'm taking—and rightfully so. This is not me. I don't boss people around, nor do I ever take control of anything—since the abduction I am not the same rebellious person I used to be. I'm the non-confrontational one—the passive aggressive girl. That's who I am now, and that's whom Brian knows. His ego is getting the better of him and he refuses to sit at the table with Cris, and just crosses his arms across his chest quietly waiting for me to continue. This would never fly with Bridgette, but based on the fact that poor Brian really is getting the shit-covered end of the stick in being an innocent bystander to MY drama, I don't ask him to sit again—this time. I continue, remembering that I have to give them completely equal treatment from here on. We are starting over. No more freebies for either of them. If I ask something of them they should respect me enough to accommodate—just as I would if the roles were reversed. Cris is obedient, but I can already see that Brian is going to give me hell. I swallow a hard lump in my throat and hold my head high, demanding their full attention just like Bridge told me to do. No fear.

"So... the truth of the matter is that I love you both very much, and in completely different ways."

"We already know that..." Brian cuts me off, planting an irritation on my tongue; which fortunately makes it a little easier to continue.

"As I was SAYING," I shoot a death glare at him, daring him to interrupt me again, causing a snicker from Cris. "I don't really know either of you the way I should. Brian, our relationship was initiated after some really harsh circumstances in my life. I treated you like you were my hero because in so many ways you were—and still are. But I never knew what it might be like to get the chance to see you as a person whom I owed nothing. I care about you, you're the sweetest, most gentle and loving person I have ever known, but deep down I don't know who you are without Cris. Would you have loved me the same? Would I have loved you the same? Haven't these questions ever occurred to you?"

"No. Love is love no matter how you got there. You of all people should know that," he replies firmly.

"I do know what you mean, but on the other hand, I really feel like how we got here does matter. I want to know you on a different level, from scratch. I want to start over."

Brian shakes his head in disbelief.

"This is the biggest heap of non-sense I have ever heard. Why are you complicating things, Kali? We were just fine until this piece of shit showed back up and ruined everything."

"Brian, that's what I am trying to tell you here. She isn't the problem. You can't wreck a happy home, no matter who you are. Do you understand?"

Cris listens attentively, absorbing everything I say and faithfully remaining quiet as I requested.

"So basically you're leaving me for her? Is that what you're trying to say Kali?" Brian asks as the anger subsides, quickly being replaced with sadness and grief.

I sigh because he's not getting it. I'm not leaving anyone.

"Just let me finish. I'm not choosing either of you right now. I want to start over and really get to know you both, as individuals."

"You want to date us both?" Cris cringes slightly, breaking her silence and finally agreeing with Brian on something. "Kali, that's just not doable. I'm sorry, and I really want to cooperate with you here, but that's a shit offer."

"Shit offer isn't even the word. It's out of the fucking question. You really think I want that girl's pussy on your lips every time you kiss me? Fuck that. You must have left your brain in Destin, Kali. Seriously…" Brian is appalled.

The statement is humiliating to me. I wasn't even talking about sex and he is already throwing in things that he has no business speaking of.

"Brian, I told you, this is a choice **you** will have to make on your own. I'm telling you what I can offer you both. If you can't do it, I completely understand. But in reference to that crude and unnecessary comment you just made, there are rules that we all must abide by, should you choose to go through with this."

"What kind of rules?" Cris asks, curiously.

"Well, one would be that there will be no sex while I am dating you both. It's not fair, nor do I think it's very lady-like to be fucking two people at the same time. Also, no overnight visits with either of you. It only increases temptation. Third, you and Brian are not to communicate at all. You hate each other; so there is absolutely no reason for you to talk. The rules are simple and clear. What do you think?"

Cris is the first to answer, as Brian begins pacing back and forth, wearing a hole in the old wooden floors of the Blue Rose.

"I don't like the idea of sharing you with anyone, but you have made a good point. You should be given time to think and consider what is right for you. I get it—don't like it—but I get it. I'm in," she agrees.

I think Brian was waiting to see what Cris was going to say first, because the moment her mouth stops moving he jumps in with his response.

"Kali, I hate your plan. I think it's selfish and destructive to the life we've built together. I'm trying so hard to be understanding here, but I've gotta tell you, I would love nothing more than to shoot this bitch in the head and go on about my afternoon. I wouldn't feel even one ounce of guilt. But unlike some people in this room, I'm no criminal. If you flash your relationship with Cris in my face I won't be responsible for what I do to her. From my perspective I am giving you freedom to an open relationship, but ONLY so you can figure out what you already know—that you belong with me. If I find out you've slept with her I'll kill you both. So my answer is yes, I will agree to this insane plan of yours. I really don't have a choice. I'm not giving you up, so I will just have to fight harder to remind you of why you love me." He smirks, feeling the adrenaline of a challenge creeping through his manly veins. "And Cris, one more thing; if you try any funny business, like taking off with Kali against her will and disappearing—I'll find you, and I will make you wish your Daddy had pulled put faster."

Cris snuffs at the remark, rolling those big brown eyes, tired of dealing with the likes of a young man who talks too damn much.

"You must love the sound of your own voice, huh? I hear your 'warnings' loud and clear. Now allow me to give you some advice of my own. The quiet one always wins. You know why? Because the quiet one listens, slipping in under the radar while the other player is too busy talking shit to notice. So keep on talking shit, Brian. Meanwhile, I'll be stealing your girl."

"You know, as thankful as I am for the wonderful advice, I'm just not sure my top source would be a mental case with a criminal record. Quiet isn't always smart. Quiet is creepy and weird—like you."

And just like that they are at it again. I think this has gone as well as can be expected. These two are like oil and water—or more like gasoline and fire. It's just not a great idea to throw them together.

"Alright, y'all, I think we have exchanged enough pleasantries for one afternoon. You can go do your thing. I'm out," I throw my hands in the air, walking towards the door.

"Wait, Kali, would you like to have coffee with me? Like now," Cris quickly catches up with me with a grin, excited to start the dating game. As tired as I am coffee actually sounds perfect, so I certainly wouldn't mind.

Brian's fists go white. He's angry, but maybe this will help him come to terms with what's going on. Still, I walk outside of the bar before answering, out of his earshot.

"Coffee sounds perfect right now. I'm exhausted from the flight. So yes, I'd love to go. But do me a favor and don't ask me on a date in front of Brian—it's rude."

"Sorry," she smirks. "Total oversight."

"Oversight my ass," I lift an accusing eyebrow. "Come on, Cris. You know all about rules. You break a rule; you get a punishment. And I promise you won't like the punishment this time."

"Sounds hot—like the old days. I knew my Bonnie was still in there somewhere," Cris's eyes light up.

A smirk emerges before I can stop it as I remember the day we daubed ourselves Bonnie and Clyde. That was the first time Cris ever referred to us as 'together'. So many memories. Though, the Clyde I know seems to have disappeared back in the mental institution.

"My Clyde is gone," I sigh involuntarily.

"Isn't that what you wanted?" she seems thrown off by my response. "Because, if it is, I have something to say…"

I cut her off; frightened that she will be upset and think that I am ungrateful for her effort to get better.

"I just have some very fond memories of Clyde. But that's all in the past. We are supposed to be getting to know each other now."

"Got cha," she smiles. "To Cris and Kali," she toasts an imaginary glass.

"Yep…"

Brian

"I swear to God I am going to lose it on that bitch one day," he tells his co-worker, Sharon, as he walks back into the police station. He is fuming after watching Cris and Kali ride off together in Cris's fancy new Mercedes.

"I'm guessing your meeting with Kali didn't go very well?" she asks.

"Yeah, you can say that again. She wants to 'date'—start over."

"That's not that bad."

"Not bad, Sharon? It's not much different than dumping me."

She sits on the corner of his desk, crossing her legs and waving her foot lightly.

"Okay, so it's a step down from what you had; but think about it; twenty-four hours ago you didn't even know if she was coming home. You should be relieved," she says, sipping a cup of steaming hot coffee.

"I don't think I made myself clear enough. Let me re-phrase; Kali wants to date us **both**…"

Her lips scrunch up as she catches the true severity of the situation. She feels for Brian, who happens to be more than her partner, he is also her best friend.

"Well shit…"

"Yeah—BULL-shit."

"I'm so sorry, B."

"Me too. The worst part is that I fucking agreed to it. I love that girl so goddamn much. I could seriously cry right now—and I don't cry. I can feel it trying to come out. It's making my throat hurt. I almost cried when she said it, but Cris was already making jokes about my age. I swear, Sharon, I want to kill her—no—torture her. How pathetic am I? I just gave permission for my girl to date her kidnapper. What the fuck is wrong with me? What kind of a man does that? I wanted to fucking marry her! Goddamn it!"

His emotions finally eject like a volcanic eruption. Sharon runs to his office door, slamming it closed before anyone comes. Sadness fills her eyes as Brian falls apart, violently flipping his desk over, sending papers, his gun, and numerous projectiles, including a photo of Kali, flying through the air and crashing with a thunderous bang into the floor.

"Brian, please don't cry," Sharon begs as the tears begin dropping from his weakened eyes.

He was able to stop it at the bar, but here, in his second home, he can no longer hold it in. Men aren't supposed to cry, but the thought of losing Kali is unbearable. He throws his glasses across the room, shattering the frames into a mangled pile of junk. He wipes the tears away with his sleeve, humiliated, refusing to make eye contact with Sharon as she kneels down in front of him, scooping up the papers he flung to the floor.

"I'm so sorry..." he looks around the room, realizing the tornado he has created.

"Just forget that for a second and listen to me—as your friend. Before you give up and convince yourself that you're losing Kali, put yourself in her shoes first. Try to think how she's thinking, and feel what she's feeling. It's a hard thing to do, especially when you're hurting. But you know as well as I do that as a sufferer of Stockholm she probably still has a mental reliance on Cris. That is NOT her fault. It's sad, actually. Give her a chance—she's a smart girl. She will figure it out. Once she sees that there was never an ounce of real love in that relationship, she will come back to you. She loves you."

"What if she doesn't?" he asks pitifully.

"She will if you give her a good reason to. If Cris wants to fight for her, you should fight even harder. To Cris, Kali was always an object; she wants the prize but she doesn't know how to play the game without breaking the law. She's proven that time and time again. Play smart. Play hard. And get your girl back. Cristina James WILL fuck up again—she always does. And guess who will be there to put her back in prison where she belongs?"

"Just give me one good reason," Brian vows.

"Exactly. Wait it out and watch her hang herself."

Brian and Sharon spend the next few hours putting his office back together. He promises himself that he will never lose it like that again. He is going to fight hard for Kali, but meanwhile, he has to keep his hatred of Cris from destroying his own good sense. Cris doesn't need any additional help in landing herself in hot water; she does a good enough job of that on her own. As Sharon said, Cris James will hang herself. And when she does, Brian will be waiting.

Cris

I can't believe she actually said yes. Now, what does one do on a date? I know she is skittish right now—we both are. Just act normal, Cris. Be natural.

"Have you been here before, Kali?" She asks, attempting to start a conversation without being awkward.

Cris is still very self-conscious in public. She has been locked away for so long that she's forgotten how to co-exist. Though, in the hospital when they were preparing her for release they did take her to a few supervised spots in Lincoln. She visited a park that Kali would have loved. There was a waterfall and flowers—it was so beautiful, just like Kali. The time she spent away from her was excruciating, but she knew it was the one sure way to make sure she was fully rehabilitated. With treatment came a lot of emotions that Cris had tucked away for so long. Learning to live with the memories of her childhood was difficult—to say the least. It was as if her body was being detoxed from harsh drugs that kept her safe. She was stripped of any protection and made to feel things as they are for the first time since she was a young child. In time she learned to deal with those feelings and accept them as part of human experience. She is finally aware and accepting of the fact that not all memories and experiences in life will be good, and you can't trick reality into being what you would prefer it to be. Life is harsh and cruel, but it can also be wonderful and fulfilling. It's all in how you look at it. Cris's first lesson after leaving the hospital was that she was going to be judged no matter how much she had changed—that's life. But as long as she continues treatment and pushes herself through the situations she used to avoid, she will be just fine.

Not running after Kali was her first test, and it sure as hell wasn't easy. But Cris decided that if she were going to ever truly be one with Kali, she would also have to allow her some space when she needed it. That's what normal couples do. If Kali wants normal, than normal Kali shall have.

51

"Of course I've been here, goof. It's the only coffee shop in town. Small talk? You nervous?" Kali responds with an awkward laugh.

"I know, I know. That was a lame conversational starter. You're forgetting, I've never really done this whole dating thing before. I'm glad you came. And fuck yes, I'm nervous as hell."

Kali places her hand atop Cris's, smiling that dazzling smile, melting Cris's heart to syrupy goo.

"I'm glad I came, too. And now that you've got a job here, I imagine I will be a frequent customer. I never could resist your cooking."

Cris blushes, staring at her brand new red converse.

"I'd like that."

"I see your choice in shoes hasn't changed," Kali giggles.

"Never will. The closest thing to a change might be a different color—and that's even pushing it. Baby steps..."

"I like your shoes anyway. Always have."

Cris and Kali order the pastry sampler, which include a cream cheese and raspberry Danish, two éclairs, and cranberry orange scones. Kali has coffee while Cris opts for chocolate milk, which she is drinking through a straw and over ice.

"Chocolate milk?" Kali laughs.

"Guilty pleasure, what can I say?"

"Ice though? Girl, I just can't..."

"Tell me you haven't fallen into the 'trendy quotes' crowd. Why is everyone saying 'I just can't'? Can't what—finish a sentence?" Cris rolls her eyes.

Kali laughs, snorting a little. "Maybe you've finally figured out the meaning of 'I just can't', because I never could. Kudos to the class smartass."

Cris can't stop her hand from falling upon Kali's cheek. She has missed the softness of her skin so much.

"Is this okay?"

"Yes, it's okay. In fact, it's perfect. I missed you. I missed this—even though I've never had it. It's exactly like I had hoped we would become one day."

"It's only the beginning, baby. I'm going to give you the world. I promise this time," Cris replies softly.

A gentleman whom Kali assumes to be Cris's new boss approaches them, asking Cris to join him in the kitchen to discuss something. Cris agrees and excuses herself from the table.

"I'll be right back, Kal."

She returns a few minutes later, scored and embarrassed.

"What's wrong?" Kali asks. "You look like your dog just died."

Cris feels like the best way to approach this new dating thing is to hide nothing from Kali—even the bad.

"Well, apparently some of the customers are uncomfortable with our touching each other in public. Don, my new boss, just asked if we could keep the touching to a minimum or hold hands under the table. He actually felt really bad about having to say anything at all. He seems like good people."

"Toto, it looks like we are back in Kansas..." Kali replies, heatedly.

"What on earth does that mean?"

"When I was in Destin I saw this couple at the airport—they were gay. I could see how happy they were. They were holding hands and kissing. He hugged his partner as he got off the plane. They were so at ease in their own skin. And nobody around them cared that they were gay. It was so different. And my friend Bridgette, I told her all about you and she was nothing but supportive. I'm telling you, I'm really starting hate this place, and all the people in it. You'll see the judge, the jury and the townsfolk at the bar every night, and then in the church house on Sunday. Some of the wives have bruises on their faces, and some of the young girls are carrying a love child by the very men who criticize us. But if you lay your hand on my cheek they want to throw bibles at us. They disgust me."

"Baby, you can't let them get to you. And honestly, I will tell them to shove this job just to be able to keep my hands on you, where they belong. The choice is yours. But don't let them make you feel uncomfortable because they're insecure with our relationship. Just be you. Fuck them."

"No, Cris. You really wanted this job. Let's just go."

"Go where? You still have no place to live and that makes me nervous."

"You don't have to worry about me. I'm a big girl. I'll figure it out."

Cris has a thought, and she might be over stepping the boundaries that Kali has created for this dating thing, but she has to offer anyway. Cris is a realist, and in reality, her idea makes sense.

"What if I get you an apartment near the school? It will save you money on gas, everything could be right there at your fingertips and you would have a safe place to live.

Kali looks torn, and asks to be excused from the table and heads for the front of the coffee shop. Cris watches her pull her phone from her pocket and dial out. She's calling someone. Cris assumes it's Brian and instantly begins beating herself up for coming on too strong with the apartment thing.

Damn it, I've pushed her too fast.

Cris is disappointed that things were going so well and now she's fucked it all up because she is trying to provide for Kali. Her intentions were genuine, but Kali might see it as controlling. If she thinks for even one moment that Cris hasn't changed, she will never choose her. Cris get's a to-go box for the desserts and a lid for Kali's coffee, knowing this date is more than likely over. The old her wants to tell Kali she is not going anywhere accept home with her where she belongs. But she knows that's just not the right thing to do anymore. It's the easy way, but not the right way. And nothing worth having comes easy. Cris fights her demons and places Kali's doggie bag on the table, walking away and giving her some space. This is going to be hard. Cris makes a mental note to keep the big guns reserved for later. Slow and steady wins the race.

Kali

I light a cigarette, falling into that old habit of calming myself when things get stressful. Accepting Cris's offer is plain wrong, but the advice I received from Bridgette earlier prompted me to give her a call and run it by her.

"Are you sure, Bridgette? It just doesn't seem right. It's like I would be taking advantage of her generosity."

"She offered. It's not like you asked or begged for her to rent you an apartment. I think she is doing it for more than one reason. First, to make sure you are safe and in a secure place to live where you don't have to trouble yourself with money. Secondly, it pretty much ensures that you won't end up having to go back to your own home—with Brian. She is offering you a huge favor. You should take it. Justify it by assuming it's in her best interest too. She will have some peace in knowing you aren't going home. It's a win-win."

"Okay, I'll accept. Let me go tell her."

"Call me tonight. I want to hear about the rest of your date."

I'm shocked to see Cris walking out the door and waving goodbye, turning in the other direction towards the parking lot. She tosses me the keys to her car so I can drive myself back to the Blue Rose. I think she's walking home.

"Bridge, she's leaving. I gotta go."

"Hey Cris, where you going?" I run towards her.

She turns, surprised that I came after her.

"I thought I upset you," she replies, confused.

"No, not at all. I had to call a friend and smoke a cigarette."

"When did you start smoking?"

"In Destin. Bridgette was quite the naughty influence. I quit long ago, as I'm sure you already know. But it seems to be like riding a bike. I'll quit again soon before it becomes a habit. I just want to finish up this pack."

"Well that's good, then you won't mind if I smoke too?"

"Since when do you smoke?" I smirk, lifting an eyebrow of curiosity.

"Always, you just didn't know it. Smoke can be offensive so I tried to make sure you never smelled it on me."

Well that was a shock. I had always seen Cris as this perfectionist with no bad habits. I suppose this dating thing will teach me a thing or two I never knew about her. At least we won't have the awkwardness of worrying about ashtray mouth. That's always a plus. Brian loathes smoke. I'm surprised he didn't say anything about it earlier when we hugged. I suppose there are more important things on his mind. Cigarette smoke is hardly a big issue.

"Ah, well fear no more. Smoke doesn't bother me," I assure her.

"Good. So who were you talking to? Brian?" She asks, instantly regretful for asking.

"No, not Brian. I had to get advice from my new friend, Bridgette. I met her in Destin. She's a riot."

"I'm glad you made a friend. That's great, Kal."

"Yeah, when you meet her you might change your mind. She's crazy and hoity-toity, definitely not like any of the people around here. It's odd how money affects some people. You have money but you still act down to earth. She—doesn't," I laugh. "And speaking of money, I have decided to accept your offer if it still stands. Especially since she assured me that you're probably doing it a little for yourself as well as me," I wink. "That makes me feel a little less moochey."

"Perhaps this friend of yours in a smart girl. And she's right, I don't want you to go back to your house, and I know you don't want to go to your parents', so it's a perfect option. I have money, so it's an easy fix. We can go tomorrow morning and check out some apartments."

"Will there be breakfast involved?"

"Without a doubt."

"Then yes. I'll see you then. Tonight I'll just get a room in town and call it a day. I'm exhausted. Can you drop me back off at my car?"

"Definitely. As for tomorrow, just call me in the morning when you're ready to go hunting and I'll pick you up. I have to work from 2:00 a.m. to 10:00 a.m. so I can be there as soon as fifteen minutes after."

"Sounds great, love-bug."

Cris kisses my cheek lightly and drops me back off at the Blue Rose. I walk to my car having thoroughly enjoyed my evening with her. I have to say; all in all, this first date was a huge success.

***

The motel of choice is the End of the Road extended stay, not that there are many choices around here. There was a fifty-fifty shot at one or the other. I chose the lesser of two roach infested evils and went with the EOR. The beds are musty and entirely too firm. I miss the California king in my home. And now that I'm alone and ready for bed, I miss Brian too. It's our ritual to grab a glass of wine—and a beer for him—and cuddle up watching Crime T.V. He should be off work. I consider calling him, but given how irritated he was when he left I figure I should give him some space. It dawns on me that this might not be the life he wants. The idea is saddening. I'm not ready to give up on Brian. I really pray he comes to terms with this.

As if it were some kind of omen, my phone rings. It's him. I find my heart jumping into my throat in excitement.

"Brian, I am so glad you called!" I squeal, thrilled to have him on the line. "How're you doing, baby?"

He sighs gently, "I've had better days, love. Coming home from work and not having you here is killing me. I miss you so fucking bad."

I think he's crying, and I hope to god I'm wrong. I couldn't take it if he were.

"Are you okay, honey? You sound so—sad."

He sniffles lightly, trying to hide the fact that I was right, he is crying.

"I would be perfectly fine if you would just come home. I'm not playing games or trying to act like a child, but you are my girl— you've officially been my girl for the last three years. I can't just let you go. I'll admit it, I am insanely jealous of Cris. She just comes back and you're right back under her spell. I knew this was coming. I was so blind to think we could survive it. I hoped that I had loved you better than her and that it would be stronger than this hold she has over you."

"Brian, you couldn't have loved me better. You've done nothing wrong. And as much as you miss me, I miss you double. This is so incredibly hard for me. I wish you could understand. Baby, I know I'm a huge asshole. I hate myself for this. But I would hate myself even more if I wasn't honest with you."

"You're not an asshole, baby. You are a wonderful woman who has been put through the emotional ringer. You didn't ask for this life—she forced it upon you. I hope you will realize through all of this who Cristina James really is. She is a mentally disturbed individual. She can't change for anyone—even you—no matter how hard she tries. She will always be **that** person—you know this, honey. You are learning about these kinds of people in school. They don't change. They are incapable of loving anyone in a normal manner."

"She's different, Brian."

"No she isn't, sweetie. She's tricking you. But this is something you need to learn for yourself in order to heal. And I will wait for you because I love you. None of this is your fault."

He is still my selfless, darling Brian. After everything I'm putting him through he still remains loyal. I need him more than ever right now. I need to feel his safe and loving arms around me. I need his comfort.

"Can you come cuddle with me and watch a movie—maybe eat a leftover scone in a nasty twenty-dollar-per-night motel?"

"Let me guess, you're at the End of the Road Motel?"

"Ding, ding, ding! And the winner gets…a lice infestation," I cheer. " "Come on, baby. You can do better than that shit-hole. Why didn't you go somewhere else?"

"I'm way too tired to drive to Lincoln. Either way, I don't care where I am. All I want right now is you. Just come on over and we can spend some time together. I miss you so much."

"I miss you too, beautiful. I'm on my way. But I'm bringing pizza, I'm not eating the leftovers from your date."

"Fair enough," I giggle at his dry and disgusted tone, though I know it's not funny.

"Is it horrible that I'm devastated that she didn't choke on them?"

"Brian…"

"Okay, okay. I'll shut up. Feta, banana peppers and onions on your side?"

"Yep. Bacon and pepperoni on yours?" I smile.

"You know it, baby. See you soon. I love you," he says sweetly.

"I love you too, honey—so much."

3
Sleepover

Brian

Having such a great time with Kali last night reminds Brian of how things used to be. They ended up watching Forensic Files instead of a movie after sharing a pizza from the Pizza Inn down the road. He hadn't expected Kali to fall asleep so fast, but he looked over and she was out like a light. He didn't want to disturb her so he stayed, moving into the spare bed. Of course this was breaking the rules, but technically she didn't ask him to leave so Brian took advantage of the opportunity. He just needed to be near her so badly. Aside from sex, the nighttime and morning traditions they have adhered to over the last three years has been one of the more difficult things he's had to sacrifice. He found himself making Kali a cup of coffee every morning over the past week, even knowing she wasn't there to enjoy it with him. The first day was just habit, but the others were more of a tribute to their relationship. He doesn't plan on giving up any of their traditions. When she finally comes home, he wants everything to be exactly as it was—but better. He wants to see to it that she never questions their relationship again. He will love her harder and better than any other person ever has or will. Not that he doesn't already, but he is going to see to it that she has no doubt about how he feels for her for the rest of her life.

Everything that's happened over the last week has made him love and cherish Kali even more. He isn't going to lose her to some psycho who won't go away. With that said, Brian feels justified in making the call to stay put for the night. He's ecstatic that he beat Cris to the punch for the first sleepover, even if it was literally just sleep. To Brian, this relationship is so much more than sex. She's a goddess with a heart of gold, and the most nurturing person he has

60

ever met. Kali is the only person he would trust to have his child one day, and the only person he could ever imagine spending the rest of his life with.

When he thinks of Cris his stomach turns to knots. He doesn't see a mentally disturbed victim of childhood abuse, or even a person who is trying to better her life through therapy. The only side of Cris he visualizes is the disgusting monster that ripped Kali to shreds. Cris doesn't love her— she is obsessed with her. She is nothing more than a perverse sexual deviant, only in it for her own sadistic pleasure. It's no secret that Brian has always felt that same-sex couples are unable to have a normal relationship with love and intimacy. To him it's all about exploring the most forbidden and unnatural desires, and blames the devil for those disgusting acts of lust. Kali did not welcome thoughts like this at all, but his beliefs aren't something he can control. He understands why it bothered her so badly now. Until tonight he wasn't really sure how far things ever went sexually with Cris and Kali. He had only asked her once and was ultimately shot down with a quickness. Now he knows the truth—thanks to Cris. They did have sex and it was obviously consensual. That is the one thing Kali had always refused to comment on. Brian wonders if the secrecy was due to the fact that Kali isn't actually sexually attracted to Cris. And if that's the case, Cris will never stand a chance with Kali—at least not on a permanent level. Kali is entirely to sexually driven. She has the sex drive of a teenaged boy. If lesbian sex is something Kali is uncomfortable with, Brian doesn't estimate their relationship will last a month. This new 'no sex' rule of hers won't last that long either. Kali couldn't go without sex for more than a couple of weeks if she tried. Brian is shocked that she's made it this long—that is— unless she slept with someone in Destin.

No, she wouldn't have…

Even the thought of it makes Brian feel anger like he's never encountered. He typically isn't the jealous type, but the thought of someone else touching Kali makes his blood boil—especially the thought of that 'someone else' being Cris James. But Cris unlocks more than just boiling blood for Brian—she actually makes him question whether he can uphold his oath to never harm another

61

human being. She brings the crazy out of him and it's frightening. Brian is no fool, however. Cris won't last long on this straight line she's walking. As Sharon said, people like her never change. What Cris needs is a whopping dose of jealousy—and this little charade will crumble faster than Rome. She needs a little dose of her own medicine. When Cris jumped right in yesterday and asked Kali out for coffee it took everything Brian had to keep it together. But after last night, he realizes more than ever that he is willing to do whatever it takes to win her back. He is going to play this little game, and come hell or high water Cris will lose. The slight bending of the rules last night couldn't have been a more perfect mistake. At first Brian was nervous about it, but the more he considered how helpful it might become in getting rid of Cris, the more he liked the idea. Pissing Cris off is pretty much what sealed the deal. Now, he just has to convince Kali to not bite his head off when she wakes up finding him here.

"Good morning, sunshine," he whispers into Kali's ear as she begins to stir.

Kali

"Brian! Are you kidding me? What the hell happened? You aren't supposed to be here."

"I guess we fell asleep. I'm really sorry, babe."

I throw the covers back and lunge out of the bed, looking towards the second bed and making sure it was slept in. I breathe a sigh of relief when it's clear that Brian had slept separately.

"I don't even remember falling asleep. The last thing I remember was eating the pizza and turning on the T.V. It's almost as if I blacked out."

"You and me both. But with all the stress floating around it's not that unusual to finally crash and burn. I haven't slept well since you left. I was so at ease being with you that I guess I just let myself relax a little too much. Again, I am really sorry."

I can't really be upset when he's right; this was both our fault. I just don't understand how the hell I remember nothing. The stress must really be doing my head in. Either way, it's not the worst offence we could have committed. At least we didn't fuck—I think.

"Brian, we didn't—you know? Did we," I ask, needing confirmation.

"I wish."

I sigh in relief. It's not that I don't want to—I just can't. I just made this rule yesterday; breaking it less than twenty-four hours later would show the weakness I am struggling so hard to disguise. Admittedly, the thought of it is tempting—really temping. Precisely why sleepovers are forbidden. This cannot happen again.

"Thank god," I mumble.

"Really, am I that bad in bed?" he gives me that sexy look with a sideways grin.

"You know damn well you aren't bad in bed. But rules are rules."

"Yeah, yeah. So what's on the agenda for today?"

"It's going to be a busy one. In fact, you're going to need to leave soon. I have to take a shower and get dressed. I'm apartment hunting today."

I feel terrible as his face sinks, finally aware that I have no intention of returning home any time soon.

"Kali, how are you going to afford that? You know I don't have the money to pay for an apartment and our mortgage, right? I wish I could help but I can't."

"I know. And I wasn't expecting you to either, baby. It's not your place to do that. I've already made arrangements."

"Are your parents going to help out?"

"No, you know they can't afford that," I reply, avoiding the question.

"Than who?" His eyes darken as it dawns on him. "Oh..."

"It's only temporary—until I can finish school. After that I will have my own money."

"Why don't you just cut my balls off and make me feel like less of a man, Kali? I'm supposed to be the provider, but yet you're letting her rent an apartment for you? In case you've forgotten, you already have a home. It's OUR home. We have a mortgage together. This is fucking ridiculous. I really thought I could do this but now I'm not so sure. I don't even feel like a man."

"Honey, please listen to me; not being able to afford two separate households doesn't make you less of a man. You are a wonderful provider. You wouldn't even let me get a part time job because you wanted me to focus souley on school. You held it down so I could better myself. Please don't doubt that you're anything less than amazing." I take his face into my hands and kiss his cheek lightly.

He gently takes my chin between his thumb and finger, shifting my face forward.

"Please let me kiss you the right way."

I don't object. The closeness I feel with Brian is pleasingly comfortable—in more ways than one.

He begins slowly, softly pressing his lips against mine, cupping his hand around the back of my head, and stroking my hair. I fall into him, like second nature. He can be so right, always knowing exactly what I need. And I need this. I need so badly to be handled like a woman. Brian has never failed to please me, even during foreplay. He is immensely intimate and always focused on pleasuring me, even more so than himself. Sex with Brian is like a perfectly delicious mixture of Heaven and Euphoria.

My lips part as the intensity rises, welcoming him to come inside. I feel his lips pull into a sexy smirk as he slowly inserts his tongue, grazing mine agonizingly slow. Our breathing quickens and my body tenses up as I try to fight the desire away. He's teasing me.

"That's not nice," I whisper.

"It feels pretty nice to me. You want me to stop?"

I shake my head, objecting to the suggestion.

"Good." His strong hands make their way up my thigh; underneath the oversized t-shirt I wore to bed. His fingers cause electric pings to jump wildly beneath my soft bare skin. He abandons the kiss, moving his wet lips to my collarbone, gently nibbling my skin, stopping every couple of seconds to kiss my shoulder. He knows that this is THE spot, and uses it against me, forcing my body to betray my mind.

"Let me make love to you," he whispers in my ear, reaching his hand up further than my thigh this time, gripping my panties and slowly tugging them down to my ankles. He runs his tongue up the entire length of my leg, bypassing my hot spot and moving upwards to my stomach. He pulls my t-shirt up to my neck, and then takes my nipple into his fingertips, manipulating it softly at first, and then harder as he listens to my body. He is so good at reading me. He moves towards the end of the bed, getting ready to go down on me.

"You ready for the good shit, baby?" He asks breathlessly.

For a moment I'm ready to cave and give in to the desire. But this isn't right. Cris should not be entering my mind right now—but she is. Brian is about to bury his face into me all I can see is Cris and the memories of that day she went down on me on her couch. That is so fucked up—and unfair to him.

"Damn it," I sigh. "I'm sorry, Brian. We can't."

As furious as my body is going to be with me for this, I manage to pull away. I can't in good conscience lead either of them on—no matter how bad I want it. I should be furious right now that he is playing my weaknesses against me. He knows every inch of my body and what spots drive me crazy. He is playing unfair. But I can't be angry; I would fight just as hard for him if the roles were reversed.

"Brian, I'm so sorry. This is exactly why I said no overnight visits. It's too hard for both of us to resist. You know sex is my kryptonite. Don't use it against me."

He sighs, turning face down in the bed. I know that sigh; he is frustrated beyond words with me.

65

"Do you have ANY fucking idea what my balls are going to feel like a couple of minutes from now?"

"Probably just as horrible as my clit feels right now. I want it—so fucking bad—but you know we can't."

"Why not? Because of her?" He demands.

"No, because of ME. When you go down on me it reminds me of her…" the words slip out before I consider what I've just said. I opt to shut the fuck up as his face goes red and angry. I wish I hadn't said that, but he was pushing me.

"What? For how long?" He glares.

I'm cornered. I've opened my fat mouth and now he is asking questions that I know he doesn't want to hear the answers to.

"Drop it, Brian."

"No. I deserve to know. How long have you thought of her while I was going down on you and never said anything; laying there pretending to enjoy it?" He yells.

"I wasn't pretending…"

"How goddamn long, Kali?"

"Always," I whisper with my head down, bursting into tears.

The moment Brian sees that I'm crying he drops to his knees beside the bed, taking my face in his hands.

"Kali, please forgive me. I shouldn't have done that. I don't ever want to force you into talking about something that makes you uncomfortable. I know you have a past with her—a sorted one at that—I won't ever demand that you tell me anything about what happened all those years ago again. I know it's hard on you."

I wipe my eyes and pretend none of this just happened. Brian should not feel guilty at all about his reaction. But I don't want to talk about it anymore so I just shift the subject quickly.

"I'm going to jump in the shower and cool off a bit, you should start getting ready for work. I will see you when I get out."

"Alright."

I need this shower to be long and hot, the bed has left me stiff and achy all over. This motel is worse than I imagined it would be. I'm surprised I was able to fall asleep at all. I must have been really out of it because I still don't remember a damn thing. I really hope I am able to find an apartment today. The thought of staying here for any extended length of time is not appealing whatsoever. In fact, I might end up going into Lincoln this afternoon to try and find better accommodations until I find my new place. This is intolerable.

As I rinse my hair I am absolutely frightened as I run my fingers through and feel something there—crawling. An ear-piercing scream bolts out of my mouth as I run from the shower, slinging my head side-to-side to try and shake it out—whatever it is. Brian busts through the door.

"What is it?"

"I don't know, I don't know. A bug or something. Get it off!"

I wrap my body in a towel after inspecting it for creepers while Brian picks through my hair.

"I don't see anything. Whatever it was, you shook it off."

He looks around the floor and notices the bug in the shower.

"Ah man, it was a fucking roach—in your hair," he laughs loudly.

"Kill it!" I order, finding no humor in this whatsoever.

He bundles a wad of cheap single-ply toilet paper in his hand and plucks the crispy oversized roach from the shower, throwing it in the toilet.

"Well, there goes their five star rating on hotels.com," he smirks.

"Oh shut up," I scowl, trying not to feed into his laughter, "I am so not staying here one more fucking night. I feel dirtier coming out of the shower than when I went in. Gross."

A knock at the door interrupts my rant, and I ask Brian to grab it so I can get dressed. Hopefully it's housekeeping and I can show them the roach that's still floating in the toilet.

"Brian, who is it?"

At this point I don't even care that I'm in nothing more than a towel. I walk out of the bathroom, angry and ready to demand that the staff bring a manager to the room and see this filth—hoping they will refund my money. But I see no hotel staff. Brian, who has since removed his soaked t-shirt, stands there with the door propped open, welcoming in the visitor. Cris stands at the door with a fresh steaming cup of coffee and a bag of donuts. The hurt look on her face is telling. She thinks something has happened between Brian and I. This really doesn't look good. I'm in a towel and Brian is here with his shirt off. The beds have been slept in and our pizza box and beer bottles from last night are still on the floor. This is bad—really bad.

"Cris…" I say quickly, fearing she will turn away from me. "Come in…"

"Um—no. I think I'm going to pass on that. I—I hope you enjoy your breakfast," she turns away, throwing the donuts and coffee on the floor and slamming the door behind her as she leaves the room.

The coffee busts open and leaves a huge brown pool in the middle of the room. I can't run after her in the parking lot with nothing more than a towel on, so I grab my phone and dial her immediately before she can leave. Brian ignores the entire scene and throws his damp shirt back on. He slips into his boots on and starts lacing them as I am repeatedly sent to voicemail by Cris. I feel so horrible. But this is not what it looked like. I need her to come back in here and talk to me.

"Babe, she's already gone. Let it go," Brian says calmly.

"Let it go? She's so hurt right now. Did you see her face?"

"Yes, I saw her face. It was wonderful."

"Damn it, Brian…"

"Calm down, she'll get over it. I'm sure she'll call you back after she cools off. But I gotta go, I'm late for work," he kisses my cheek and I angrily pull back.

"I'm glad you think this is funny," I mumble.

"I don't think it's funny, baby," he kisses my nose. "I think it's fucking hilarious."

"Bye Brian," I hold the door open, as he walks out.

Cris

There hasn't been a single instance in Cris's entire life that she has felt an emotion that she simply could not identify. She's angry of course, hurt, and sad—but there is no name for what is going on deep down inside the depths of her heart right now. Usually there would be nothing in this world that would stop Cris from accepting Kali's phone calls, but right now she isn't sure what to even say to her. She doesn't want to hear Kali reveal what Cris already believes to be the truth—that Brian spent the night and they had a sweet little date with pizza and drinks, and then somehow they ended up fucking. In Cris's mind that's bad enough, but even worse than that is the thought of Brian 'making love' to Kali. Soft, romantic and gentle—all the things Cris has never had the chance to give Kali yet. The thought makes her ache to kill him. Literally kill him—just like she wanted to kill Danny all those times she watched him sweating like a disgusting pig on top of Kali.

"I just can't," she says, irritated that she herself used the very words she made fun of Kali for using yesterday on their date. If nothing else, the memory makes her smile a little. Still, she can't erase the image of Kali coming out of that bathroom undressed and seeing Brian standing there with no shirt on. Cris isn't stupid. The whole 'it's not what it looks like' bullshit only happens in the movies. It **is** what it looked like—and she's absolutely crushed. She respected Kali. She followed the rules she was given. But not Brian. Brian's a cop. Brian's a leader. He doesn't have to follow anyone's rules, because he's a **man**—and no woman tells a man what to do. Cris's male chauvinistic opinion of Brian isn't helping to settle the rolling waves of nausea that keep hitting her in the stomach when the images of his smug face keeping creeping back into her mind. Kali deserves so much better than him. She deserves an equal partner, not a father who feels the need to dictate every move she makes. Kali deserves to speak on her own behalf. With that said, Cris knows it's not her place to make assumptions regarding what she saw this morning. Kali called her repeatedly and wanted to explain, but Cris took that right away from her when she blanked her phone calls. That makes her no better than Brian. Though, her reasons were very different than Brian's. When Cris walked out of that room she absolutely lost it for the first time in six years. She lost control of her own actions. Today was the first time she has had to use her breathing techniques in years. Even with the assistance of breathing, she blanked out. It wasn't for long, but it was definitely enough to frighten the fuck out of her. This cannot start happening again. This is not what she promised Kali when she returned. She has to be stronger than that. For herself and for Kali.

"Face the music, even when you don't like the song," her new psychiatrist's words of wisdom come back to her. And he couldn't be more correct. It is time to face the music. She can't change the station and she can't fast forward. The only way she will properly deal with her problems and be normal is to face everything head on. No more fuck ups, no more blackouts and certainly no more mishaps like what happened this morning. She promised Kali a new person, and she has to deliver or she will lose her forever this time.

She turns the car around, heading back to the motel. When she reaches the parking lot she sees that Brian's car is still there. Instead of further escalating the situation, she keeps on going in the opposite direction. She will just leave Kali a message and they can meet up later to talk. When she dials out it's Kali who sends her straight to voicemail this time, which ultimately peaks her interest. The thoughts going through her head are distracting from what she is trying to do here. People only dodge calls when they're sleeping, screwing, or angry. Kali certainly isn't sleeping right now. The other options suck. Cris ignores her own screeching mind and leaves her a message, hoping she is wrong about why Kali didn't answer.

"Kal, it's me. Um—I wanted to apologize for putting you in voicemail. I just kinda' lost it for a second. A message is no real place to discuss this, but I'm supposed to talk about my feelings as they happen—doctor's orders—so I have to be honest with you about something. I blacked out for a second in the parking lot, but don't freak out. I came right back. I'm so much better than I used to be. I'm telling you because I didn't want you to think I was running away like I used to. I just needed to cool off for a minute. I'm here if you want to talk later. I was going to come back to the motel but I saw that you still had company. And…that's none of my business, I know. As for the coffee I threw on the floor, I am giving my information to the manager of the hotel and having them bill me for

70

the cleaning—as if it weren't already vile to begin with. I'm still available if you want to go find an apartment. I don't want you staying there any longer than you have to—it's in the slums. Um— anyway, just call me back when you're done doing whatever you're doing. I'm rambling, aren't I? Talk to you later."

She sits in a parking lot across the street—waiting for Kali to call back. Hopefully she will still want to go apartment shopping. Cris was really looking forward to spending some time with her. They could be scrubbing floors together and Cris would still be happy. I suppose some things never change.

Kali

"Cris wouldn't have fucking done that, Brian. She's not stupid. You are crossing the line here. You know this is a skanky hotel with no security, and we are in the druggie zone. You're wrong about her," I angrily shout.

As Brian left for work I began cramming my few things inside a duffle bag so I could check out of this dump. In a matter of moments he busted back in, yelling something about Cris slashing his tires—which is total bullshit. Any other time he would have recognized the fact that we are in the shittiest part of Humboldt and that it was more than likely teens or druggies acting a fool. But not this time—no—this time he pointed his finger directly at her.

"So you expect me to believe that my tires just happened to get slashed right after Cris nearly hit me with a cup of scalding hot coffee, and went storming out of here? Open your eyes, Kali. You won't even consider that she was the one who did it. You always protect her," he sneers.

"Because she didn't do it. I know her. And you're exaggerating too; that coffee landed no where near you."

"Yeah, I don't need a reminder every fucking moment of the fact that you **know** her better than anyone knows her. Of course you do, she's a freak who never left her dungeon until now. All she wants to do is come back and fuck everyone's life up. I'm sorry if you don't like it, but I'm filing a report."

"You have no goddamn proof."

"Technically, I don't need proof to file a report. All I need is probable…"

"Don't you feed me this bullshit. I know the fucking law. You're crossing the line. You don't have a single shred of evidence that she had anything to do with this. You're making this personal, which is illegal and morally disgusting."

He shakes his head, arrogantly. He doesn't give a flying fuck about morality. This **is** personal and he isn't denying it. He simply doesn't care.

"Okay, Kal, let's say she didn't slash my tires, I still have cause to file a report. She damaged hotel property. If they happen to press charges I won't be complaining. And I will give a witness statement."

His cocky attitude is really starting to infuriate me. He is looking for a reason—any reason at all—to throw Cris in jail. And it pisses me off to no end that he would use such unsavory tactics to try and win. If he thinks throwing Cris in the pen is going to increase his chances of getting me back he has another thing coming. The only thing he is accomplishing right now is pushing me away, and showing me who he really is when things don't go HIS way. It's not very becoming on him. He can threaten to abuse his power all he likes, but I'm not going to just sit back and take it.

"Fine. Waste your time convincing them to file a report. But keep in mind that this little game of yours won't end in your favor. If they go after Cris I will have the health department shut them down for unsanitary conditions. Now, you can call a friend for a ride, or a cab for all I care. I'm finished with this conversation and you need to leave before I say something I will hate myself for later."

"Why do you want me gone so bad all of the sudden when you practically begged me to come here last night? Let me guess, you're done with me for now and you're dying to call your pathetic little puppy dog back here and lick her wounds for her? Fine."

"Fine."

"Last thing, Kali, I can't charge Cris for what happened with my tires, but I will be watching every move she makes. And if she comes near my property again, I will arrest her so fast your head will spin."

"Noted. Get out."

Feeling any degree of sympathy for Brian is growing harder minute-by-minute. I understand that he's upset about his tires, but he can't just go around accusing Cris of every bad thing that happens to him. She was literally here for less than a minute. She bolted. There is no way she did this. She would never risk getting in trouble with the law so soon after she was released. Plus, she is different now. I can see it. I only wish Brian could be fair enough to see it too.

I put Cris in voicemail while Brian and I were fussing, I sure as hell didn't want to add fuel to the fire. She left a message, but I want to catch her before she goes out of reach again so I don't even listen to the message, I just call her back directly.

"Hello," she answers quietly.

"No 'hey babe'? Just hello?" I ask, trying to sense her mood.

She sighs, remaining quiet for a moment searching for words. She is very angry—or just very upset. Either way, I think I've made the shit list.

"Sorry BABE, I am not going to lie, I'm kind of—upset. Well actually, I'm more than kind of upset. I'm really upset," she sarcastically replies.

"And I totally understand why. But can you please just hear me out? Come get me. I'm dressed and ready for you."

"Well, I'm glad you're dressed..." she sasses. "Is officer ass-hat gone now?"

"Yes, the ass-hat has left the building—thank God. But for your information, I didn't sleep with him. You have my word."

"I'm at your door," she says dryly.

"How can you be here so fast?"

"I was across the street waiting for him to dip. Why is his car still here?"

"You were spying? That's naughty," I tease, though I can tell she's in no mood for humor. "His car is still here because it was having—issues," I omit the story, in no mood to revisit that conversation.

"Oh. And by the way, I was **waiting**—not spying. Big difference. But if you prefer the old me..." she begins.

"No, no, no. That's okay," I hang up, opening the door for her. She is still smiling.

"You sure about that?" She grabs the back of my head, pulling me into a deliciously deep kiss. "You know you're still mine, right?" she asks breathlessly. "No matter what happened with Brian last night, I just can't stay mad at you. It's like cutting off my oxygen."

"This side of you is still my favorite kind of poison," I whisper, as my own breathing is more of a pant than actual breaths. I miss this—I miss her intensity. That certainly hasn't changed.

"Good," she backs away gently. "We should probably step back from each other a little bit before we end up breaking rule number one—I really want to be a good girl. So, let's stop all this

74

kissing nonsense and talk about why the fuck Brian was here this morning half dressed," she frowns.

"Good idea, we should talk about it because it's not what you think. Let's get out of this shit hole. I'm groggy, sore and starving. Those donuts on the dirty floor are even starting to look good at this point."

She scowls at the thought, shaking her head briskly.

"God no. We don't do eat off the floor young lady. You're making my OCD go off just thinking about it. How about I buy my Queen some lunch?"

"Not arguing."

"Arguing with what, exactly? Being my Queen or me buying you lunch?" She lifts an eyebrow.

"At this point, neither," I kiss her, softly this time; enjoying the thump I've stirred in her chest.

"You drive me fucking crazy, Kali James."

"I'm still Kali Ness."

"Come on baby, you have to admit it, Kali James sounds so much better."

"Perhaps so."

***

"Seriously, you chose this place for lunch? The food sucks," I say plainly. "Plus, they were rude to you last time when you showed up looking for a job the night you got out of the hospital."

"It's more of a statement, really. I want them to know you're with me—even if it is only for the day," she smirks.

"But seriously, they refused you a job and their enchiladas blow. I swore I would never come back here."

"I'll order for you—something that won't suck. Trust me," she promises.

"Okay, order for me then. But don't say I didn't warn you."

The waitress approaches, recognizing us both from last week when Brian caused a huge scene. She doesn't say anything, but it's clear she's uncomfortable, as she refuses to make direct eye contact. I wouldn't call her rude, but ashamed of baring witness our previous experience here.

75

"I'm not going to bite you. What's your name?" Cris asks pleasantly, causing the waitress look up and smile a bit.

"My name is Abby. Can I get you two something to drink?" she relaxes slightly.

"Absolutely, but let me go ahead and inform you that I am a chef, which means I'm picky—and annoying to servers. I'm very specific, but I tip really well so I'm worth the trouble. You like money, right?"

"That's why I'm here," she warms up.

"Good. I have lots of it. So, we will start with a pitcher filled with ice but no liquids; top shelf liquor on the side—six ounces—Patron only. Five limes uncut, three ounces of Triple Sec, three of sour mix, and five ounces of strawberry puree, all on the side. Heavily salted chilled mugs, and a shaker. Are you following?" Cris asks confidently, as the waitress frantically writes all the items down on a small white note pad.

"Absolutely. I think I've got it."

"Sweet. If not I will just remind you. I'm not a difficult customer—just particular. We will give you a moment to recover and then order. That will be even worse," Cris laughs. "It seems my beautiful lady is unimpressed with your cuisine. I will have a special request for the chef."

"I will be the first to admit that I leave work and pick up McDonalds. I hear you loud and clear. " Abby quickly makes her way to the bar, and we immediately begin getting shitty looks from the bartender.

"I think the bartender hates us," I giggle.

"He'll live."

"What is all that crap you ordered anyway? I'm baffled."

"Really, Kal? Margarita's."

"I don't like them from here. They're too sweet."

"Yeah, babe. I know. That's why I ordered everything I need to make our own. Good ones."

"Show off."

"I'm trying to impress my future wife. Is that bad?"

"No, not at all," I blush.

After the insanely amazing Margaritas Cris handmade for us, she gives a mile long list of specific instructions to Abby, which seems amused and takes it in stride, repeating back our order.

"So, you would like the chef to prepare two steaks, Philadelphia style, with fresh grilled onions, peppers, and mushrooms with adobo sauce. Anything else?"

"Tortillas, sour cream, guacamole, salsa fresco, and the typical veg, like lettuce and tomato," Cris adds.

"Can I sit and eat with you guys?" she jokes.

"Absolutely, the more the merrier. In fact, before you put in our order, grab me a to-go cup. I want you to try something," Cris says cheerfully as I sit back, amazed at how charming Cris can actually be when she lets her guard down. I like it.

Abby returns and Cris pours a generous amount of our Margarita pitcher into the to-go cup. "Go take a break. After you drink it chew on a wad of cilantro—it's a natural breath cleanser. They will never smell it on you."

"Seriously? " She smiles, looking around for a manager before accepting the cup.

"Go for it. We are in no hurry. Grab a cigarette, and have a decent drink on us."

Whatever idea she had about Cris when we came in has disappeared. It's nice to see someone else enjoying her company and letting go of everything from the past. Abby seems like a good person—very down to earth and open-minded. These are the kinds of people Cris needs in her life.

"You two are the most fucking awesome customers ever! Shit, I said 'fucking'. And now I said 'shit'. Damn it…"

I laugh loudly at the silly girl. I wonder how awful the customers are to her here in this asshole town. She seems so happy with us. Cris's generosity makes me look at her in a different light. I knew I loved her for a reason.

"Are you sure, y'all? Do you need anything first?" She confirms before heading off.

"You're good, dude. Go do your thing. I'm busy looking at this pretty lady anyway. Food can wait," Cris takes my hand, looking into my eyes and ignoring everything else in the room while Abby bounces off excitedly, cup in hand.

"Okay, I'm impressed. You just made that girl's day. You are so—different. You are fun and easy going and you're letting people in. I'm so proud of you, Cris. Doesn't it feel good?"

"What?"

"Knowing that Abby is going to have a better day because of you."

She contemplates for a moment recognizing her own behavior for a change. "It does, actually," she blushes.

After about twenty minutes Abby has to return to the table to ask Cris what a Philadelphia style steak is, which I learn is a steak that has been seared heavily by the grill, yet remains rare in the center. Whatever the fuck it is, it was so worth the special request. The meat was cooked perfectly and the accompaniments are on point. I have a small amount of pride as the manager approaches the table, greeting Cris in an entirely different manner this time around.

"How is everything tonight?" She asks, staring at Cris.

"Perfect, thank you," she responds with a full mouth.

"I don't want to interrupt your dinner, but I would like to reconsider your employment application."

Cris smiles at me and waves a tipsy smirking Abby away from the table, as to not involve her in this awkward conversation.

"I'm sorry, I have already found another position. But I would be glad to lend some advice to the chef any time. Thanks, but no thanks."

"What if we offered you twice your current salary?" She counters.

Cris stops eating and looks seriously at the manager, who is clearly regretting her decision. "I tried to politely decline, so that I wouldn't be forced into informing you of why I would never work for you. As for money, it wouldn't matter if you offered me six figures. Your establishment is crude and unwelcoming. The only thing you have going for you is Abby. I wouldn't work here if I was starving and eating baked beans from a can every night to stay alive. So again, thanks, but no thanks."

"I understand," the manager walks away with her tail tucked.

"Cris!" I gasp.

"What? They are rude here. They can crash and burn for all I care. The only person here worth saving is our waitress. And she won't have to work for a while after the tip I leave her. It's called karma. And karma is a horrible little bitch. That is all."

"Fair enough," I shrug, enjoying Cris's small victory.

Cris pays the tab and we walk out to the parking lot. She opens the door for me as I lean against the car, enjoying the afternoon sun. Abby runs out to the parking lot, stopping us.

"Cristina James. That's what it said on the receipt," she says frantically.

"That's me," Cris replies nonchalantly."

"I think you made a mistake on the tip. I wanted to catch you before you left."

"There is no mistake," she winks, and closes me in the car.

As we leave the parking lot I see Abby crying in the distance.

"Cris, please tell me you tipped her well… she's crying. We ran her to death tonight. Don't blame her for the manager's bad karma," I say firmly.

"I didn't."

"Why is she crying then?"

"Because I left her ten-thousand dollars."

My eyes have widened to the size of volleyballs. She can't be serious…

"Wow, Cris."

"What?" She smiles.

"You are without a doubt the most beautiful person I have ever met. I absolutely adore you."

"I adore you more, Mrs. James," she says.

"I must to admit, that is starting to sound nice," I smile.

4
Breaking the Habit

Kali

After lunch Cris and I look at a minimum of four apartment complexes; most of which are only striking me as 'okay'. I'm perfectly content with 'okay' but Cris is entirely more persnickety than I am—of course. Nothing has quite met her standards yet.

"It's your choice, Kal. I just think that these are a little too far away from your school. Not to mention, the kitchens are way too small and there haven't been any units with garden tubs available until next month. You know how much you love your baths."

"I know, but honestly I just need somewhere to lay my head at night and a place to shower where roaches won't drop into my hair from the ceiling."

"Eew—what?"

"Okay, last night Brian came over, just to watch some T.V. and have a pizza. We ended up completely crashing out—sleeping. When I woke up I was irritated that he slept over and broke a rule, but it was an accident so I said fuck it and moved on. I went to take a shower because my body hurt so badly from that stiff bed. While I was washing my hair I felt a bug crawling through my hair. I flipped out. Brian came in and killed it. That's why he was shirtless; he took it off because it was wet from the roach drama in the bathroom. We were not having sex or having playtime in the shower. I know what it looked like, but I'm telling you that's not what happened. We honestly just fell asleep."

Cris gives me a suspicious look and sighs slightly.

"I thought part of your schooling was training you on how to spot the truth from bullshit," she says with a hint of arrogance.

"I don't know what you mean by that, but I am assuming you are saying that I should know how to lie better since I'm learning about it in school. You don't believe me..."

"Oh, I believe **YOU**."

"What is that supposed to mean, Cris?" I cross my arms defensively. "Brian fell asleep too. He works long shifts and he gets tired just like any other person. We were sitting together on the bed eating pizza and watching Forensic Files. That's the last thing I remember. We both zonked out. End of story. Sorry if you aren't buying it, but I've got nothing to sell you other than the truth."

"Kali, I already said I believe you."

"Well, you keep emphasizing the **YOU** part. You are clearly unconvinced of something."

"You're right, I am. I find it hard to believe that you and Brian both passed out accidentally. The covers were wrecked on both of the beds."

"Yeah, even more proof that we didn't do anything."

"More like proof that you fell asleep and HE didn't. He stayed deliberately; otherwise he would have 'accidentally' fallen asleep in the same bed that you two were watching TV on. Plus, when I got there he was only wearing boxers. Did his jeans get wet in the bathroom too?"

I stop and think for a moment. She is completely fucking right. He woke up that way, in a t-shirt and boxers. When we were eating he had flat out refused to take his shoes off because of the nasty carpet in the room. If he had really just fallen asleep along with me, he still would have been dressed and had his shoes on. Motherfucker. As much as I hate to admit it, she's right on this. How could I have overlooked something so blatant? I feel like an idiot, and worse yet, Brian lied straight to my face. This makes me wonder something else, something I hadn't thought of until now.

"Speaking of odd. How did you know where I was? I never mentioned where I was staying. Were you watching me again?" I accuse her, feeling betrayal creeping up on me from both ends.

"Um—no," Cris looks baffled. "You're the one who texted me and said you were ready for me to come get you. So I grabbed some breakfast from work and headed right over. You gave me your room number and everything."

"No I didn't," I argue back, defensively. "If you are trying to mess with my head it's not happening again, Cris. I never texted you. Tell me how you knew where I was—the truth this time."

You know what? I am doing my best to be upfront and honest with you about everything, including the fact that I blanked out this morning in the parking lot. If I will admit that, why would I not admit to this? Even if I had been looking for you, it wouldn't have been that difficult considering there are literally two motels in town… Just saying."

Either she's a really great liar or she's telling the truth. But there is one very easy way to figure it out for myself. I open the text messages in my phone, going back into the last conversation that Cris and I had.

"The last text I sent you was to meet me at the bar when I got home. Look for yourself. There is no text asking you to come to the hotel."

She doesn't even bother to look; she only counters me by opening her own messages and putting it directly in front of my face.

"See for yourself. This message came from YOUR number. Sorry, baby. It looks like we got punked."

She's right. I can't deny what I see with my own eyes. I remember looking at the clock right before I went into the shower, because I told Brian he was going to be late for work. It was exactly, 9:56 a.m. when I went into the restroom. The text was received by Cris at 10:02 a.m. Brian sent it. And then deleted it. He fucking set it up to have Cris stumble into a scene where I wasn't dressed and he was standing there with no shirt on. It was all a ploy to try and one-up Cris. I am livid right now—absolutely livid.

"Wow," is all I can muster.

"Well, what can you say? That's what you get when you're in a relationship with a kid. He is of legal age right?" She laughs, as if it's a joke, but I know she's serious.

"Oh shut up, he's twenty-four. Twenty-four going on thirteen," I sulk. "I should call his ass right now and give him a piece of my mind."

Cris shakes her head adamantly. "Not on my watch. This is my time-slot remember? Plus, give the kid a break; it was actually a pretty ingenious plan. Props. He wants you back and he's trying with everything he has. Even I can't blame him for that. But don't be shocked if I have to play a little harder to get back in that game. I want you just as badly—probably more. After that little stunt he pulled this morning, the gloves are off."

"I didn't hear that. You two keep your petty games to yourself. If you want to act like children I will simply disappear and leave you two on a play-date. I'm not going to be referee or mommy to either of you. Keep it clean and keep it fair. That's the only time I'm going to say it."

"Yes ma'am."

"Cris, there is one more thing about this morning I wanted to talk about. You said you blacked out in the parking lot. What happened there? Is that still happening frequently?"

"Didn't you get my message?"

"No, I just called you back instead. I don't typically listen to my messages. I'm lazy like that."

"Alright. I'll keep that in mind next time I leave a five hour-long voicemail. Anyway, no, it was the first blackout I've had in years. I was so upset. It just happened. But I came right back out of it. I'm doing a lot better now."

"That's great Cris. Again, I am so proud of how far you've come."

"Me too, but I can't let those things start creeping back up on me. If I'm faced with a situation like that, it's better for me to stay and talk it out."

"Absolutely. As I told you six years ago, I will help you."

"I know you will, baby. Now then," she moves on from the conversation and pulls into another apartment complex, "this is our last viewing of the day. It's walking distance to your school. That's an automatic plus. And it's gated access—even better. This might just be the one," she grins.

I smile back at her, but my mind isn't into this viewing right now. As proud of her as I am, I still know that when she has these blackouts she does things—sometimes bad things. I really hope she had nothing to do with Brian's tires being slashed this morning. I know she would never do that under normal circumstances, but what if she did it during a blackout? I don't even want to confront her about it because I don't want her to feel like her progress is unseen or unappreciated. However, I am going to have to keep a close eye on her. The fact that this is the only one she's had in years is very reassuring. I'm still convinced it wasn't her. In that area of town it really could have been anyone. And I should be shot for thinking this way; but if she did flip out because of what Brian pulled on us this morning and end up blacking out and doing this, than he deserved his tires to be slashed. I'm going to keep quiet on this with both of them. I won't tell Brian that I know what he schemed up this morning, and I won't tell Cris about Brian's tires. I'm calling an eye for an eye situation on this one. That's the best I can do.

Cris walks inside the apartment's management clubhouse, quickly returning with keys swinging around her finger.

"Keys?" I ask curiously.

"The manager was busy with another couple so she just went ahead just gave us the keys to view it ourselves."

"They do that?"

"I guess so. I had to leave my license to ensure that we returned the keys. You ready? This is the last one, I hope it's a little more acceptable."

"I hope so too. I'm beat."

During the walk through I notice the fine details of this apartment compared to the others. The kitchen is larger by at least a hundred square feet, with beautiful hand crafted butcher-block countertops. An oversized basin sink with a separate food washing station is a fantastic addition to the more standard apartment kitchen. The backsplash is created of distressed copper. It's not something I ever would have chosen off a sales shelf but it's actually beautiful and gives a charming and fashionable feel to the entire kitchen. Cris is smiling widely; she's in heaven.

"Someone likes this kitchen," I tease, "You're kinda drooling, Cris."

"It's definitely my style. But the question is; is it yours?"

"I adore it. But I am not renting a place based on a kitchen that I'll hardly ever use."

"But you love to cook," Cris reminds me.

"I do, but now that I've had your cooking mine doesn't seem quite as delectable. It's like comparing a burger to a filet mignon."

She wraps her arms around my waist and kisses my nose, "I could always give you some private lessons. You can pay me in kisses or something."

"Deal," I lay quick and simple peck right on her warm lips.

"Shit…that kind of kiss wouldn't even get you a meatloaf recipe. But it's a start, I suppose."

We browse the rest of the apartment and find all the amenities that were on my basic list of wants and needs.

"I really like this one. It's close to school; there is a balcony so I can smoke outside—just in case I don't quit right away. Garden tub, walk in closet, spare bedroom, formal dining room and an office where I can do my homework—it's perfect. If I were to choose this place would this be the exact unit I get? I assume this is a model apartment since it's furnished with all this beautiful furniture."

"Well…actually…" Cris blushes. "I kinda knew you would like this one. After you agreed to let me help you find a place I went ahead and got a head start on my search yesterday. I scouted it after we left the coffee shop—you know I like to do my research."

"Get to the point, sneaky snake," I lift an eyebrow.

"Well, I kinda already signed the lease. And I had it furnished. And the utilities are all turned on. Everything in here is yours."

As with most—if not all—times Cris has decided to do something—this is completely over the top. I don't know if I should be angry or grateful. I'm definitely excited, but how can one person pull off something so huge in a matter of hours?

"You did all of this in one afternoon? It hasn't even been twenty-four hours since I agreed to let you get me a place."

"What can I say? Money talks. I didn't want you having to shack up in a hotel too long. Are you mad?" She squints.

"Um—I should be. You should have talked to me first. However, I would have chosen it anyway. So you're off the hook," I shrug happily.

"Yay!" She cheers.

"So the manager wasn't really too busy to show us the apartment?"

"No ma'am. These belong to you," she hands me the keys and I jump excitedly into her arms.

"You are simply amazing, Cris. And overbearing, sexy, thoughtful, and just absolutely insane!"

"I guess that's what love does to me."

The afternoon flies by. After she and I rearrange the furniture to my liking Cris looks totally beat.

"You're tired, huh?"

"Yes Ma'am, it's been a very busy few days. Working miracles can really wear you out," she smirks.

Her phone rings and she excuses herself to the balcony while I lie down on the couch for a moment. When she returns she seems rushed.

"Everything alright?"

"Yeah, something has come up. I gotta go. But I'll call you later."

"Okay."

"Here, take this and go load up with groceries. The fridge is empty," Cris hands off her credit card.

I feel like I am taking advantage. Of course I know she has plenty to spare, but still, I can't shake the freeloader feeling away. She is already sensing my reluctance as her eyes begin rolling in her head.

"Kali, don't start. Just get some food. Maybe I can give you that cooking lesson tonight."

This is just like Cris. She makes it into an offer that will benefit us both so I won't feel guilty. She's clever, but I see right though her intent. Be that as it may, denying her company is something I wouldn't dream of doing tonight. And not because of all she's done, but because getting to know her over the last couple of days has been interesting and fun. With Brian it's as if we are going backwards. The more I learn about this new attitude and the sneaky behavior he's been up to, the more I forget about the good things we used to share. Pressure and competition does not bring out his good side. This is honestly the first time I can say that I am turned off by him. His young age is radiating brightly in this situation. That bullshit he pulled this morning is absolutely unacceptable and immature. At least Cris is an admitted manipulator—and even she has her limits. Company with a person of likened age would be great tonight.

"So a cooking lesson, aye? Alright… I'm down."

Her eyes sparkle in excitement. I like this look on her, she's so happy—so different from the reserved and inverted person I used to know. If I could just have this side of her, and she could still maintain that intense and kinky naughtiness on the inside, it would be a perfect balance. Though, I know I can't have my cake and eat it too. I wanted her to get better, and she seems to have accomplished that. I'm proud of her. But I would be fibbing if I didn't admit that I miss the old her just a little bit.

"It's a date. I will see your hot ass later," she smirks, kissing me goodbye.

As she leaves I wonder for a moment how it would feel to be intimate with her again. Maybe, if things go well, we can give it a shot. Of course sex is forbidden, but I never said we couldn't fool around. I need to see if that intensity still lies underneath her creamy white skin. I'm willing to bet she's still in there somewhere.

***

At the market I hit a brick wall. What kind of food does a plain-o like myself buy for a chef? I imagine it would have to be nothing processed, nothing frozen, and nothing pre-made. That narrows my options substantially and leaves me staring blankly at the shelves for nearly an hour. I suppose the first place to start would be the meat options—which are plentiful. I recall the Kraken I ate in Destin with Bridge, and steer clear of anything outside of the norm. There are some scary choices here in the meat case; such as beef tongue, which looks vile and caught my eye with its putrid greenish-pink color. Worse yet, the fucking taste buds are still attached. Who the fuck eats shit like this? And pig feet too? Dear god, I thought grocery stores would have reduced the need for primitive eating. I could understand eating these things out of survival—but to willing choose and pay for this monstrosity of disgustingness—no way. Chicken, beef, or pork it is. Since we had steak at the Mexican restaurant earlier I go with the chicken. I snatch up all the fresh produce and herbs I can find, as well as seasonings and spices.

I also get my own typical munchies for the rest of the week, loading up with the junk I'll be eating in between meals when Cris isn't around to coach me. My typical food fare is ramen noodles, chips and dip, roasted peanuts, veggies and ranch, and a handful of frozen pizzas. Cris won't love these choices, but these are the things I have time for during my typically busy schedule, which resumes tomorrow. The vacation is coming to a close quickly and it's balls to the wall again. From what I hear, professor Denali is going hard on us this upcoming week, though he won't reveal the assignment until class tomorrow. I'm excited and worried that he is going to work the hell out of us. Usually I live for deadlines; it keeps me focused, but currently my focus is on Cris and Brian. I wanted to squeeze as much time in with them as possible before I went back to my hardcore routine.

That's why I hated that Cris had to go so suddenly earlier. I wasn't ready for her to go. It was probably the coffee shop calling her in for work early. Her schedule usually has her working in the wee hours of the morning, but maybe they were short staffed. Perhaps I will pop in for a latte on the way back from the grocery store and surprise her. She would like that. I just can't seem to break away from her. I think I've caught the sickness.

Three hundred guilty bucks later, my car is fully bogged down with food and several other items such as candles and air fresheners—things that I love in my space. I'm actually pretty excited. This is my very own place alone—ever. It might be fun. I can do whatever I want. That might sound childish, but it's new to me and I like it.

I don't see Cris's car at the coffee shop but I know sometimes she walks there so I go in anyway and order a white chocolate latte. I try to peek around the counter to see if she's in the back but I can't really see much from here. The barista sees me looking and curiously waits for me to speak.

"Hey, is Cris working?" I ask quietly, afraid of getting Cris into trouble for having visitors.

The young and very polite and flamboyant male barista replies with a smile, "Oh no, honey, she won't come in until 2:00 a.m. I'll be tucked away in my jammies by then."

"Those hours suck," I reply.

"Girl I know that's right. You couldn't pay me to work a pastry chef's hours. I would just hang myself if I had to be up that late. Bags under the eyes are a no-no for this boy. Uh-uh."

After hearing this young man speak I can tell we have a kindred in the coffee house. He is definitely gay. Naturally, like most gay men he is beautiful and clean cut with sparkling blue eyes and perfectly highlighted blonde hair. His personality is bursting with sunshine. Just his presence alone makes you feel happy. It's odd, but true.

"Well, that's cool. I'll just take my latte to go. I have groceries in the car."

"You're Kali, aren't you?" Cris just goes on and on about you," he beams.

"Yes, I'm Kali. And your name is?"

"Lawrence. So nice to meet you," he leans over the counter hugging me as if we've known each other for years.

"Well, Lawrence, I will see you soon. If Cris happens to come in let her know I stopped by."

"Girl, you know I will. Don't you even worry. Worrying causes premature wrinkling, and we simply can't have that, now can we? I'll see your little sweet self later," he waves.

***

I'm ever grateful for a ground floor apartment, as lugging all these groceries up two flights of stairs would kill me. I easily manage to get them all in and put away exactly the way I like them. I don't know what the hell Cris is going to make with all this shit, but I'm confident it will be amazing—as long as I don't ruin it.

I skip happily to my new bathroom, setting my latte on the side of the huge garden tub and begin running water. I pour in the bubble bath that I just bought and turn on the jets. In a matter of moments I have a huge bubble mountain. I am just dying to jump in.

It's so nice to soak and relax for a while. This couldn't be any more perfect and I don't think today could have been any better. I wasn't so sure how today would turn out considering this morning's drama. Thankfully it's all worked out now and Cris knows the truth. Brian is still an issue, however. I will be waiting patiently for an apology for the way he treated me. Also, I would love to know if he ever plans on telling me that he set me up to get 'caught' with him by Cris. I won't mention it for now, as I see no point in rehashing it. But I really hope he knocks this shit off. As much as I love him, his behavior is pushing me away—fast—and right into Cris's arms. I'm nowhere near making a choice yet, but he isn't pleading his case very well, that's for damn sure.

Brian

"You should really tell her what you've done, Brian. That was a sleaze-ball move. Plus, you know she's going to find out soon enough. You're digging your own grave," Sharon lectures as she and Brian ride in the squad car, leaving the scene of a nasty accident on Hwy 12.

"Technically yes, I should tell her. But I wasn't thinking. I had just found out that Cris had come to her rescue—as always—and offered to cough up the money for Kali's new place. I was jealous. I had the perfect opportunity to piss Cris off so I took it. Not one of my best moments, but I did it just the same. And I didn't lie to Kali—I omitted."

"You sent a text from her phone and then deleted it so she wouldn't see it. That is lying and you know damned well that was a shitty thing to do, Officer McDowell," Sharon raises a disapproving eyebrow. "But hey, that's none of my business. I'm just throwing in my two cents worth."

"Nah, I appreciate your advice. You're a great friend. Just like one of the guys."

"You know, I am like one of the guys. With that said, I have to ask, did you sleep with her last night, or was it really just a ploy to get to Cris?"

"No. Almost had her, though."

"Well, maybe next time. So, what about Cris? How did she react?"

"She pitched a toddler fit and threw her coffee across the room."

"I have to tell you, though; you are really walking a fine line with Kali. Cris is getting the majority of her attention and all you're doing is pissing her off. Let me lend you some more unwanted advice; stop fighting with Kali over Cris. Work smart, hot hard."

"Yes ma'am. Smart, not hard."

Cris

She is so fucking beautiful…

Cris watches Kali as she shows off the goodies she found at the store. She doesn't have the heart to tell her that some frozen vegetables can be just as good as fresh, and at half the price. She just let's her show off her bounty with pride.

"So I don't really know how to cook these, or what they are but I thought maybe you could show me."

"Well, baby, these are actually called Fiddlehead Ferns, and they are good sautéed with some garlic and olive oil. Simple to make, and a very healthy choice. Nice. What else have you got in there?"

"Well, there are these things…" Kali holds up a bag of frozen Edemame with sea salt. "Okay, I know—they're frozen…"

"There's nothing wrong with frozen."

"Good to know. I have no fucking clue what Edemame are and I can't even pronounce the name, but I figured you could." She shrugs. "So, wow me with your mad cooking skills, Crissy Pooh. What are you teaching me to cook tonight?"

"Good god, don't ever call me that again," she shakes her head, laughing.

"Okie dokie. I will just call you shit-brick instead," Kali sasses.

"That's better than the alternative. Now then, let's see what we've got here."

Cris rises from her position on the couch, joining Kali in her beautiful new kitchen, digging around the spacious pantry and fridge. Kali is so excited; Cris could just eat her up right now. She is so in love with her. It feels so good to finally acknowledge it. Kali is wearing a white camisole that tightly hugs her breasts. It's taking everything Cris has to stop herself from staring as Kali speaks. Keeping eye contact is difficult. The only way she can distract herself is by pulling Kali by her waist and indulging in another deep passionate kiss. Kali doesn't resist, but instead presses harder against Cris.

"How about I teach you to cook another night and I can just have you for dinner?" She continues, gently sweeping Kali's hair to the side, kissing her bare collarbone.

"Don't do that. I can't take it. That's—one of **those** places. We need to be good—for now," Kali whispers, breathlessly. "But I was thinking, maybe after dinner we could fool around a little. Just no sex."

"You think I've forgotten?" Cris stops for a moment, staring deeply into Kali's eyes and biting her lower lip. "I know where **those** places are. All of them."

"Oh…my…god. Cris… please."

"You really want me to stop?" she continues, pressing her lips harder against Kali's warm skin.

"No—but yes—and no—ugh!" Kali whines.

Cris's heart is racing. Just hearing Kali's pleasure thrusts her desire into overdrive. She isn't supposed to be doing this, but she can't stop herself. Kali wants it, and she wants to please her more than anything. Still, she better not push it. Baby steps.

"Okay, baby, I'll stop," Cris turns away, filling her lungs with a heaping dose of much needed oxygen. "Yeah, so…um—we can start with the Edemame. We can snack on it as we cook. Go ahead and pop it in the microwave for 5 minutes."

"I'm getting a lesson in microwaving? I feel jipped," Kali scowls and crosses her arms jokingly.

"The bag says 'steam-ables', so steam it," Cris sasses.

"Okay," she says, popping it in the over-the-range microwave. "What now?"

"So we are going to do Chicken Kiev. Chicken breast stuffed with a flavored butter—in this case; a lemon and thyme butter. Good choice, baby. We can make the fiddlehead ferns and some roasted garlic couscous. Sound good?"

"Uh, yes. Way better than the Kraken or Beef tongue."

"Kraken? Do I even want to know?" Cris asks.

"Nope."

Kali

Cris walks me through everything, including pounding out the chicken breast, making an herb butter, and cooking the Fiddlehead Ferns, which look like something that grew right out of Alice in Wonderland's ass. Either way, we are in waiting mode right now. Apparently the butter must be frozen in order to properly incorporate for stuffing the chicken breast. But I'm not complaining. It gives us a chance to catch up and grab a glass of wine on the sofa while the butter freezes—which Cris assures me will only take a half-hour or so.

"Grab your glass and come out to the balcony. I need a cigarette, watching you cook is making me hot—literally," Cris pants.

"You're really passionate about your career, huh?" I smile; walking her outside, glad to have a cigarette myself.

"I am. I know it's not important, like a cop or anything—such as Brian. But food is important. Think about it, when you're sad you eat, when you're happy you eat, when you celebrate you eat. Food is comfort. I like to be comforting, especially for you."

She's right. I suppose I never thought of it that way. I love her passion, it replicates my own.

"I know exactly what you mean. Do you know what I am studying?"

"Law enforcement—forensics on the backside. I wasn't surprised to find out. You love forensics. What inspired you to turn it into a career?" Cris asks as she lights her cigarette.

"Finding **her** is my inspiration. And of course other criminals. But she is my main focus. She is my lifetime goal."

"She? As in Val?"

"Yeah. Her."

Cris looks away, exhaling a long stream of smoke into the warm May air. "Babe, I get it, I really get it. But it's not healthy."

"How so?"

"Going to school for years with only one goal in mind is unhealthy. I want her caught too, but where will you go after that? And more importantly, what if you never catch her?"

93

"I will. There is no 'what if' in this situation. I will. That's all."

"Do you want to hire Derek again and see if he can help?"

"No. Just me. Or…just US."

"Noted," she smirks.

A knock at the door stuns me. Nobody knows I live here yet so I wasn't expecting any visitors. Plus, having Valentina in the topic of discussion makes me edgy to begin with.

"Cris, can you get it?"

"Yeah, baby. Of course," she puts her cigarette out and walks to the door, leaving me on the balcony lost in my thoughts.

"Kal," she calls. "Brian is here to see you."

Brian? How the hell does Brian know where I live already? Oh right, he is a cop. Cops know everything…

I walk into the living room to find he and Cris standing there quietly next to each other. The two don't speak, which is nice for a change, but I am feeling the pressure like an elephant on my chest.

"Brian, what are you doing here?"

"We need to talk. Now."

Just as I'm about to ask him to come back later after Cris and I are finished with our date, he shoots daggers at Cris again. She politely remains calm, for my sake I'm sure.

"Kali, I will excuse myself to the guest bedroom, baby," Cris offers, kissing my cheek on the way through, causing Brian's eyes to roll back and his head to shake.

"Oh isn't that just fucking sweet? And Cris—you can actually stay put. Where were you this afternoon around 5:00 p.m.?"

"I don't have to answer your fucking questions, Brian. I know my rights," Cris replies.

"Why are you questioning her, Brian? What's going on?" I ask, confused.

He stands, arms crossed and angry. "Because our home was broken into this afternoon around that time. It's funny, she's released from the hospital and all of the sudden my tires are slashed in the parking lot this morning and now our home was burglarized. Where were you, Cris? The alarm company pegged it at 5:03. Where were you?"

"Bye, Brian," instead of going to the other room she leaves the apartment, food and all behind.

I am furious right now. Cris has no reason to break into the house—none. He is just grasping at straws at this point. I think he's making this shit up to make Cris look bad. I won't have it. That's taking things way too fucking far.

"It's over, Brian. Officially over. Cris was able to play by the rules, but you—every chance you get you try to implicate her in something. This is so childish, and unfair. Cris is trying to build a new life for herself and you are doing nothing but trying to destroy her. I can't do this. I'm done."

"Kali, I have proof, the alarm was set off by an intruder. Check it for yourself.

"And where were you?"

"Sharon and I were actually coming back from an accident on 12. I got a call from Briggs."

"Than why automatically blame Cris. She was with me most of the day—apartment hunting."

"Was she with you around that time?"

"Well—no. She had to run out for a little while. But I know for sure she wasn't breaking into our house."

Brian pulls his phone from his pocket; opening up a photo he took in my former master bathroom.

"What is that?" I ask.

"You see it for yourself. There is a message written on our mirror. It says 'she's mine'. Kali please, use your common sense. Who else would have done that?" Brian pleads.

"Not her," I argue, though unsure of the truth behind my own words.

"Just humor me. Call her right here, right now in front of me and ask her where she was at 5:00."

What he's asking of me is despicable. Whatever small doubts I have regarding her whereabouts are completely unfounded and unfair. I want to prove to that he is dead wrong about Cris. She's different now. If this is what it finally takes, I'll do it.

"Fine! I'll call her, but only because she would never lie to me and I am tired of you being on her back and looking for a reason to put her in jail. I'll call her now."

It rings only once.

"Kali, I'm sorry I left. I'll come back as soon as he is gone. I just can't deal with his bullshit. The only reason I haven't drop kicked him is because it's disrespectful to you. And I don't want to go back to jail."

"I understand, Cris. Just answer me this one question."

"Anything."

"Where were you this afternoon?"

After a long period of silence she finally replies. "I was at work."

I try to hide the devastation in my eyes, but Brian picks up on it instantly.

"Okay, Cris. I'll call you back."

I sit on the couch and light a cigarette; I don't give a fuck that there is no smoking allowed inside. At this point I can't even move. I know for a fact Cris is lying to me. She was not at work. I was there. What if Brian was right? No, I won't believe it.

"Are you okay?" he asks.

"Um—yeah. I am just tired," I lie.

"You shouldn't be smoking, Kali. Come on now."

"I don't need another Daddy, Brian."

"Okay, I get it. Listen, I know you're upset and I will leave in a minute so you can get some sleep. But aside from the break-in, and the tires, there is something else I think you should know."

"What now?" I sigh.

"In case you weren't already aware of it, Cris lives in the building."

"What?" I gasp.

"I put an APB out on your car earlier—I wanted to know where you were. I know it's wrong and I'm sorry. But I was worried after the incident with my tires this morning. Cris is unstable."

"What is your point, Brian?"

"I was told by a source that Cris has lived here since she was released. She purposely brought you here so she could keep you in her sights. I'm sorry to tell you, but this was all planned. She is playing you like a fiddle."

I begin sobbing—like a child who has been betrayed by the only person I trusted.

"Just get out. I don't want to see either of you again."

"Babe, I was just trying to protect you. You know I would do anything for you. I am terrified that she is going to kidnap you and run away and I will never find you."

"You're no better! I know what you did too, Brian. You set me up this morning."

His head sags but it's clear that he is holding tight to his justified reasoning.

"I admit it, I set you up. But it was only for your own good."

"Get out of my apartment! Now!" I scream.

"I'm so sorry, Kali," he says, walking out with his tail tucked, leaving me crying like the fool I am on the living room floor.

"Fuck the both of you."

5

Opportunity Knocks

Kali

"I hadn't heard from you in a bit so I was just checking in. How is my darling protégé? Bridgette asks after Kali tearfully answers her cell phone.

"Bad. Things are really bad, Bridge. I'm finished with both of them."

"Whoa, back up a bit. What happened?"

I spend the better part of two hours on the phone with Bridge, going over every little detail of what's been going on here; the apartment—the tires, the break in, and now the fact that Cris has been lying to me about work and living here in the building.

"You know, it doesn't even bother me that she lives here. It's the fact that I had to find out from Brian. It made me look like a fool. I'm just done. I've lost everything."

"Well, why are you finished with Brian? All he did was try to show you the truth that was right in front of your face. If anything, you should be thanking him."

"Hell no! What he did at the motel was underhanded and completely immature. It proves that he is too young for me. I'm smart enough to make my own conclusions regarding Cris. I don't need his interference."

"Yes, but if he hadn't interfered you wouldn't know that Cris has not reformed as she'd claimed to. She is the same psycho she's always been. She is playing with your head."

I'm not even sad that Cris has hurt me, yet again. I'm angry that I was dumb enough to trust her, no questions asked. It makes me look like a naïve idiot.

"I should have known. That's all it ever was with Cris—head games. It's so fucking hard with her. I still want to believe that she had a good reason for lying. I'm angry right now. I don't know what to do," I sigh, ready to scream.

"I have a brilliant idea," Bridge announces.

"Hopefully more brilliant than this dating game idea. It was a disaster from the start," I sneer.

"How about some distraction? A visit?"

"Oh, Bridge, I would love to…but I have school. I only had the one-week off and this passing weekend off. School is back in on Monday—tomorrow. I'm stuck here for now."

"No, dear. I was talking about me—coming there. Tomorrow."

My heart pounds with excitement at the thought. I would love to see her, and truth be told, I need a friend now more than ever.

"Yes! Yes, yes, yes!"

"Great, I shall make the arrangements. Do you have any good accommodations nearby? Preferably with a spa on-site."

"Um—no, this is Humboldt…" I nearly choke on my wine as I laugh. "You can stay with me. I have a spare bedroom," I offer.

"Hmm, alright. I will have a limousine service delivery me to your residence promptly at 7:00 p.m. Is the timing acceptable?"

"Of course, fancy lady. You're gonna stick out like a bright red thumb here."

"A lady always makes a grand entrance."

"Oh, Bridge…"

**

Night comes and goes in a blur as rising sun peers its unwelcome way through my bedroom window. I'll have to shower fast if I'm going to make it to school on time. With all this shit going on it's no surprise that I am losing hours of time here and there without recollection. Again, I don't remember falling asleep or anything in between. If this keeps up I will either have to do the impossible and erase both Brian and Cris from my mind, or otherwise start drugging myself up with anxiety medication. Seriously, my mind isn't working right, and that is a definite no-no this week. I have to concentrate on school or I'm fucked.

After getting ready I notice something odd in the kitchen. The food, all of it, has been put away in the refrigerator. Last night I was too exhausted to do it and I really didn't give a shit if it went to waste or not. Cris and I won't be cooking dinner together—ever. The thought leaves a sickly feeling in my stomach, literally. I grab my keys and race out the door, now having to make yet another stop before school. I am going to be late now—without a doubt—so I don't see what a few more minutes will matter. I'm going to that damned coffee shop. It was bad enough that I caught her in a lie last night, but now that she's taken it upon herself to enter my home and clean up for me, she will have to answer for it. I just can't let this one go. Coming into my space without permission is yet another indicator that she has not changed.

***

As I walk through the front door of the Coffee shop I see Lawrence cheerfully wave. I'm in no mood for cordial greetings, but I do my best not to take it out on him.

"Kali! It's great to see you again! Guess who's here this time?" He chimes, pointing towards the kitchen.

"Good morning, Lawrence. Can you tell Cris I am here to see her, please? It's important."

"Yes, girl. Be right back."

Cris walks out from the kitchen, covered in white powdery flour and looking tired. Her face lights up into a huge smile as she sees me standing there.

"White chocolate latte for my baby, please, Lawrence, Cris says as she walks past the counter with a goofy grin.

"Already brewing, Cris, I remembered from yesterday when she stopped by to see you and you weren't here."

Cris looks like a deer in headlights, and proceeds towards me cautiously. She knows her lie is out in the open now.

100

"Lawrence, I won't be needing that Latte after all. I just came to talk to Cris. Outside," I stare her down with a scowl.

"Kali, I have scones baking, I can't go outside right now. Can we talk about this later? I can explain," she nervously fiddles with her hair.

I keep my voice at a lowered tone as to not cause a scene, but this cannot wait.

"Explain which part, Cris? The fact that you live in the same building as I do and I had to find out from Brian of all people? Or maybe you're referring to the part where you lied to me and said you were working, all the while my house is being broken into and someone leaves a nasty message for Brian on the mirror? And Brian's tires…did you need to explain about that too?"

"Baby, hear me, please. I didn't tell you I lived there because I wanted you to feel like you had your own space. I didn't want to overcrowd you. The apartments are the nicest in town; I wanted you to have the best too. I had planned on telling you during dinner. I swear."

"No you wanted to spy on me—like always," I retort angrily.

"No, please, it's not like that at all."

"Really? Than why were you in my apartment last night while I was sleeping? Just like the old days, huh, Cris?"

She looks stunned and taken aback.

"Someone was in your apartment? Are you sure?"

"Unless all that food we laid out magically put its self away and all the dishes washed themselves, then hell yes I'm sure someone was in there. And I'm also sure that someone was you. You are the only one aside from me who had your hands on my keys."

She rolls her eyes, "I was **not** in your apartment, Kali," she becomes irritated. "And the fact that someone was in there makes me nervous. We need to get you a security alarm."

"**We** aren't doing anything. Plus, security alarms don't seem to bother intruders. Much like the one that broke into Brian's house yesterday during the time you 'claimed' you were working. Yeah, you didn't know stupid old me had come to visit you, huh? You weren't here. You straight lied to me. You broke into Brian's house, just like you slashed his tires in the parking lot yesterday morning at the motel."

"I didn't do anything to Brian's house or his car. I didn't even know about it until last night when he accused me."

"Right, Cris. You already admitted that you blacked out in the parking lot. How do you know for a fact that you didn't do it?" I challenge, raising my voice.

"Please stop yelling at me," she starts tearing up and fiddling nervously with her earlobe. "I didn't do it."

"And Brian's house? Where the fuck were you, Cris? I know you weren't working. Tell me the truth this time."

"If I told you it would make me look even worse at this point. Just let me promise you that I didn't do anything. Trust in me. Please believe me."

Watching her so upset is hard for me. I have always trusted in Cris. And she continues to prove me wrong each and every time. I can't let her do this to me anymore.

"Cris, it's over."

She falls to her knees, placing her hands over my feet.

"Don't walk away. Don't quit me, please."

"Cris you're at work. Don't do this here. Just let me go."

She grips my ankles tighter this time, refusing to let me walk out. "Kali, don't do this to me. I love you. Don't leave me. I'm begging you. I'll tell you where I was. Just don't go," she is sobbing at this point, drawing attention from not only the customers, but her managers and the staff as well. Lawrence has a look of devastation on his face as he approaches Cris, lightly pulling her hands off my ankles.

"Cris, come on, honey. Let's go to the back," Lawrence whispers.

Cris is inconsolable as Lawrence gently leads her away from me; he turns back around to wave me off and out the door while Cris's back is turned. Her whaling screeches through the swinging kitchen door, shattering my heart in to jagged angry shards of glass. The guilt is overwhelming—I should never have done this here. Cris is still obviously very sick. She needs to stay away from me. I make her worse. I can't look back. As hurt as I am, I have to keep walking.

***

"Professor Denali, I'm so sorry I'm late," I walk into class, disheveled and clumsily disrupting the class by pulling out the nosiest chair on God's green earth.

"Ten minutes...I'll forgive you," he smiles.

Professor Denali is the head of the Forensics team here at Lanier Tech. I adore his easygoing attitude and expertise. I couldn't have landed a better teacher. But even his bright demeanor does little for my mood.

"We are discussing fingerprints today, Kali. I was going over the value of the human fingerprint. The technical aspects will come later, where you will learn to identify certain trademarks of an individual person's fingerprints. Yes, we have machines to do that for us now, but back in my day, The Jurassic Era, we had forensic technicians who were specially trained to identify 'markers'. These markers are what separate your fingerprint from that of your mother, son, father, etc. No one person in existence has identical markers, and this includes identical twins."

"Professor Denali, I've heard of people who burned their fingerprints off, or even cut them off to avoid being caught. Is this myth or is it really an effective way of avoiding identification?" Jesse Donovan, a twenty-something kid asks.

"I suppose it depends on how you look at it, Jesse. Think of fingerprint evidence as if it were only one tiny piece in a much larger puzzle containing millions of pieces. Years ago, the big puzzle had a lot fewer pieces, so fingerprints were your main go-to for identifying a suspect. Fingerprint evidence was about the best you could have in a crime scene—then. Now, with modern technology, there are many other ways of identifying a person—including DNA. Removing your fingerprints does not ensure that you'll leave no trace evidence and DNA behind. You can accomplish the same thing by wearing a standard everyday pair of latex gloves, as opposed to burning your fingerprints off, and with substantially less pain involved. DNA is our major identity tracker in this day and age. Though, fingerprints remain important to crime scene analysis as well."

"Ah, got cha'," Jesse replies.

"So, with that said, this week we are going to be focusing on proper collection and analysis of crime scene evidence. We will be using the evidence you collect to identify the 'Perp'. Our science team has seen to it that the evidence you need to solve your crime is all here in the scene and in the system for comparison, should you find it. We are splitting into groups of two, meaning there will be five groups total. There are five different mock crime scene rooms we have created for you. It will be one group per room to ensure the scene remains untainted by too many people—also another very important key in evidence collection. Pick your partner and go over your strategy so tomorrow you can begin the treasure hunt. You will have to identify the means of death/and or crime, time, method, and probable suspects based on the evidence you find in the rooms. You will each be allowed unlimited access to the lab for the week, and also have full privileges for testing equipment, as long as you passed the equipment functionality and safety class from the beginning of the semester—which all of you have. I will need a report on Friday containing all the evidence you've found as well as your pick on the Perp. Good luck and have fun with it—this is a huge part of your grade. So go ahead and partner up, it's my coffee time," he winks.

Professor Denali takes a seat at his desk and pulls out a news paper and a cup of coffee, which came from none other than Cris's coffee shop… Damn it, I can't think about her right now. This is a huge assignment and I really need to focus. Knowing what a huge week this is going to be, I'm not so sure that this is the greatest time for Bridge to visit. I look at the clock and it's too late to cancel now. I will just have to do my best with it.

"Do you have a partner yet?" Jesse asks. "I know you're the best in class and I don't want to get stuck with one of these kids who aren't taking it seriously and end up doing all the work myself."

"I hear you on that. Sure, we can team up. Sit down; we can start plotting our strategy. How are you with the lab equipment—what are your strengths?" I ask.

"Hair and fibers. I'm great with that. I'm still iffy on fluids and blood. Fingerprints are hard as hell, but I'm trying."

"Yeah, the fingerprints are tricky, but I managed to master the markers already. I did a lot of research at home. So I'll handle the prints and you can handle fibers. I doubt they used blood in the mock-scenes, but just in case we can work on that together. We can also work together on DNA extraction; I'm lagging in that. How does that sound?"

"Sounds perfect. When did you want to go over how to approach the crime scene?"

"Uh—well I have a visitor coming over at 7:00 tonight, but you could stop by my place around 5:00 and we can plan. I live at Kensington Creek apartments. Apartment 124."

"Wow, fancy apartments."

"I ain't paying for it," I mumble.

"Double score. I'll see you later then."

Professor Denali stops me before I leave.

"Kalista, you seem off today. Is everything alright?"

"Not really. But I'm hoping school will help me refocus a little. Having a week off left me with way too much time on my hands."

"Not anymore. We are going to be busting tail until graduation. This is where we separate the boys from the men— figuratively speaking. That's actually what I wanted to talk to you about."

"What exactly? My grades are perfect. I mean, I know I need to work on my extraction some but…"

"Relax, we will revisit extraction soon. That was just a beginning course. You will learn a LOT this week. But it's fun as hell."

"That's a relief."

"So what I was getting at is that I was approached last week about a position that's opened up in Seattle. It's come to me through a friend of a friend."

"You're leaving us? No… I don't approve," I cross my arms childishly.

"Oh heck no! I'm no city dweller. This is an intern position for their CSI team. They would like to know if I had any worthy recruits. And that's why I am coming to you."

My jaw hits the floor. This is something I have wanted my entire life. But there are no opportunities for a woman here in the Humboldt department. In all likelihood, I would become a paper pusher like Sharon. I am honored and ecstatic by the possibility.

"Wow! I'm flattered."

"Are you interested? I know some people wouldn't relocate for an intern position, but you've got something I see in very few students. This is your calling."

"Of course I would relocate. And hell yes I'm interested! What do I have to do?"

"This week's assignment is somewhat of a contest. Win it."

"But there are others in the class who are just as good as I am."

"There are definitely some good ones. And I have designed these crime scenes at a master level—this is going to be the hardest case you will ever solve. But Kali, you are the best here. In fact, you are my best student ever. You can win this. Remember, I have given you access to every lab and study room in this building for the next week. Day or night. Use it to your advantage. Practice. Work the hell out of that crime scene. Find the criminal using nothing but intuition, skill, and the available technology. You've got this in the bag."

"I guess all of those Forensic Files over the years have paid off," I laugh. "Will my partner have a shot at the position as well?"

"No, this is just a regular old assignment for the entire class. But I am testing YOU personally so I can give a recommendation. All I have to do is say the word and the job is yours after graduation. And all you have to do to get me to say the word is win. Easy enough."

"No pressure, huh?"

"This job is nothing but pressure. Get used to it."

"Yes, sir."

I all but skip to my car, where I find Brian waiting. Seeing him isn't exactly what I was hoping for but just like Cris, he always seems to turn up like a bad penny even after I've flung him away. After everything that's happened lately, I find myself wondering what's happened now? What is he here to accuse Cris of this time?

"You're glowing," he says, suspiciously.

"I was, until I saw you standing here," I scowl. "What do you want?"

He sighs heavily, taking my hand into his softly.

"I'm here because I want to call a truce. This has gotten completely out of hand."

"No can do, Brian. And I don't have time for this shit right now. I have a huge project for school and it needs my full attention."

"What's the assignment? I would love to help."

"The assignment is called, none of your goddamn business."

"Wow, Kali. You always share your day with me. And you always let me help you with your assignments. Why are you pushing me away?"

"You know why. And we can talk about that another time. Right now I have things that I have to do. I need to go to the house and pick up my school laptop and the rest of my clothes. Did you need to escort me or can I just go?"

"It's your house, too. I don't need to escort you anywhere. I did change the code for the alarm though, since Cris broke in. I tightened the security. The code is the numerical date of the day we met, the best day of my life," he says sadly.

I look into his eyes, feeling his pain shooting straight through my heart. Somehow I can be so angry and yet Brian and Cris both have the ability to turn me to mush with nothing more than a saddened look or a few short words. And I know Bridgette is right about one thing, Brian hasn't done anything other than love and protect me. Did he go about it the wrong way? Absolutely. But in the end, none of us are perfect. At least he never lied to me, and with Cris, that's all she's done from the beginning it seems. I don't know if she is responsible for the things Brian claims she's done, but I do know for a fact that she lied to me. That doesn't plead well for her case. I'm not ready to make any sudden promises to Brian yet, but I do owe him an apology for being so harsh with him. If he is acting erratic and mean, it's only because I have put him in an impossible position. I am even changing myself. I am being ugly and flying off the handle, flip-flopping back and forth and toying with the emotions of two people who want nothing more than a shot at loving me for the rest of my life. The stress is making me question my own sanity. I feel like we are all walking circles and repeatedly tripping each other up and pointing the finger at each other to avoid the fact that none of us know what the fuck we're doing or which direction to go in. This dating idea was bad—and it's bringing out the claws in all of us.

"I just want to say something that you deserve to hear, Bri. I am sorry for my behavior. I really am. The pressure is doing me in. I know you're just trying to protect me and I love you for it. I really do."

"I love you too, Kali, more than ever. And I don't want to add any extra stress to your life. So as hard as it is and as much as I miss you, I'm really trying to give you some space. I went about everything all wrong and I ended up pushing you away. I hope in time you will come back to me. I'll never stop waiting. I've loved you for a thousand years, and I'll love you for a thousand more," he recites our song, tugging at my heart strings.

I nod, trying to shake the song lyrics from my head. But it's there now, and beginning to seep its way out of my tear ducts.

"I—I need to go Brian. Have a good day at work, okay? Please be safe."

"Always."

I take him in my arms, squeezing tightly, imagining if he were to go to work tonight and something happen to him. Knowing how much he loves me and how I've treated him—I could never forgive myself. I find myself unable to let go. Somewhere in the middle of all this the words of our song begin leaving my lips into his listening ear.

"Heart beats fast, colors and promises. How to be brave. How can I love when I'm afraid to fall? But watching you stand alone, all of my doubt suddenly goes away somehow. One step closer...." I feel his tears soaking through my shirt, dampening my shoulder where his face is buried. This is the first time I have ever seen him cry. Two of the people I love have cried for the first time in front of me today. I can't bare it.

"I have to go, Brian."

He only nods, watching me drive away. Watching from my rearview mirror, I am forced to look away as I see him emotionally slamming his fist into the hood of his squad car and painfully slumping down, sinking his head into his hands in tears. My poor Brian.

***

Walking into my old home was hard. Packing was even harder. Pictures of Brian and I are scattered throughout the entire house. The photo of us on our last anniversary, which was only a few short weeks ago, has been placed on his bedside table. We were so happy then. Everything was normal. Now—I don't know if anything will ever be the same again. I have treated him so badly. He might still love me, but I'm not sure he can ever truly forgive me.

I walk into the bathroom to get a few other things, such as my perfume, makeup, and flat iron. The first thing I see it that damn message on the mirror. As if you could miss it. It's in bright red lipstick. My lipstick—which happens to be still lying there on the counter. If it was Cris, she certainly didn't take much care to cover her tracks. I don't think Brian intends to press charges, which is good for her. But something seems odd to me. Cris was never that careless. She knows evidence like this could easily be linked back to her with modern technology. Why would she leave this here? Did she want to be caught?

I don't know why, but I take the lipstick, grabbing a plastic bag from under the counter and gently scooting the tube into the bag, careful not to touch it. I can analyze this lipstick. I wonder if it's my own subconscious way of still trying to protect Cris, and clear her of responsibility for this little shenanigan. But on the other hand, if this lipstick proves that she is responsible, there would be no doubt whatsoever that she crossed the line and broke into our home. That could very well be the one thing that would help me walk away from her mentally, once and for all. After Bridge arrives tonight and she is asleep, I will go to the lab and analyze the lipstick. I need the practice anyway. Aside from the personal reasons for going tonight, I really want this position in Seattle—I need this position. The thought of it leaves me ecstatic, and reminds me that Jesse is going to be at my apartment any minute to study. I really need to hurry and get back.

I leave my old home behind, dropping a small note on Brian's pillow as I go, just to cheer him up when he gets home. I can see him losing it. He needs a small glimmer of hope that whether he ends up with me or not, everything will be okay again. Someday.

***

Jesse is already waiting by my door when I get home.

"I'm sorry, Jesse, I had to go get my laptop."

"It's cool. I literally just got here."

"How did you get in the gate?"

"My mom works on the police force, remember? They have codes they use to get in the gate. I called her and she gave it to me," he winks.

109

That could explain how Brian ended up here last night without me even having to buzz him in. I completely forgot about police access to the gates.

"Come on in, have a seat," I lead him through the door and we sit at the dining table. I grab us a couple of beers from the fridge that I had initially bought for Cris. I guess she won't be drinking these.

"So your mom works for Humboldt PD? Must be Sharon. She is the only woman on the force. I didn't even realize you were **that** Jesse. Shows how oblivious I am," I laugh. "Your mother and I go way back. It's weird that I never made the connection that you were her son."

"Yeah, well you don't seem to notice anyone in class. You are in a zone while you're there. That's why I chose you as my partner. Being a friend of the family is just a bonus."

"Small world, I guess," I smile and get right down to business, eager to ace this assignment. "So, I was thinking we would both go into the crime scene separately at first, in full gear so we don't contaminate the scene. We give it a good once over and then compare notes. Every eye is different. You'll see things that I miss and I will see things that you miss. Then after comparing notes, we can go back in together and establish what type of crime scene we are looking at and then begin collecting evidence."

"Sounds good," he agrees casually, anxiously handing over the reigns.

"But listen, we need to be thorough. The more we go in that room, the more we compromise the scene. We need to try to get everything in ONE shot, even if it takes hours," I reiterate.

"Yes ma'am. You're the boss."

"What makes me the boss?" I laugh.

His eyebrows lift slightly.

"Because you're the best. It's common knowledge. Did you not see all the disappointed faces when I got to you first for partner? The moment Denali said we were teaming up I was ready to run for you."

"Shut up, you're making me blush. And you are very capable as well. Your mom is a cop, and I've learned a lot from Brian and his dad—but we are not going for regular law enforcement. We are specializing in forensics. We have to do double work. We are going

110

to have to work twice as hard as everyone else. Gotta keep my reputation up to par, you know?" I joke.

"True, true. So what about our uniforms?"

"I think we should go all the way. Full body suits, goggles and footies. We don't want to miss anything. And after we come out of that room, we will even go over the clothes we wore in case we picked anything up while we were in there—hairs, fibers, etc. No half assed work. I want to find that Perp. And word is, Professor has made it extremely difficult."

A knock at the door disrupts us and I'm irritated. I'm in my school zone and I hate distractions. I see that it's Cris and become even more agitated.

"Kali, can I come in for a second?"

"Cris, I'm in the middle of studying."

"Seriously, it will only take a second."

I sigh, not wanting another scene, especially in front of my classmate.

"Just for a minute. I have a huge assignment," I inform her. "Jesse, I am going to step out to the balcony and have a smoke. You go ahead and continue considering the different possibilities for the crime scene. It could be murder, or even a burglary. We have no way of knowing what we're walking into tomorrow."

"You've got it, boss."

As I light up I realize that I was supposed to quit when I finished my pack—four packs ago. Right now I don't care all that much, but I do need to keep a mental note. It was hard enough quitting the first time. Now that Cris smokes in front of me I notice that she chain smokes—badly. It's not healthy.

"You smoke way too much," I comment, out of nowhere.

"Not usually. It's been—stressful."

"Why are you here, Cris?"

"First of all I came to tell you that I don't accept the whole 'it's over' thing. I also wanted to explain why I lied about being at work. I figure, I am supposed to talk about these things, not hold them in. This is what I'm supposed to do. So I'm doing it."

"I'm listening."

"I had to go to a hypnotherapy session."

I look at her, not quite understanding the reason why she would lie about that.

"I already knew you were continuing treatment, Cris. There was no reason to lie."

"But there was. I had no clue what I had done in that few minutes when I blacked out at the motel. I had to find out."

"And what did you find out during your therapy—assuming you're telling the truth?"

"Honestly, nothing. I was unable to regress what happened."

"Then how are you so sure you didn't do it?"

"Because I can feel it. Please just trust me. I think someone is setting me up, or trying to."

I roll my eyes, and look down at my watch. Bridgette will be here in an hour and I still have work to do on this assignment. Cris is lying—and wasting my time. I can't do this right now.

"Cris. You need to go. As much as I want to believe you, I don't. Unfortunately you have lied to me so many times that I don't know truth from fiction with you. Please go. If I fuck this assignment up I will never have this opportunity again."

"Alright. I'm in 123. In case you ever decide to talk to me."

"Right next door, Cris? Jesus."

"I don't like stairs… I'm leaving. Good luck with your assignment."

Cris sees herself out while I take a seat at the table again.

"Sorry about that, Jesse."

"No problem, I was just wrapping up. We can meet up in the supply room tomorrow at 10:00 a.m. All the suits are in there."

"Absolutely. I'll see you then."

***

The apartment is gleaming, still perfectly spotless since I've been here for a mere twenty-four hours. Everything is ready for Bridge. I'm excited, but with this new assignment I feel as if the timing is horrible. When my phone rings I see Bridgette's name pop up and wonder if she was unable to secure her limo—this is Nebraska after all.

"Hey Bridge. How are you?" I answer.

"Just dreadful, darling. I have decided to stay over in Lincoln tonight. I am frazzled and exhausted."

"Oh hun, I'm sorry. Are you sure?"

"Yes, I simply couldn't go any farther. To top it off I'm famished. The food in first class was simply unacceptable. Disastrous, I tell you. This better not cause a wrinkle or I will sue Delta Airlines."

I burst into laughter; she is such a diva.

"Sue them for bad food?"

"Not just that, don't be ridiculous, child; for pain, suffering AND starvation. As well as post traumatic stress. There was a bump, I was certain we would crash. I saw my life flash before my eyes, and I imagined I was buried in Wal-Mart clothing. It was a nightmare—a dreadful horrible nightmare. I need a massage and a martini," she sighs. "Worst day of my life—aside from the time my liposuction doctor was unavailable. Can you imagine; he left me high and dry because his mother died. I needed him more. His mother was decaying while I had to show up at the Miracle Gala looking like a bowl of pudding poured inside a polyester pillow case—it was dreadfully humiliating. I know Wilma Higgins had a riot with that one…"

"You are fucking crazy, Bridge, but damn you make me laugh. You are so gonna hate it here."

"I know…"

"Well listen, I have to go to school in the morning so I am leaving a key with the front desk so you can let yourself in. I'm walking to school so you can take my car if you want to sight see; though, I warn you, there is nothing but corn around here. Welcome to Hell."

"I'm frightened. I will just find somewhere to get a facial and a manicure while you're at school."

I laugh under my breath; knowing she will not find a place for a facial here in Humboldt, but I omit it.

"See you then."

"Goodbye, darling."

I shake my head at her over dramatized events of the day. She really would have died on the flight I experienced to

113

Destin. But there again, I flew coach—no frills. I was grateful for my honey-roasted peanuts.

Since she isn't coming until tomorrow I can go get some practice in at the lab. I am unbelievably excited to have the opportunity for this internship. For a moment I want to call and share it with Brian, but I shouldn't get my hopes up. I have a lot to learn yet. I will start practicing with that lipstick. I grab Cris's cigarette butt from the ashtray, as well as the lighter she accidentally left on the balcony for fingerprints.

"Alright, Cris. Time to separate fact from fiction."

6

Questionable Evidence

<u>Kali</u>

Now that Bridgette has decided to head in tomorrow instead I can't make it to the lab fast enough. Walking in, I am already so excited I can't even contain myself. I can't stay long because I have such a huge day tomorrow, but hopefully I can lift some prints off this lipstick and Cris's lighter.

"Well aren't you just the eager little beaver, Kali? Come to get some practice in?" Professor Denali asks as he fiddles with a microscope.

"Yes, actually I brought some personal items I want to look at. It's a little more than just practice—someone broke into my old house and left a message on the mirror with this lipstick. They left it at the scene."

"Interesting. Was it collected properly?"

"Not exactly. I didn't touch it, though. I pushed it into the bag with an eyeliner pen."

"Well, that will do. Question though, why didn't the police collect it?"

"Brian never reported it."

"Alright…" His eyebrow lifts slightly.

"Well, he's an officer. I suppose he thinks he has the security covered."

"Hey, it isn't my home. No judgment here. Was anything taken?" He wonders.

"Not that I know of. Apparently Brian thinks it might be a stalker."

"In that case, I want to help. I haven't worked on real honest to goodness evidence in a while. Do you mind?" He perks up. How lucky am I? I have one of the best in this field willing to help me.

"Hell no I don't mind."

He puts gloves on carefully before removing the lipstick from the bag and placing it on a sterile towel. I observe every move he makes without a word. This is going to come in handy tomorrow. I watch as he lifts two sets of fingerprints from the lipstick like second nature. He questions me as he's working them.

"Okay, Kali, what kind of prints did I just find? Patent or Latent?"

I go back to the lesson we studied a couple of weeks ago.

"Um, they were Latent."

"Why?"

"Because they weren't raised or highly visible to the naked eye. You had to use black magnetic dust to see them, and then you used clear adhesive tape to lift it, securing them to a latent lift card for preservation and further analysis."

"Star student. What's next?"

"Just like patent prints, you will still need to photograph them so they may be enlarged and entered into the police database to look for matches. Upon entering the print into the system it will do the hard work for you and begin identifying specific markers, in case you need them for comparison," I reply with confidence.

"You are doing great," he replies. "You are going to ace this assignment this week."

"I hope like hell you're right."

He continues quietly for a few minutes, which is all it takes for him to enter the print into the database.

"It's searching," he informs me.

"Well, I actually had one more thing I wanted to look at—for comparison actually. A suspect. But I'm not sure I can adequately make the call on whether they match or not. Can you help me with that once we lift the print? It should be a good one. This person directly touched the item and didn't wipe it off."

116

"Why don't you lift the print and I can help with the comparison. I'll walk you through it. But remember; if it's someone in the database we won't have to compare it manually. Has your suspect ever been arrested?"

"Yes."

"Well, we can do it anyway for practice if you want. But the DB should pick it up if he or she has been arrested or fingerprinted in the past for any reason."

"Am I keeping you from anything," I ask, feeling kind of guilty to come in here and unload all this work on him.

"Yeah, my couch and frozen dinner will be pissed when I get home," he laughs. "No, I was just here making sure everything was up to par for tomorrow."

"Cool."

It only takes me a moment for me to lift the print having just watched Professor Denali. It was my first time actually doing it and I am proud of myself. This was way easier than I expected. Professor Denali quickly enters it into the system for me. I don't have access to the police database as a student.

"After the database finishes its search what do we do?" I ask, curious about the next step.

"Well, it will either give you a name, or not. Some people have their children fingerprinted while they're young as a safety precaution against kidnapping, etc. Some people in the database are people who have been arrested previously. It stores it in the system—just like the system we have for DNA now. Once it's in the system it stays there forever."

"And what if there is no match in the database?"

"It will be filed away as evidence until a suspect is printed for comparison. Once we identify the source, it will be added to the database for future usage."

A sound comes from the computer, making my heart jump into my chest.

"It found someone?"

"Two of the prints have been identified so far. One of them is yours, from the lipstick, and the other belongs to a Cristina James, from the lighter."

I had forgotten that the police had fingerprinted me once I was found after the kidnapping. It's strange to know that I am on the

117

radar now. Not that I would ever do anything to where they would need my fingerprints, it's just fascinating how far science has come. "What about the third print?" I ask impatiently.

"Actually, it just finished up. No match on the other print from the lipstick. Damn…" he's visibly disappointed that he couldn't solve my mystery.

"So you're saying that Cristina James' fingerprints are not the prints found on the lipstick?" I repeat just to confirm.

"Nope. The other set could belong to any other person who ever touched the outer case of the lipstick—other household residents or, maybe someone whom you loaned it to at some point."

I'm so confused. After Cris lied to me I was convinced it was her who had been in the house.

"So Professor Denali, would it be possible that she could have wiped her prints from the lipstick?"

"No. There was no smudging, plus it would have wiped the other prints away as well. They were actually in perfect condition. Even if she had worn gloves it would have smudged the prints that I lifted. She's not the one."

"And you're sure?"

"There is never any way to completely eliminate a person. But with the evidence you have right here it is showing that another person used this lipstick to write on that mirror. And whoever it was is not in our database. Keep sorting through your suspect list and start making comparisons. You can store these here in the lab for safe keeping if you like. They are essentially useless to the police now that we've tampered with them anyway."

"Right. Well thank you so much for your help."

"No problem, it was fun. Go home, get some rest and get ready for the big day tomorrow."

"Yes, sir."

***

As I get home and lie down I'm completely consumed by my thoughts. If I was wrong about everything and treated Cris the way I did for no reason I will never forgive myself. After finding out the she never touched that lipstick it automatically makes me wonder what else I was wrong about. I consider calling Brian and telling him what I've done, but it will lead into a long conversation that I don't have the energy or the time for tonight. If I am ever going to get out of this hellhole of a town I have to get this job. I will never find another opportunity to go straight into that position. It would take years to get there, and I'm certainly not getting any younger. Boy trouble should be the last thing on my mind right now. I have to focus. I can't blow this.

I had taken a couple of over the counter sleeping pills when I got home to make sure my mind will release all my troubles and allow me to fall asleep easily. Thank God they are kicking in fast.

***

Morning comes too fast as my alarm pulls me from a dreamless sleep and reminds me of the treacherous schedule I will face today. Nothing else matters more than school today, but I did set my alarm an hour early so I could stop by the coffee shop and talk to Cris before school. I want to ask her a few questions. As important as school is, I also can't let this go undone. If she is innocent, I need to apologize, but more importantly, Brian might be in some kind of danger. As far as I know he has no enemies, but with all the people he has put in jail you just never know. It's all part of the business. This has to be resolved—soon.

I feel awkward walking into the coffee shop. Yesterday was horrible and Cris was so devastated. I am embarrassed to even show back up. I just can't let this wait until this afternoon when I leave school. We need to talk now.

Lawrence greets me with a nervous smile.

"Hey Kali."

"Hey… I know I caused a bit of a ruckus yesterday, but could you please get Cris for me? I swear, there will be no scene today."

Lawrence looks at me oddly.

"Honey, Cris was fired yesterday. She flipped once you left and destroyed the entire kitchen. We don't know what happened, she was usually so mild mannered…"

119

"Oh god, she must have tranced out," I speak aloud, knowing that Lawrence will have no idea what I'm referring to. They don't know her like I do.

"They decided not to press charges because she agreed to pay the damages and walk away quietly. You haven't seen her?" Lawrence asks worriedly.

"Last night—briefly. But she didn't say a word about it."

"You might want to go check up on her, Kali. Something just wasn't right."

"Don't worry. I know what to do. Thank you, Lawrence."

She doesn't reply to my text and I don't want to bombard her with a million things so I keep it simple, only asking her if she's okay. Usually she responds within seconds, but as I arrive at school I've still heard nothing. I'm beginning to get worried. This cannot be happening today. If I don't get my shit together and walk through that door I will fuck everything up. Why does this have to be happening right now? I'm worried—equally concerned for Cris and Brian. Cris swore faithfully that she had nothing to do with this and I blew her off without a second thought. And Brian is so convinced that this is Cris that he hasn't even reported the break in—which is more than likely my own fault. I pretty much told him in a nutshell that if he reported Cris I would never speak to him again. That's why he won't report it. Now, there could be someone out there after him—and trying to set Cris up. It makes no sense. Who would do something like this? I have to find out.

"Kali, I was just looking for you. I'm glad you're here early," Professor Denali greets me with a smile. "Come into my office."

I walk in with my mind swarming with a million other things aside from school. "What's up?"

"After you left last night I did some further testing on the lipstick. There was DNA. That means we can cross reference it in the system once the results come back and see if we can start making some links."

"What?" I gasp excitedly. "But if the prints weren't in the system than the DNA wouldn't be either—right?"

"Not necessarily. But if DNA was ever found from another crime scene and not matched to a specific person it will still remain in the database—nameless. That means we will have a place to begin searching."

"I don't get it. We would still have no name."

"No, but if it was in the database we would have information on the origin of the criminal. Say there was DNA at a murder scene, and it was still unsolved because they didn't have a suspect to compare it to, the DNA would still show up in an active case. You would have a location—a starting point of where to being looking for suspects. A city—a state—it's enough to get it started."

"Hot damn, you're right! What type of DNA did you find exactly?" I ask excitedly.

"A hair. Stuck on the inside of the lid."

I cringe before asking, but out of curiosity, I ask anyway. "What color?"

"Dark."

Cris's hair is blonde… It definitely clarifies that it was not her. I am such an asshole. Now we have to figure out who has a vendetta against us. This hair could be hugely important.

"How long until we get results?"

"Fortunately, I have connections. A few days."

"Thank you so much, Professor."

"You can start calling me Frankie while we aren't in class."

"Okay—Frankie. Let me know when you hear something."

After leaving Frankie's office I catch a hundred dagger stares from my jealous classmates, as if people actually think I'm one of those 'under the desk' kinds of students. Eew. I stare right back and remind myself that in the very near future I will never have to see these assholes again.

"Alright class. Are you ready for the ride of your life? Let's get it on," Professor Denali announces, sending us off to our crime scenes.

Jesse and I are suited up in a matter of minutes. I'm so ready to get this assignment over with.

Fucking focus, Kali. Everything is riding on this…

Brian

"Dude, why the fuck are you here?" Cris asks as she answers her door, seeing Brian propped against the trim.

"I'm here because of Kali."

"Well, she isn't here. In fact, she doesn't ever want to see me again because of you. I played fair, you are the one who decided to break her rules. She really deserved a chance to make her own decision. You took it upon yourself to deny her that because you seem to think she's your property. Have you forgotten she was mine first?"

Brian is in no mood for this. It took a lot of soul searching for him to do what he's doing, and he really didn't come here to fight.

"Can I just come in?"

Cris stands to the side, allowing him inside. The first thing he sees is pictures of Kali everywhere, including a framed photo they must have snapped during their last date while they were getting ready to cook the other night at Kali's new apartment. The apartment is a mess, which contradicts everything Kali has ever told him about Cris. He was under the assumption that Cris was some kind of neat freak. This place is a tornado.

"Every heard of Merry Maids?" Brian asks, sarcastically.

"It's for therapy, asshole. Not that it's any of your business."

"Alright, listen. I'm here for a reason."

"Clearly. What do you want?"

I want you to back away from Kali. I am asking as a man. I have offered her a truce. You need to walk away. She needs me. I don't think you understand what kind of shape you left her in when you went into that hospital. I put her back together. She still isn't right. I keep her sane."

Cris rolls her eyes, laughing under her breath. She knows Kali had a hard time when she left, but she hardly has challenged sanity. Brian is once again exaggerating his worth, and only to make himself feel better.

"She doesn't need you and she doesn't need me. She is a fully capable woman if you haven't noticed."

"Even if you cast her mental state aside, which is selfish and wrong in itself, also consider the fact that she has no income and you and I are the only people able to take care of her. Do you really want that kind of responsibility right now, just having got out of the hospital yourself? That's a lot to take on."

"I appreciate your heartwarming and genuine concern for my health, but I'm good."

"What if we made some sort of deal? I am willing to sell my house for the money to settle this. What if I paid you—all of the profit from the sale—as compensation for everything you've done for Kali? I appreciate you stepping in and helping her get a place to live. But I can take it from here. You and I both know you haven't changed and you're still a very sick woman. She doesn't need your mental issues disrupting her life. She is almost finished with school and she's already said that once she graduates she would consider marriage and starting a family. These are things you can't give Kali, legally or physically. Your marriage wouldn't even be valid in this state."

"There are other states, Brian."

"Why don't you just take the money and go find a woman more suitable for you. Our house is worth at least one hundred and seventy thousand dollars—I will profit at least fifty thousand of that. It's all yours if you'll have it."

Cris bursts into laughter.

"Do you not know who I am? I have enough money in the bank to buy one hundred of your houses. And last time I checked, Kali is not for sale. You're a piece of work, Brian. I am going to be the good-guy here and not mention this to Kali, because it's absolutely degrading to her. But no, as long as she wants me here, I am not going anywhere. No amount of money would ever make me leave her."

Brian's frustration is building quickly. He is trying to be reasonable and Cris is being uncooperative, as always. He thinks on his feet, willing to try anything, even to the point of lying. He needs her gone—now.

"What if I told you she's pregnant?"

"I would say you're grasping at straws and trying everything you can to get your way. Kali is definitely not pregnant. She's still smoking and drinking, she would never do that if she were pregnant. You know this."

Brian considers his words carefully before continuing.

"She could be… We had sex at the motel that night. No matter what she told you—it happened. So yes, she actually **could** be pregnant. So back up and let us move on from all of this."

"Nice try. I know what happened that night and I know Kali. She didn't sleep with you and you know it. You think because I have a mental disorder that I'm of lesser intelligence than you. I get it. But you're way off. I'm not even close to ignorant, and I am sure as hell not as naïve as you were hoping when you came here tonight to try and lie your way back into Kali's life. You just keep doing what you're doing, Bro. You're only hurting yourself."

"I figured you would put your own happiness over what's best for Kali. I don't know why I even bothered to try and reason with you."

"Anything else?" Cris holds the door open, letting Brian know it's time to go.

"Yeah, and stay away from my car and my house. Next prank you pull will land your ass in jail. No more freebies," Brian warns, walking out the door.

As Brian pulls out of the complex he wonders if he has just made another huge mistake. Going to see Cris accomplished nothing—aside from further irritating himself. Why can't she just see that Kali is better off without her? Kali's life would be torture if she were to end up with Cris. The stares—the lack of children or a normal family—she deserves better than that. Cris has nothing to offer her.

There is one last thing that might work. It's worth a shot. Brian is running out of options.

Cris

"What a fucking idiot," Cris scoffs as she lights a cigarette and watches Brian pull away from the parking lot. "You just fucked up bad."

Cris's phone rings and she runs back inside for it, hoping it's Kali. After all, she is the only person who ever calls her. But she doesn't recognize the number.

"Hello," she answers.

"Hey girl, it's Lawrence. How ya' holding up, darlin'?"

Cris is surprised to be getting a call, but it's not an unpleasant shock—just different. A friend would be nice.

"I've been better."

"Have you seen Kali yet?"

"No," Cris answers in a dull disappointed sigh. "Even if she wanted to see me, she is at school today anyway. Apparently something big is going on—some huge assignment."

"Oh yes, girl. I totally forgot she said she had to get to school," Lawrence remembers.

"You've seen her?" Cris's interest peaks.

"She came to see you this morning, and she was pretty disappointed that you weren't here. She looked like she needed to talk to you."

"Damn it! Why didn't you call me right away?"

"Uh—because she left. I'm sure she'll come by again later. With those bags under her eyes I can tell that girl will be needing a latte this afternoon."

"Bags?"

"She looked like she hadn't slept all night. Probably from studying, but bags are just a no-no on those pretty blue eyes of hers."

"She's beautiful regardless," Cris says with an unintended aggravation in her tone.

"I know, don't get bitchy. Anyway, I just wanted to let you know she was looking for you."

"Thanks Lawrence. Can you do me a favor?"

"Sure."

"Deliver her a latte. I'll swing by later and give you a huge tip for your trouble. If she's that tired I don't want her doing badly on her assignment today."

"Girl, no tip necessary. I'll do anything to get you two lovebirds back together. I can't be the only gay in this town. I liked having another couple. You know what I mean."

"Absolutely."

Cris hangs up with Lawrence feeling nice about having someone on her side for a change. It gives her hope that maybe someday things can change and that she might have a shot at a normal future. She only prays that Kali is part of that future. She has to be. Brian has got to go.

Kali

I realize quickly just how brutal the crime scene Professor Denali created actually is. Jesse was supposed to go in first but he backed out quickly, nervous that he was going to screw something up. I went in myself an immediately figured out the source of his intimidation. The mock-bedroom crime scene is ransacked. Every inch of the floor was strewn with clothing, jewelry, an overturned and shattered television, and many other items that contain evidence that might be altered if we stepped on it. I did my best mission impossible moves, trying to step around the props. I remember from an earlier briefing in class that the first thing to do is stand in the center of the room and give it a nice 360 degree look. There are just so many things that immediately jump out at me; it's overwhelming. I have no clue where to even begin. For a moment I forget everything I've learned in class and go blank. The pressure is heavier for me than for any other person in this class. If I don't get this right I have more to lose—a lot more. After taking a deep breath and trying to relax and focus on everything I've been taught, I finally begin piecing my thoughts together. In a real crime scene you would use experience to guide you—as well as instinct. Today I have nothing more to rely on that what I've recently learned in class, as well as my own instinct.

Jesse is a little more comfortable once I return and inform him of which exact path to follow. He wasn't in there long, and returned anxious to see what my assessment was. I'm beginning to see why he chose me as his partner—the kid is essentially clueless, and I don't mean that in an ugly way. I feel bad for thinking it, but it's pretty much obvious. His mother is a cop and he is trying to follow family tradition. Though, he doesn't seem to have the skill level to back up what he will need to know. We have all already passed through the Police Academy, so he will still go on to be a great officer; I'm just not sure he has a future in detective work or forensics. It looks like I will be solving this crime all by my lonesome.

"Alright, Jesse let's go over the mock-up police report again. It says the burglary took place while the victim, a single mother of twin toddlers, was on a date with her new boyfriend. The kids were visiting their fathers home—the ex-husband—for the weekend. The break-in took place somewhere between 8:00 p.m. and 11:30 p.m. and there was no forced entry through the front door, nor was there any other part of the apartment disturbed or disrupted. Now, after viewing the scene and knowing more about the crime what is the first thing you noticed?" I ask, hoping it's something worthy.

"It was extremely messy in the room," he replies, prompting a sigh from me. "What about you? What did you see?"

"Well, the first thing I noticed was the lack of forced entry from any of the bedroom windows. Since there was no forced entry throughout the rest of the house we have to assume it was someone she knew, or someone who had a key. Single mothers don't go around leaving their doors unlocked. Remember that even though we are only analyzing the bedroom itself, the faux police report has all the necessary details regarding the rest of the residence—which are just as important as the room itself. So when you're considering how someone entered, remember it was an apartment, and on the third level. There are only two entrances—front door or bedroom window, which would have been inaccessible from that height. Definitely someone with a key—no question. The next thing we need to do is read through the list the victim has made of missing items. It will be crucial, seeing as how there was an abundance of valuable items left in the room—watches, jewelry, the TV was smashed, cash on the nightstand. Either the Perp was looking for something specific, or they were trying to stage the scene to look like a burglary. Are you following me?"

"Yes ma'am. So what do we do next?"

"I personally think we should go over all the documents first before we re-enter the scene. We need to look over the reported missing items, create a suspect list, and establish a motive. Say the only item reported missing was a gun; we would focus in around the nightstand or under the mattress. It helps us determine the best approach. If we go in without a strategy we might destroy evidence in the process. Since we have no dead person to worry about, the timing isn't quite as sensitive."

"I think you're right. Good plan," he says.

My late night is catching up with me. And just as I walk out of the classroom and into the hall lobby to find a cup of nasty school-brew I see Lawrence standing there with a smile.

"Someone thought you might need a refreshment," he passes a steaming cup of coffee and a bag of brownies to me.

"I could just kiss you right now!" I plant one on his perfectly bronzed skin. "What made you think to come by and bring me this?" I blush.

"I can't take the credit. I was actually talking to Cris. I mentioned that you had bags under your eyes from a sleepless night—no offence but you do—and she asked me to bring you a recharge."

"She's too good to me," I grin softly. "Tell her I said thank you. And also tell her that I'm not happy that she didn't respond to my text. I was worried sick. I need to apologize too—can you tell her I'm sorry and I'll get with her soon?"

"Uh-uh girl, you tell her yourself," Lawrence winks. "And FYI, she probably didn't get your text. When she found out you came by and I didn't let her know right away she was pissed. She was waiting to hear from you. She wouldn't have dodged your text. I'm sure of it. Just stop by and see her on the way home."

"I might just do that. Thanks again, duty calls. I better get back in there."

"Come see me soon, sweet-face," he kisses my cheek goodbye. "And get some sleep tonight, yes?"

"Will do."

***

As little as Jesse and I accomplish forensically today, we do manage to come up with a list of three possible subjects after detailing the police report and the insurance claim for the property loss. We read through witness statements and the account from the victim and her boyfriend upon entering the house.

"Okay, so we know that the only item claimed to be missing was a gun. I don't get it," Jesse says, confused. "All that mess for a gun?"

"Denali said this was going to be difficult. We still have way more material to cover, but it will have to be tomorrow. Class ended an hour ago—everyone else is gone. Just go home and absorb everything we found today. Use your instinct to make sense of it. Right now it seems like a jumbled mess, but trust me the answer is in these papers and in that room. We will find it."

"I have no doubt in you," Jesse says.

"Thanks, but get your brain flowing too. I need your help."

"Yes Captain! See you tomorrow."

***

I see that my car is gone when I arrive home. That must mean that Bridgette has arrived and is out sweeping the town. I wonder what kind of trouble she will find herself in today. I can't wait to see that nut of a lady. Since she's out it's the perfect opportunity to stop by and see Cris for a moment while I have time. I want to talk to her about what I found—and apologize for accusing her. I feel like such a dick for the way I've acted. After she tried so hard to change I treated her just as badly as Brian. I couldn't be more ashamed of myself right now. I realize just how nervous I am as I knock on the door, and stop breathing for a moment as I hear her footsteps coming in my direction.

She opens the door in her red converse, jeans, and a black wife beater that fits snugly against her sturdy frame.

"Hey, Kid," she looks bashfully at the floor, not knowing what type of mood I might be in today and still visibly scorned from the confrontation at the coffee house yesterday.

"It seems we always meet like this lately," I reply, horrified by my actions and but more so concerned with the condition of this apartment. Even from outside the door it looks like a hurricane has struck. I don't mention it, however. It's not my place to call her out on it.

"We always meet like what?" she looks up.

"With me coming to beg your forgiveness for being such a bitch."

She shrugs and opens the door further, welcoming me inside.

"I'm really sorry for everything, Cris. And I am mortified that I got you fired. I'm just—there are no words."

She sits on the couch and watches me quietly.

"I don't care about that job, you know it was just a time killer. What changed your mind though about the other stuff, if you don't mind my asking?"

"Well, a lot has happened in the last twenty-four hours. Do you remember I told you I have a huge assignment?"

"Of course."

"Well basically we have been given a crime scene to analyze and find the criminal. It's very realistic, not to mention fucking hard as hell. Anyway, they have given us unlimited usage of the lab for studying and practice. When I went to Brian's yesterday to get some clothes I saw the lipstick that was used to write on the mirror in the bathroom. So I took it."

"Why did you do that? The message on the mirror said, 'she's mine'. Aren't you even worried that someone might be after you? The police should have been notified."

"Never mind that. I am going to find out who it is myself. I took it to the lab at school. Whoever wrote that left their DNA on the lipstick—and fingerprints. My professor helped me analyze it. The prints did not belong to you."

"Yeah…I know that, dip-shit. I really just wished you had trusted in my word from the beginning. It's offensive that you think I would do something like that. Maybe I would have before—but I'm not the same person I used to be. It just makes me wonder if you will ever believe in me. No matter how hard I try people still view me as a monster. I just didn't think you would be one of those people," she looks at the floor, saddened.

I don't think I could feel any guiltier at this point. She's right, and I'm feeling it—hard.

"Cris, you're right, and I am so sorry. It's just—the pressure has been unbelievable. I'm being tugged from all directions here. Now with Bridgette here to visit and this assignment…I just can't handle any more. I'm on the brink of losing it. If I don't get this job I will be forever disappointed in myself."

"What job?"

"Professor Denali has offered me a recommendation for an internship on a CSI team in Seattle. All I have to do is ace this assignment and the job is mine after graduation. Is that amazing or what?" I beam.

"Seattle?" Cris is heartbroken.

"Honey, I haven't even gotten the job yet."

"But you will because you're amazing at everything you do," she replies quietly. "And you will force me to…"

"To what?" I wonder aloud.

"Follow you there," she smirks, reminding me of that devious girl she once was.

"Time will tell," I reply. "But I suppose if not for your much-needed help today I would have probably failed miserably anyway, so letting you come along is only fair. I owe my success to you today." I grin.

"Huh? What did I do?"

"I would have fallen asleep today if you hadn't sent me that little pick me up from the coffee house. Thank you."

"You're welcome, Kali. Anything you need. All you have to do is ask."

This is the first time I have been the one in the position of needing forgiveness. As hard as it is to let my guard down and stop struggling to be so strong, I can't leave things off this way. She seems to be over it, but I need to say the words.

"Cris, I want to promise you something. If Brian comes to me with any more bullshit I will talk to you first and we will work it out. I am putting my trust in you. I know it's probably too late and you won't believe it, but I do believe you have changed. And I do trust you. Please forgive me for doubting you."

She stands, wrapping her gentle hand behind my neck and pulling me into a soft kiss. "Forgotten."

I breathe a sigh of relief. "But this means we have to be completely honest with each other from now on. No secrets. No lies. No omissions. Someone is stirring things up and we need to find out who. Brian could be in danger, we all could. Especially if you think someone is trying to set you up."

"About that…"

"What about it?" I ask curiously.

"The day I blacked out in the parking lot, I found something in my car. I had to go to hypnotherapy to make sure that I hadn't done anything. I couldn't recall the memory, but I know it's not mine. Someone put something in my car."

"What was it?"

She walks into her bedroom and brings out a plastic bag with a switchblade knife inside. "I think this is the knife that was used to slash Brian's tires. But I swear, it's not mine."

"Cris, I believe you." I take the bag from her and begin asking questions. "Did you touch it?"

"No, I picked it up with the bag and sealed it inside."

"Good. Do you mind if I take this to the lab?"

"Be my guest. I would like to know where it came from myself."

"Excellent. One more thing, I need to analyze your car."

She stands, handing me to keys.

"Anything else you need?"

"Yes, I need some rubber gloves, some paper bags and some tape to collect fibers. You know what? Scratch that, what are you doing later?"

"The usual. Nothing."

"Well listen, I have company from out of town. I am going to try and pawn her off on someone so we can just take your car to school. I have access to the lab. It will be easier to get the supplies from there."

Cris agrees and walks me to the door. She has gone quiet and seems to want to tell me something.

"What is it, Cris?"

"You said no more lies and no more secrets. I wasn't going to say anything because I found it pointless. But it's about Brian. He was here earlier."

"What? I said no contact," I reply, irritated that Brian has yet again broken the rules. "What did he want?"

"He tried to pay me off to leave you alone. And then proceeded to tell me that you're pregnant with his child. And please don't think I'm accusing you of anything—I know it's all bullshit and I called him out on it."

I laugh out loud, shocked that he would go to such lengths.

"Um, I can assure you I am not pregnant. What a fucking liar. And to try and sell me… Wow—new level of low. I'm about tired of his bullshit to be honest with you."

"So I am correct in assuming that you really didn't sleep with him at the motel, right?" Cris lifts an eyebrow. "Again, I'm not accusing, I'm asking."

"No, Cris. I did not. Honestly, I don't remember anything at all that happened at the motel after a certain point. I think I had some sort of stress induced sleep coma. But I do know I didn't sleep with him."

"I figured you didn't; I just had to ask for the record."

"Fair enough," I shrug. "As much as I would love to hang out with you right now, I have a guest who will be back shortly. Mind if I pop in a little bit later so we can work out the details on getting your car to the lab?" I ask.

"Definitely," she kisses my cheek, walking me to the door. "Kali, there was one more thing I wanted to ask really quickly. Brian said you have mental issues that I seem to be setting off. I'm not really making you sick am I?"

"No honey. I'm perfectly fine. Those days—as dark as they were—are over. We can talk about that another time. But be assured, I'm fine. And I want you in my life—always."

***

Instead of going right in to my apartment I take a seat on the curb for a moment, lighting a cigarette and reflecting on the information I've just been handed. Brian trying to sell me is disgusting enough, but having him reference my former mental state in order to fulfill his own wishes is despicable. My mind wanders back to that cold December morning in the City Night Diner off Broad Street, where Brian and I sat together discussing our future, three short years ago...

"Do you really think you're better this time?" Brian asks with a worried crease forming between his eyes.

"They released me, so I assume so," I reply half-heartedly as I push my eggs around with my fork.

"I really think we should talk to your parents about this. You can't keep fighting this battle alone. I'm losing you, you're losing yourself, baby. You walk around here like everything is fine, yet all the while I am forced to keep this charade up with you. I'm the one who has to lie to your family when you go into hiding. I'm the one who's had to rush you to the hospital after two suicide attempts. I am the one who has to lie to the doctors and nurses,

134

making excuses for how you accidentally overdosed yourself on painkillers. This has to stop. I'm putting my foot down with you."

"I'm better now, Brian. I promise. Just trust me. I won't do it again."

"You said that last time."

"But it was an accident this time for real."

"You keep saying that, but I'm not buying it. How do you accidentally strangle yourself with a belt? If I hadn't come home early…" He cringes.

I hang my head, humiliated by the fact that I'm going to have to tell the truth this time.

"Brian, this is embarrassing for me…"

"There is no room for embarrassment. We are talking about your fucking life here!"

"Fine," I reply angrily, feeling trapped. "I use the belt to choke myself when I'm masturbating. It reminds me of her. I like it. I like the way it makes me feel. I wasn't trying to kill myself; I was trying to bring her back—to keep her memory alive. You don't understand, you'll never understand."

His face shows his appall. He doesn't quite know how to respond and I can't blame him. I know I'm fucked up and he will never understand why—I don't even understand it.

"Why do you feel like you have to do that? Do I not please you sexually?" He asks, confused. "Don't you understand that love is gentle and caring—not like that."

"It's where I first found love."

"That wasn't love, baby. I know it feels like it was, but it's not. I can show you love. Let me. I want to replace that need for pain with a need for love."

"I am what I am. I'm sorry," I whisper, defeated.

"I hate that it's come to this, but the reason I brought you here this morning was to give you an ultimatum. I would like to spend my life with you. Move in with me, go back to school and see a counselor. I need you to let Cris die. If you can't do that, I am walking away from you and I will make sure your parents know that you need help. I can't be in a relationship where there are three people. Let me love you—the right way. The choice is yours. Me or Cris."

135

As I put my cigarette out I realize just how ironic my life is and how I am currently in no better predicament than I was three years ago. In the end a choice must be made. The only difference is, Brian was never willing to fight against Cris—until now. And this time he's the one playing dirty. He doesn't feel like it's my right to choose any longer. He has taken the same approach as Cris had six years ago—he wants me and he will do anything to have me, even if that means lying, cheating or compromising his morals. People do change and it's not always for the better. As sick as Cris made me, I am getting the feeling it's becoming contagious. Brian is changing. And it's because of me.

7
Well…That Was Interesting

Kali

It's no secret that I am beginning to lose it after everything that's happening around me. Until now I have tried to keep the hellatious issues of my life quarantined in their separate corners, but I'm encountering the impossible. Brian and Cris are grown adults. I can't ban contact between them. Nor can I stop them from killing each other if that's what they choose to do. My life has become an indescribable mess—to the point that I can't even concentrate on what I need to be doing for school. My memory is failing; I figured that out from the moment I walk inside my apartment. I must have left the coffee pot on this morning, as the scent of scorched bitterness fills the entire space. I don't even remember making fucking coffee this morning. Yeah, I'm definitely losing it. Either that or I'm just tired as hell. It certainly doesn't feel like I just arrived back home from vacation less than a week ago.

I barely have a moment to sit on the couch before a knock at the door shakes me from my thoughts. I look through the peephole, currently disinterested in seeing anyone. I realize I have forgotten yet another thing—Bridgette. Shit!

She stands tapping her foot at the stoop as I welcome her in, hardly impressed at having to wait for nearly two minutes while I scrambled around picking up a few loose items of clothing and an ashtray from the table before opening the door. I assume she didn't use the key I left for her because she knows I'm home, or more likely because her hands are loaded down with several shopping bags.

"Bridgette let me help you. I'm so sorry, sweetie," I take two large bags from her hands, relieving her underworked arms of the pressure.

"You look like shit on toast, Kali," she gawks as she observes my disheveled uncombed hair and tired unmade up face.

"It's wonderful to see you too! I've missed you, and your incredibly rude insults," I sass.

"Oh how I've missed you too, darling. I have spent the better—or should I say worse—part of my afternoon looking for a spa salon. This town is barren."

"Warned you."

"Indeed. Never mind that for now, where do you keep the booze in this place? I need to wind down."

I feel awful. I had meant to stop in at the store and grab some wine and cheese so we would have happy hour when she arrived. But that, among many other things has also slipped my mind.

"Shit, I meant to go get us some goodies but I've been so busy. Brian and Cris are driving me insane, and now I have a huge business prospect on the horizon. I'm stoked, and yet completely overwhelmed at the same time. I think I should just come back to Destin with you and float out to sea and never show my face here again," I sigh loudly, plopping down on the sofa.

Bridge shakes her head and offers her typical unsolicited advice.

"My sweet child, why work when you can just marry well? I know it sounds bad, but honestly it's not that bad. Pick a nice old and well off gentleman with no children. It's the best business prospect you will ever have. Usually they are impotent, which is fantastic. You have so much to learn."

I roll my eyes and hug her tight. As much as I am dreading the distraction from school, this is a much-needed break from Cris and Brian.

"What on earth am I going to do with you, Bridge?"

"Take me out for a drink since you are simply dreadful with entertaining."

"You're such a lush. My life is going down the toilet and you wanna go slosh it up."

"I know…I'm a selfish bitch. But on the bright side, I make an absolutely gorgeous lush…" she smirks.

"Indeed you are. I know the perfect place for a drink—it's nothing posh, I warn you. But if I can recreate the drink I had the other night that Cris made, you will absolutely die!"

"In that case—cheers! To death, may it be wonderful and prosperous!" She toasts an imaginary glass.

***

"Abby, please meet my friend Bridgette. She is visiting from Florida."

I introduce my two newest friends. Abby was ecstatic to see me walk through the door. Though, I hope she isn't expecting a tip like Cris left last time. The best she can hope for with me is twenty percent. I'm all kinds of broke.

"Nice to meet you, Bridgette. Any friend of Cris and Kali's is a friend of mine."

"Really? In that case bring your new friend a drink," she smiles widely, revealing a surgically perfect set of sparkling teeth surrounded by her trademark crimson red lipstick.

I observe the rest of her for a moment, admiring her charcoal pencil skirt and mile high black stilettos. Her beautiful blonde locks are pulled into a tight bun. I wish I could look that posh. I feel like a homely housewife in my tiny cut off shorts, sleeveless faded Paramour baby doll tee and sockless black converse. I did manage to pull my hair into a sloppy ponytail before we left, but I still look like a lump of dirty charcoal sitting next to a pristine diamond. I wouldn't call it jealousy—but I certainly feel less than acceptable in her presence. Maybe a drink would do me a little good too.

"Abby, do you remember what Cris ordered last time? I might be able to recreate it if I saw all the ingredients."

"Uh—no. Your Cris is a master. I don't know what she made but it was amazing. Why don't you call her to come out?" Abby suggests.

"I think that is a splendid idea, Abby. Go ahead, Kali. Call her. I know she'll come."

"I thought this was a girls night out," I reply.

"She is a girl—unless we are talking about another Cris…"

"You know what I mean. But alright, you twisted my arm," I smirk, pulling out my phone.

139

"Yay!" Abby replies. "In the meantime I will bring you two a glass of wine on me—that way the bartender can't screw it up," she winks.

"That would be fabulous, darling," Bridge perks up.

Cris answers faithfully on the first ring.

"Hi baby-licious."

I blush and Bridge notices instantly, smiling.

"Hey—sweetie. Um, Bridgette would like you to meet us at La Cazuela. Are you available? Abby is working and she wants you to come hang with us too."

I wonder for a moment if she will accept. She is hesitating but finally responds.

"Thank you for the offer, Kal, but you know how I am around people. I can be really socially awkward... I don't want to make a bad impression with the first friend of yours who actually wants to meet me."

"Nobody is socially awkward after a few drinks," I counter, unable to finish my sentence as Bridgette grabs the phone from my hands.

"Cris, this is Bridgette. I am the one requesting your presence. I came all the way from Florida to meet Kali's friends; it would be impolite to decline. I won't take no for an answer..." she hands the phone back with a smile.

"Uh—don't mind her, Cris. She just needs a good stiff drink and she'll relax," I make a face at Bridge, stunned that she was so forward with Cris. Cris is NOT receptive to people ordering her around—obviously.

"What the actual fuck is wrong with that woman? Have you not told her who I am? I don't take orders from people. How did you meet her again?"

At this point I don't really care if Cris joins us or not. Call me spoiled, but I have never had to beg Cris to come to me. If I have to beg for her attention it's not even worth my time to have her here—she'll only sulk the entire time anyway. This new Cris... I just don't know. I liked it better when she actually NEEDED to see me. Things are just not the same. Or perhaps my expectations were unrealistic when she came back home. Either way, I'm slightly disappointed and I have no real reason to feel that way.

"Okay, well I understand. I'll just see you another time," I shrug nonchalantly, causing a slight shift from Bridge in her seat.

Cris sighs heavily.

"Do you **really** want me there?"

"Not really. I can tell you don't want to be here," my tone comes out sharper than I would have expected. Her reluctance has placed me in a rotten mood.

"Alright, I'll be there in ten minutes," she replies, irritated.

I lay my phone down just as Abby returns with our wine.

"She'll be here soon," I inform them.

Bridgette sips for a moment before the interrogation begins.

"What happened there?" She asks. "You're irritated."

"She isn't a people person. But before…back in the day…she just… oh never mind."

"What? Finish. You don't have to hold back your feelings with me."

"This is the person who stalked me—for ten years—and then went to the lengths of kidnapping me. Now she won't even join us upon invitation. It's as if she doesn't really care as much as she used to. I know it sounds weird, it's just—she isn't the same person I fell in love with. It's hard to explain. The intensity that pulled us together like a magnetic force is disappearing."

"I understand—I think. Women have the need to feel wanted at all times. You feel rejected right now. It's not that strange. You're just over analyzing the situation," she assesses. "Maybe you should dress yourself up a bit more—up the ante."

"So you're saying she's losing interest because I've let myself go? It doesn't seem to be the case with Brian. It's as if they are switching roles. It's fucking weird."

"And that's not what you want?"

"No. I want them back the way they were. I'm losing it for both of them. Or maybe I'm not—I don't flipping know. I don't know what I want."

"Well, let's just not think about it tonight."

I look down at myself and wonder if Bridge is on to something. I am a mess. I look like a thrift store clearance item. But there isn't anything I can do now. Cris is already on her way.

"I don't want her to see me like this. You're right."

"I planned for this—just in case we decided to paint the town tonight. Your makeup bag and some supplies are in the trunk of your car. You'll also find a package. I saw the most hideous dress at some store called 'Hot Topic' today while I was shopping. It looked like you. It's too Goth for me, but you would look sexy in it."

"Seriously?" I perk up.

"Yes. It's all in the trunk. Hurry up before she gets here. And you're welcome."

***

When I return to the table I have a brand new attitude. It's amazing how makeup and nice clothes can improve your mood. There isn't a lot I could do with my hair, but luckily the punkish style of the dress is just casual enough to afford the shaggy ponytail. My converse pair well with it as well. Naturally, the dress is black and extremely short. It has a corset bodice and a petticoat style attached skirt. The cut is perfect for my thin yet curvy body shape. I go hard on the makeup, wondering if the shift in appearance will rekindle the fire Cris used to radiate for me. I suppose we'll see.

"Well look at you. I had my doubts that anyone could make this ugly dress presentable. I stand happily corrected. You look hot—really," Bridge gloriously smirks.

"I feel better, so that's good. Since we are inviting guests we should invite Lawrence as well," I send him a text asking him to meet us here as well.

"Who is Lawrence? Tell me there isn't another man in the mix… If so, you are going to have to start sharing. I'm getting the itch."

"No. Bad Bridgette. No itch. You just came out of a divorce. You have plenty of money. Try love for a change," I suggest, sipping an ice-cold glass of Pinot Grigio.

"The very situation you're in is why love is not worth the trouble. Thanks, but I whole-heartedly reject that suggestion."

"You're going straight to hell," I giggle.

"I hope so. It's warm there—not to mention all the naughty men. I'll take it—with a side of martini."

She is so beautiful she makes me sick. Even if she has had enough plastic surgery to make Michael Jackson look like a knife-virgin—it has paid off for her. I suppose I am a wee bit jealous. I can only hope to look as good at her age. She could have any man she wants and it seems so wasteful to throw her life away on money. I just can't understand why she is so coy about traditional relationships. Perhaps she was hurt and no longer wants that type of situation in her life. Who knows? I suppose everyone has a story to tell. It's not my place to intrude on her past.

Cris walks in and quietly and makes a face I can't describe as she takes a seat at the table without even introducing herself to Bridgette. Bridge is automatically offended, but she doesn't know how incredibly shy Cris can be. So I try to warm them up a bit.

"Cris, meet Bridgette. Bridgette, Cris."

She holds her hand out for Cris to take. Given that her hand is palm down Cris is supposed to kiss it—that's how introductions go in the presence of the higher elite, but Cris doesn't take the cue and awkwardly shakes her hand, then pulls away, briskly smearing her hands in liquid sanitizer from her pocket. My eyes are gaping at this point. I really hope Bridgette didn't notice. Cris might have changed somewhat, but there are things I'm sure she will never overcome. She still doesn't like touching strangers.

"You have no manners, Cris," Bridgette says casually, but since you are a friend of Kali's I shall forgive you."

Cris makes a humored face and slightly rolls her eyes, "I always appreciate forgiveness from strangers, because their opinions are so important to me. Again, thank you. If you hadn't forgiven me I might have slit my wrists tonight..."

Bridgette chuckles a smidge, "I like you. You're a smart ass."

"Whenever possible. Nice to meet you," Cris replies. "So, Kali, what the fuck is all that makeup on your face?"

I wanted a reaction, but not this type of reaction. She hates it. I want to crawl under the table.

"Um—I was just kind of thinking that..."

Cris cuts me off abruptly, literally throwing a napkin across the table at me, causing me to jump.

"Wipe that shit off. I don't like it. You're ruining your face," she scowls.

"Whoa! She looks gorgeous. You have a lot of nerve," Bridge steps in, aggravated.

"She does—without all that shit on her face. Take it off, Kali," she repeats, more demanding this time.

THIS is the Cris is know. I realize that this is more than likely just a slip up on her part—of course these things will happen occasionally. Nobody changes overnight, but I am running with it. Just having her bossing me around for the first time in ages makes me wet between the legs. That's MY Cris. I shouldn't feed the fire, but I can't stop myself.

"No. I'm not taking it off," I lift an eyebrow, firmly refusing her order.

She closes her eyes and takes a deep breath—several of them—just like she used to, and returns to her calm state.

"You're right. Sorry, Kal."

No! Don't be sorry...

"So girls. What are you two up to tonight," Cris continues quietly.

I'm still slightly sullen that she has somehow managed to tame herself—which is fucked up beyond words on my part. But I step over it and try to do the decent thing and be happy for her that she's making huge mental strides.

"We wanted to come out for a decent drink and I wanted the one you made me the other day. But I couldn't remember what you put in it," I admit.

"Ahh, so you're using me for my bartending skills and not calling me here for my sparkling personality? Seems kind of selfish. What do I get out of the deal?"

Bridgette is less than impressed. She's already irritated by the way Cris spoke to me. Knowing her, she will be knit picking everything move Cris makes for the rest of the night.

"Oh, no, no, no. See Cris, when a lady is present you do as your told. End of discussion. I give you this tidbit of advice because I like you—very much, actually."

144

"You just called me rude a moment ago. Now you like me? Make up your mind," Cris replies dryly.

I'm not sure that Cris cares very much for my new buddy, but she's trying her best to be polite. Bridge's personality can be a bit abrasive. But once you get to know her she is hilarious.

"Well, you **are** rude. But I couldn't help but to be impressed when I heard that you gave that waitress quite a large sum of money last time you were here. You know how to treat a woman; we simply need to work on your manners. Kali has bad manners as well. It must be this backwards town."

Cris's eyes widen, as if to say that Bridgette is the rude one, but she keeps her thoughts to herself. I lay my hand atop hers to keep her tamed. She gives me a long and deep glance, accompanied by a sigh. If I could accurately read minds I would assume she is wondering how long I am going to make her stay in the company of this woman. I was right. She doesn't like Bridge—not even a little. And when Cris doesn't like a person, she has a hard time hiding it.

"Well, on that note. I'm going to the bar to get you ladies your drinks. I will just instruct him on how to make them this time. After that I think I'll be on my way."

"No, you can't go. Lawrence is coming to hang out," I tell her.

"Kali, can I talk to you for a moment—outside?" Cris says, pulling me out of my chair and away from the table before I can even answer.

She takes me out the front door and lights a cigarette.

"Kal...I'm not having a good night as you can see. I've already yelled at you and I am on my last breath with that woman. She is arrogant and vile. I know she's your friend but the first thing she did was insult me and then turn around and tell me she only likes me because I have money. That woman is a snake—and she dresses like Cruella Deville. I was never a fan of Cruella Deville. She reminds me of my mother. I'll bet she smokes those long ass cigarettes too doesn't she?"

I can't help but to burst into a laughing fit because she's right. I nod, confirming Cris's suspicions.

"Ha! I knew it."

"Cris, please just stay with me. I'm really not upset about the makeup thing. You're right; it is a bit much. I'll take it off if you want."

"No Kali. This is not the way it works. I was wrong and you do not have to follow my rules or my orders anymore. You are a grown woman. I had no right to act that way. I don't want you to take it off."

"Can I be honest with you? It made me so fucking hot when you yelled at me. I know I'm weird, but it reminded me of the good old days."

She rests her forehead against mine. I can feel her heart racing.

"Kali... I am going to pretend that hearing you say that didn't just make me hot too. Be careful what you wish for... I'm warning you. Just stop."

Now my heart is racing and the wet spot between my legs is quickly returning. "Why don't you feel how wet I am and then tell me again that you want me to stop."

"Jesus..." she rests her face in the crook of my neck, panting. "We are going back inside to your friend now. I'll stay. But you need to be good. I'm starting to think you're the bad influence."

"You have no idea..."

***

"I'm going to the bar for your drinks. You and Cruella can do without me for a little bit right?"

"Yeah, I think we'll live. Try to ease up on Bridge though; she really isn't bad she just has a strong personality. Give her a chance. She'll rub off on you."

"Yeah, like wiping with a brillo pad," she grins. "But, I could never leave you if you wanted me to stay. Plus, once Lawrence gets here I will just talk to him. Abby still here?"

"Yeah, she's at the bar."

"Perfect, just where I was headed. I'll go chill with her for a minute."

For a moment I feel a twinge of jealousy. Cris wants to hang out with Abby over me. She sees the change in my expression.

"Kali… don't be silly. It's not like that."

I cross my arms and give her a glare.

"No funny business, or…"

"Or what?" she wraps her arms around my waist, and plants a quick peck on my lips.

"Or I'll… um…I'll be very mad. And sad too."

"Like I am every time you're with Brian?" she says seriously.

The words hit me hard. I know I explained the situation to them both and they accepted it. But I never considered how jealous the other might feel—or how sad. I don't want to make them feel that way. Thinking of Cris sad makes my heart hurt. Brian too.

"Noted."

I notice Bridgette is on my phone. I had left it on the table when Cris and I went to smoke. She promptly hangs up when I sit back down. Cris has made her way to the bar and she is giving the bartender orders on how to make our drinks. She said hello to Abby, but took a seat on the other side of the bar—away from her. I know what she's doing. She's making sure I don't get jealous. She is thoughtful and she does have manners—contrary to what Bridgette might think. I feel bad, though. I don't want Cris to think she can't have friends. I was only halfway kidding about Abby anyway. I know Cris would never cheat on me. I mean, if we were actually together.

"Who were you talking to?" I ask Bridgette curiously.

"Well, I thought this would be a perfect opportunity to meet both of the loves of your life so I called and invited Brian. That's alright, yes?"

Fuck no that is not alright. Brian and Cris are at each other's throats right now and this is just a recipe for disaster. Why would she do this to me?

"Seriously, you didn't… Brian and Cris will kill each other. Plus, Lawrence is coming and Brian is weird around gays. You should have asked me, Bridge. Why couldn't I have just introduced you to him alone tomorrow?"

She shrugs, and takes the last sip of her wine.

"Because I am only staying the night. I have a date with a new prospect back in Florida tomorrow evening—it can't wait. He is

147

only in town for a couple of days on business and then it's back to Napa. That gives me a very short time to reel him in. As for Brian and Cris, I am trying to help matters. You need to be done with this situation. It's driving you crazy, and it's driving them crazy as well. I've met Cris and I don't see what all the fuss is about. She's cute, but she has absolutely no manners. The only thing going for her is money. For me, she would be the sure choice, but you aren't interested in money. You're looking for love—which I will never understand. So I need to do an assessment of Brian so I can give you my suggestion. I am here to save the day."

"Well you better save them from killing each other while you're at it."

"We'll see."

Brian arrives shortly after Cris disappears to the bar and he and Bridgette hit it off like peanut butter and jelly. Apparently his manners are more refined to her liking. Lawrence has since shown up and joins Cris promptly—which is a great distraction between the two enemies in the house. Cris is calm and collected, but keeps a close eye on every move I make while Brian is in my company. He has taken the seat next to mine and draped his arm around my shoulder casually, like he always does. Cris doesn't like it, but she is holding up like a champ. She and Lawrence must be talking about us because they are both smirking and looking at Brian. I probably don't even want to know what fun they are poking at Brian's expense.

"You look damn good tonight, babe," Brian says, pulling my hand to his lips and kissing it softly.

Sadly, as good as his lips feel on my skin I want to pull away. Cris shakes her head and turns around, unable to watch any further. It feels so dirty. This is weird—too weird for me.

"I have a great idea," Bridgette says, summoning Cris and Lawrence down to our table. Brian and Lawrence make an awkward introduction, and he slinks closer to me—afraid to catch the gay disease.

"So this is getting stale. Let's all go to Lincoln. There was this really great nightclub I read about," Bridge continues, trying to break the ice.

"Uh—nightclub?" Cris asks, disinterested.

"Bridgette, I'm sure you weren't aware, but Cris is afraid of crowds, she has—issues," Brian smirks.

"Enough, Brian," I warn.

Lawrence takes this as his cue to leave—this is too uncomfortable even for him.

"As much as I would love to join you all, I have to go to work in the morning. I was about to head out anyway. You guys have fun, though," Lawrence gives me a tight hug and whispers in my ear.

"Good luck. I know this sucks, but a club will be better. It's less intimate of a setting. Trust me."

"Thanks, Lawrence," I kiss his cheek.

Bridgette does her normal thing and takes over the conversation, offering Cris a glass of the margaritas that she had the bartender specially make for us.

"No thanks. I'm good with my Dr. Pepper. Not much of a drinker," she replies as politely as possible.

"More for us then. Brian, would you like some?" Bridge smiles.

"Absolutely. Every party has a pooper and Cris seems to have filled that position. Fill me up, buttercup."

Jesus, could this get any worse? Brian needs to grow the fuck up. I choose to keep my comments to myself, but instead I show my displease by shrugging his arm harshly off my shoulder. Cris snickers and Brian shoots daggers at her.

"I'll have a refill please," I push my glass towards her, eager to eliminate at least a small portion of this awkwardness.

"So, I still vote for a club. Let me be blunt here. I know what's going on and I think you are all playing nasty little games with each other. Let go of some of the stress and let's have fun. Consider it a date double."

"What the fuck is a date double?" I giggle, feeling the warmth of the alcohol soothing my nerves.

"Kind of like a double date, except it's one woman and two men. Let them vie for you. A little competition never hurt anyone. And all I see is two pansies that have become spoiled by your generous notion to hurt no one's feelings. I see no 'team Kali' spirit. They are going back and forth like schoolboys. Stick your chests out and show her who the man is—pardon the terminology, Cris—you know what I mean."

"You want us to go on dates together? Do you seriously not find any of this weird?" Brian asks.

"The entire situation is weird, starting with the fact that Kali is in love with her kidnapper—no offense Cris."

"None taken, for the fiftieth time tonight," she sighs. "So, I will be the first one to step up and be a 'man' as you call it and accept the date double challenge. I have no problem with competition. In fact, I know the perfect club for us to go to. Though, it's slightly unconventional."

"Unconventional how?" I ask, intrigued.

Cris takes my face into her hands and runs her tongue across my lips; right in front of Brian. I know I should pull away, but I can't.

Brian stands and Bridgette grabs him by the arm, sitting him down.

"It's a place you will like—trust me," Cris finishes. "S&M."

Bridge and Brian both look as if they are coming head to head with the plague, but neither of them argues. Bridge gives Brian a nod of approval and he falls into place like an obedient soldier. Why don't I have that effect on men? I don't get it, but Cris is right. I am stoked. I have never been to an S&M club in my life. I'm certainly intrigued—especially about how Brian will handle it. Honestly, the thought of them competing is turning me on. Lately all I can think about is school and this non-sense going on with Brian and Cris. I need to take a break.

"I want to go," I reply breathlessly, as Cris pulls her tongue away from my lips, smirking in that devious sexy way she always did when she had badness on her mind.

"I'm in," Brian replies, coming behind me touching his mouth to my neck, sucking lightly, capturing that spot that drives me insane.

My eyes roll back involuntarily. If these two don't stop I will explode. Cris leans back in her chair, folding her hands behind her head and crossing her legs, plotting her next move. I know her. She is patient and strategic. Her eyes don't leave mine. She is sending me those same mental messages I was forced to decode for so long while in under her rules six years ago. Right now, I'm being bad—

and to her—unfaithful. The feeling makes my insides scream with excitement. MY Cris is back, and this new and different Brian is willing to go head to head with her.

"And that's what I call competition. Much better. Let's go," Bridgette says, giving me a wink of approval as I finally come back down to Earth.

***

"You've got to be kidding me," Brian says as we walk through the door to the club.

I am absolutely intrigued. It's dark, almost pitch black, and there are dancers in bondage and chains. It's hot—hotter than I ever thought I would ever expect. The girls are on podiums in all corners of the room—chained up and undergoing torturous sexual acts. They like it—but don't. It's awesomely twisted.

Cris seems right at home, comfortably walking through, familiar with the entire set up of the place. A man greets her and she slips him a one hundred dollar bill. We are escorted to a private VIP room in the back of the club. She has obviously been here before.

"Kali, you can't be serious?" Brian screams over the seductive music selection.

"Give it a shot. You might like it," I beg him. "Look over there, Bridgette has already found herself a nice gentlemen to talk to."

"Give it a shot? I'm stuck here with freaks in masks and a dyke who wants to get in your pants. This is weird shit, Kal. You can't honestly be into this."

"You have a lot to learn about me—about my past. I'm not sure I'm into the whole bondage thing, but I do like a little rough play every now and then."

Brian is shocked by my admission, and shakes his head, joining us in a VIP lounge that holds maybe fifty people. It's a more private setting than the rest of the club.

"I thought you were over this shit, Kali. Three years ago you said you were going to tone it down on all this kinky shit. Do you not remember what happened last time with the belt?"

"I try not to. Drop it. This is not the time."

Cris is confused by the conversation but goes on about her business, thankfully. This is not something I want to discuss with her—not while she's trying to correct herself. Knowing what a mental wreck I became after she left will do no good. But Brian seems hell bent that she be aware of everything.

"Three jungle juices, my style, please, " Cris asks the bartender.

"You've got it, Cris."

"Oh shit, she's a regular here. How do you know she hasn't got diseases?" Brian asks.

"She has never slept with another person aside from me. Truth," I reply, as Brian tries to hide the fact that he is sickened by the mere thought of Cris touching me.

"So you're finally admitting it out loud? You did fuck her. Or did she force you?"

Cris looks back waiting for me to answer, trying to hide the snide grin on her face. She is enjoying this way too much. She loves that she and I have secrets, and she is soaking in the joy of Brian being the outsider for once. I don't see the point in lying. Now that they are both back in my life there should be no secrets. He wants to know, so he will have to deal with the truth whether he likes it or not.

"Both. Kind of," I smirk, infuriating him. Bridgette is right; I'm so ready for the tears and sadness to end. I want fun and excitement. I want them to show me how far they are willing to go for me. Cris is working on it, but Brian is still uptight. Perhaps the jungle juice Cris ordered will loosen him up, because I am ready for a break from the sulking.

When it arrives at the table Brian chugs it, while I have to sip. This shit is fucking strong.

"Cris, what the fuck is in this drink? I feel like I am drinking fruity rubbing alcohol."

"A little of this, a little of that," she shrugs. "Just drink it. You'll forget about the taste in about a minute. Then we can play."

"You're drinking too?" I ask, shocked that Cris is actually going to party with us. Though, under the circumstances it might be the only way she will be able to tolerate Brian and Bridgette, considering she can't stand either of them.

"Fuck yeah, baby. We are gonna have some fun tonight. Plus, I can't deal with that douche unless I am plastered. I'm trying—for you. If not, I would have stabbed him in the throat for kissing your neck earlier. I've changed—but not that much," she grabs my ass, squeezing hard enough to bruise.

As much as I don't want to admit it, Cris is turning me on with her threats. Of course I don't want her to hurt Brian, but her intensity is mind-blowing; just like the person I fell in love with so long ago. I need this and she knows I needed this. I need the intensity. I suppose my words resonated hard with her earlier. She is giving me what I want from her—even if it is only for the night.

I drink up the jungle juice just as Cris instructed. And she was right. After a few harsh sips I don't care which way is left or right. And apparently neither does Brian, as he has taken to the dance floor, groping on some woman in full bondage. The drink certainly did the trick on him. I am pleased so much that he has relaxed that I actually join him on the floor. Cris stays planted at the table watching my every move—sipping her cocktail.

I like the music here. Closer, by Nine Inch Nails is playing. It's danceable with enough alcohol in your system. Brian certainly isn't having any problems moving to the slow seductive tune. It lures me in, and he pulls me closer against him, slowly pushing his bulging jeans against me. I hold his hair with one hand and wrap my other around his waist, moving slowly into him. If I can't have sex, I will at least try to feel something. The moves alone are torture. And the drink has made me looser than I would typically act in a public place. I notice Bridgette has returned, joining Cris who has another round waiting on the table. She's finished her first drink and seems to be downing another. Even while grinding Brian I can't take my eyes off her. Seeing her face enraged and enthralled with jealousy and passion is sexy. Pairing that with the feeling of Brian's body eagerly pushing into me has created a dangerous combination of hormonal overdrive. This dry period has to end—soon. Bridgette leans down, whispering into Cris's ear, pulling a smirk to the corners of her lips. She chugs the last of what's in her glass and starts moving slowly towards me. When I turn to face her Brian begins dancing behind me, drilling the hard knot in his pants into my thin petticoat. Cris takes me from the front, this time locking eyes with Brian. She begins moving with us, running her hands into my hair and taking a sweet lick to my collar bone before she drops lower to the ground, slowly dragging her body back up, pressing against me—hard. Brian grinds harder with every move Cris makes, trying to out do her. He knows he has something I can feel, Cris is going to have to work harder—but she seems up to the challenge. Bridgette dances over holding our drinks, waterfalling it into Brian's mouth and then repeating the same gesture with Cris and myself. She see's what's happening and for some reason, this insane gold digger is fueling it. The song isn't helping matters either. It's so sexual. Even the other people around us are feeling the same effect, as they all seem to be getting as dirty as we are. In this moment I am probably more turned on than I have ever been in my life. I have them both. And they aren't even fighting each other anymore; they are just trying to be the person who pleases me the most. Bridgette goes back to talking to her new boy-toy, who has joined her at our VIP table.

The music has completely shifted from alternative to rap as the song ends. It's odd how even a change in music can increase the electricity between us. The lyrics are about sex and even through the dizzying effect of the drinks the one word that keeps jumping out to me from the song is 'wet'. All I can think of is how wet Cris might be right now. The thought alone makes me drenched. I felt her once, and I have never been able to forget to sensation of my fingers sliding in and out of her so easily. It is like no other feeling I've experienced from a man. It was exhilarating. I want it again.

Our movements slow, becoming more sensual by the second. Brian is the first to take it to the next level, wrapping his arms around me from behind and fondling my breasts. I don't stop him. Cris just keeps moving, though fully aware of what's going on. I know what's about to happen when she places two fingers in her mouth, soaking them in warm spit. She runs her fingers inside my inner thigh, getting higher until she is touching my clit. Her eyes close and a minty burst of air leaves her lips, sighing upon my face. Just touching me is driving Cris to that place—the ecstasy zone. I don't have to touch either of them and yet they are both completely captivated in the moment. When Brian sees what Cris is doing his grip tightens on my breast. The drinks have hit us all hard. Brian is unstably swaying and Cris's head is buried in my shoulder, holding her up as she continues playing with me. Brian sucks that place on my neck—driving me mad. He falls into a chair that is resting directly behind us, pulling my ass down hard on top of his dick. His hips move against me. He can't stop himself from dry fucking; it's that naughty involuntary reflex your body plays on you in a moment of passion. Cris follows suit and kneels down to chair level, meeting my face, thrusting her tongue in my mouth and driving her fingers deep inside me. Every person in the room has disappeared to the three of us. There is only me and my toys, nobody and nothing else matters. I want them—both. My body betrays me, allowing me to wait no longer. Cris pulls her fingers out and traces her lips with my wetness. I reach underneath, unzipping Brian, releasing his fully hard dick. I pull my panties to the side, slipping him into me—hard. I'm still facing Cris who has a devilish grin on her face. She pulls my dress up from the front as I ride Brian backwards, and starts going down on me making an even wetter mess all over Brian. He thrusts underneath me, as it gets more slippery. I know his movements—he's about to cum. We both are. Cris's tongue is going wild and I slam harder and harder into Brian. I feel his cum burst inside me and come oozing back out as I still work it hard. Cris knows I'm cumming and reaches up for my throat, choking me like she did the first time. The orgasm is mind-blowing—so mind-blowing that I have two back to back. But during the second one Brian jerks up, ripping Cris's hand from my throat.

"What the fuck are you doing?" Brian yells.

"Giving her what she likes," she pulls her head out from under my dress, ruining my last orgasm."

"No, you were trying to do some of your freak shit on her."

"Brian," I reply breathlessly, lifting myself off of him and readjusting my panties and dress. "You know damn well that I do like it. Calm down."

"Wait, you let Brian choke you?" Cris replies angrily. "That's our thing, Kali."

"No he hasn't. I—um—I used to use a belt when I would masturbate. I would choke myself. Brian knows this."

Cris relaxes again, completely okay with my explanation.

"This is sick. The bondage, the choking—all of it. You know that right?" He smarts in disgust.

"Yeah, that's why I like it," I grin at Cris who ignores Brian and begins kissing me from my hand all the way up to my shoulder.

"I love you," she whispers in my ear.

"I love you too. Both of you," I call Brian closer with my finger, kissing him hard this time.

"What the fuck is wrong with us?" Brian sighs, placing a hand on my flushed red face, and shaking his head.

***

Bridgette drives us all home in a completely silent car. We are all still buzzed and also feeling the twinges of awkwardness. A threesome was not exactly what we had expected to happen tonight. I'm not complaining, but from the looks on Cris and Brian's faces, they are not happy with their behavior.

After dropping them off, Bridgette and I take a seat on the couch in our robes and slippers—a girl's favorite ensemble. I don't say anything for a moment, until she bursts into laughter.

"What are you laughing at?" A guilty grin forces its way to my lips.

"That was—quite a show. It was twisted and bizarre—and just so wrong. But I couldn't stop watching. No one could, actually."

"Oh god, people were watching?" I ask, yet caring less in the moment.

"More like drooling. It was pretty hot. Even the bartender stopped working to watch. You are a bad bad girl."

"I wish I could be more ladylike and say I shouldn't have done that. But damn it, I couldn't help it. I love sex. I haven't had any in a couple of weeks now. I was horny. And the two of them kept playing with me. It just happened. And I'm not sorry."

"So, I do have to ask; you really liked that thing Cris was doing to your throat?"

"Oh Bridge—you have no fucking idea…" I flop backwards on the couch, letting my eyes roll back with a smile.

***

Bridge wakes me up early, knowing I have to be at school soon, and because she is gathering her things to get ready for her flight home in an hour. I'm so grateful she is here because I totally would have overslept. I had no business going out last night. Be that as it may, here I am tired and hung-over—and somehow in my room.

156

Again, I have no idea how the fuck I got there. I need to lay off the booze.

"Oh, you aren't looking so good, dear. Can I make you some of my famous hot tea before I head out? It usually fixes me right up," Bridge offers.

"Would you please? I feel like shit and today is going to be horrible."

When Bridge goes to the kitchen I hear a gasp, "Kali! Come in here."

I walk in with no clue of what to expect, and hoping like hell I don't have bugs in the apartment. I would be humiliated to find that Ms. Fancy-Pants has seen a roach in my place. But it's no roach. There, carved into my beautiful brand new countertop, is a message. The word 'whore' has been scratched in by a knife. I go to the front door, finding that it is locked and there is no sign that anyone forced themselves in, just like when someone came in before. I had thought it was Cris, but she would never do something like this. Whoever did this has to have been the person who came into my house before. Cris would never call me a whore.

"What is going on here, Kali? I know for a fact that this was not here last night," Bridge asks, terrified.

"I don't know. But this is not the first time someone has been in my home. Something fucking crazy is going on here. First Brian, then Cris, and now me."

"Kali, this is frightening. The whore reference can't just be a coincidence. What if this creep was at the club last night?"

"It's possible. I need to call Brian and Cris over here. Things have gone beyond creepy now. Someone in our circle is playing games. And I want to know who it is."

I pace for a moment, trying to figure out my next move. I'm frightened, panicked, and also feeling guilty—as if the intruder read my mind. I am a whore.

8

Blank Spaces

Kali

I choose to drive to school today even though I could walk in less than five minutes. I have found myself with a threatened and uneasy feeling for the first time in years.

For a long time I honestly thought Valentina was coming back for me, but Brian helped ease those fears into memories of the past. Valentina is never coming back here—it's too dangerous for her. She was into self-preservation to a degree that she was willing to kill for it. She knows she wouldn't make it into city limits before the police got their hands on her. Especially since it's common knowledge that my boyfriend is an officer. He would protect me from her or anything.

Now, with all this new non-sense going on I don't know what to think. Much like in the case I'm working on in school right now, there is no motive here. Brian blames Cris for everything, and Cris seems indifferent and unbothered by the whole situation. I was convinced in my head that they were fucking with each other because of a rivalry fueled by jealousy. But if that were the case, why would I be brought into it—unless one of them was furious about what happened last night? But really, would either of them actually be so childish as to come to my apartment and damage my things in order to make a point? I really don't know. I have no enemies, so that's what makes this even more of a mystery. And none of this started happening until Cris came back. I hate to say it, but I really am starting to wonder if it's one of them trying to use me as a way of getting rid of the other—even if it means scaring me to death. Right now my main focus is going to be developing a motive—just like in class. I have to connect the puzzle somehow—the tire slashing—the break in at Brian's house—my own home invasion—and most importantly, the supposed planted evidence Cris found in her car. Anyone who would go to such lengths is a danger to society—whether it be a person I love or not. The mental instability is something I wasn't displeased to let go of after the Valentina situation resolved. I've had enough of that to last a lifetime and then some. I need normalcy—or at least something close to it.

"Good morning, Kali," Professor Denali greets me as I walk into class. "First to arrive, last to leave, as always," he smiles.

"Always. This is why I have earned a reputation as the teachers pet. I'm not that popular in this class."

"Well, popularity doesn't land you an internship, does it now?"

"Point noted. And I concur."

He stands and walks over to the table in which I've sat down at.

"So I haven't gotten any word back on the DNA yet. I'm hoping for this afternoon or tomorrow at the latest."

"That would be awesome, especially seeing as how..." I stop, wondering if this is appropriate to discuss such personal business with my teacher.

"Go on."

I sigh. "So the situation is complicated. To make a long story short I am dating two people right now—both of which are at each other's throats. I thought one or the other might be behind all of this. But whoever is doing this has come into my house now—twice. It's no longer a feud between the two of them. Now it's involving me. The problem is I am trying to use my experience and knowledge from what you've taught me to help me solve this mystery. But I'm stuck. I can't find my motive in my faux crime scene, and I can't find it in my own dilemma."

He takes his glasses off and lays them on the table, looking me in the eye.

"Sometimes the key to solving a crime is the simplicity. Take away the complicated stuff—the evidence and the DNA—fingerprints—and go back to the basics. Sometimes when you're looking too hard at something you can completely miss what is right in front of you. The one bit of advice I can give you as far as finding motive is to look beyond your suspects. Sometimes we are so busy looking at the suspect that we forget to look deep into the life of the victim. How can you establish motive if you don't even know anything about your victim? Ask yourself that."

I'm confused. It was my home that was invaded—twice. That would make me the victim—and I know everything about myself. His theory might work for my crime scene, but it doesn't apply here.

"I don't get it, Brian's tires were slashed, and then evidence was said to be planted in Cris's car—which I happened to bring in today for analysis if I have time. Brian's home was broken into, and then my own. Who is the victim here?" I ask.

"It seems that Brian is a target—his personal property was the first one damaged. Even if the evidence was planted in Cris's car by another person, technically Brian is the victim until that is a proven fact."

"And what about me? Am I am victim since someone scratched the word 'whore' into my countertop?"

"If it were isolated I would say yes, but since the other crimes were committed previously, you are being used as an extra."

"An extra?"

"Yes. Basically whoever is committing these acts of crime against Brian is screaming at him through you. Obviously, he didn't get the message from the first incident or even the second. The suspect is basically saying, *if you didn't hear me before, you will certainly hear me now.*"

"So I'm just a pawn to get to Brian?"

"That's what experience would tell me."

"So you're saying that it's probably Cris?" I ask bluntly.

"Absolutely not. I am only saying your victim appears to be Brian right now. If this so called planted evidence in Cris's car happens to be legit, than you will have the job of deciding who your victim really is. Not everything is as it seems at face value. Look into Brian and his past a little more. Try to figure out why someone would want to threaten him. You already have a head start. Whoever it is left their DNA behind on that lipstick, as well as on the new evidence from Cris's car. But more importantly, you already know that it's someone directly connected to you as well. Otherwise, why would they use you as a pawn to grab Brian's attention?"

"Well, I haven't even told Brian or Cris yet."

"Good. Since you have no intention of taking this to the police than there is no need at this point to tell either of them. Your suspect could be staring you right in the face. Don't give either of them any information. Play the case like you would play poker. If you show your hand, they will take everything you've got and run."

"You're right. Thank you so much for everything."

"No problem. Did you want to analyze that evidence Cris found in the car? I know you're slammed today with your assignment."

"That would be amazing!"

"And what about the car where it was found?"

"Cris and I were actually planning to do it together. I wanted to bring her car here so we could look for fibers, hairs, and lift some prints."

"Good idea. But like I said, just keep it quiet. Can you come up tonight by yourself?"

"I don't think it will be a problem."

"Okay, 'borrow' her car and I will meet you here with the collection kits. And Kali, one more thing," he looks concerned, "if this escalates any further, I suggest you alert the authorities. If Brian is your victim here and they see that they are getting to him successfully through you, it could put you at risk."

"Yes, sir. I understand."

It doesn't take long for the rest of my classmates to start piling in and teaming up with their partners. Jesse comes in sporting my favorite drink, a white chocolate latte from Café Briscoe.

"Good memory, Jesse. You remembered my favorite drink," I smile, holding my hand out gratefully.

"Well, I can't take the credit. When the little blonde gay boy at the counter asked if I was on my way to school I told him I was and he asked me to bring this to you."

"That's Lawrence. He is such a doll."

"Sweet as a little fairy," Jesse jokes.

"Hey now, be nice."

"I'm kidding. Sensitive much?"

"No. It's just—I'm kind of dating a woman myself. I'm no different than Lawrence."

He looks confused, and stunned at the same time.

"Hey, different strokes for different folks. I was just under the impression that you were exclusively dating Officer McDowell, my mom's partner. At least, that what she told me when I mentioned that you were my team mate for this assignment."

"Well, I'm sure she just didn't want to give away my personal business. I like your mother; she has always been a kind person and a great partner to Brian. She's a good woman."

Jesse rolls his eyes.

"Yeah, she has her moments. The fact that she's still single is telling," he laughs.

"That's your mom you're talking about, dude. Be nice. Plus, we women all have our moments. We aren't the easiest people to get along with, trust me I know. I'm on the other side of it now. But for the record, I am still seeing Brian as well. We can just leave it at that."

"Sure thing. I don't even want to know."

"Good," I smile. "Let's get to work."

There are simply not enough hours in the day. After letting Professor Denali's advice sink in I requested additional reports regarding the victim of my crime scene. She has been named 'Colleen Marcus.' After reading some of the background reports and new information I realize very quickly that my suspect pops right out at me. All along I had suspected the husband, wondering if he were looking for some kind of incriminating papers that the ex-wife might have had hidden out in her room. But he has been eliminated easily. I know exactly who did it. Now I just have to prove it. I look to Jesse, who is finishing up reading the reports for himself.

"So, what do you think?" I ask, indulging in the fact that I basically get to play the role of teacher when it comes to Jesse. It feels good to be the one with the insight.

"I think it's the husband. He was looking for something and he didn't find it. He took a couple of items just so she would report something missing and not suspect him," he replies.

"Um—I don't think so. You read the background reports and previous police records for our victim, Colleen, right?"

162

"Well, I breezed through it. Honestly, there wasn't anything that really grabbed my attention about it. She is a single mom, she works as a real estate agent, makes good money, and has a new boyfriend she has been seeing for around six-months. There is nothing extraordinary about her."

I sigh loudly, I had really hoped that I could teach him a thing or two and that he might actually be able to pass this class. Since I know his mother, it almost feels like a kid brother that I'm trying to mentor. But sadly, he is just not grasping it.

"Jesse, if you go back in the file you will see that this is the fifth report filed in the last month. Four previous times Colleen had summoned the police saying someone was trying to break in to her home. In the notes the officers always documented that she acted erratically during questioning, never fully giving them the details they needed. The only thing she would consistently ask for was her ex-husband—not the boyfriend."

"And?"

"And each time that this happen it was documented that once the ex-husband arrived Colleen would suddenly stop cooperating with police and ask them to leave."

"Yeah, she's scared of him. She might have thought it was him breaking in, panicked and called the police, then regretted it when he showed up fearing that he would retaliate if she implicated him."

"Your theory is flawed. You're forgetting the fact that she's the one who had him called there—each and every time. She didn't want the police to search the house, she didn't want a guard—which was offered and refused. All she wanted was for her ex-husband to come to the rescue—which is very odd considering the fact that documents prove that she fought the divorce tooth and nail. She should have wanted nothing to do with him after he left her high and dry. She had a new boyfriend and no reason to call her ex for protection."

"I see what you're saying. But calling a person who you've been with for most of your life for protection is hardly incriminating. It's a reflex."

"True, but on the forth report of an attempted break-in there was something very different. This time, the ex-husband refused to come."

"And?"

"She had to up the ante. They were becoming suspicious because of her pattern of crying wolf. This time it *was* a break in— not an attempted break in. She took it to the next level because she had cried wolf too many times and people were starting to notice— including the ex-husband that she was still desperately trying to hold on to. She staged this burglary herself. This was all a ploy to get him back in her life and it failed. She was grasping at straws."

"Is that enough of a motive to do something like that?"

I consider my own situation and think about his question. Would Brian be desperate enough to stage being stalked simply so I would run back to him? It seems excessive, sure, but it's possible. This case seems to be tying way more into my personal situation than I realized.

"It depends on how much she wanted him back. If she fought that divorce as hard as the documents say, then I say yes; that was certainly enough for a motive—for her. Now, that we've established that, we can go in tomorrow and begin collecting evidence. Assuming you agree with my theory. If not, please throw something else out there."

"I am going with you on this. But something tells me there is something we are missing. That was too simple. Denali wouldn't have given you something so cut and dry. I think we need to keep an open mind. We can start with her, and if we can prove it than great. If not, we will need to think outside of the box. I do agree that we should eliminate the husband as a suspect, though. You made a good point. He just seems to want to move on and visit with his children on the weekends. He ain't studying her."

I love the way he put that. At least we agree on that part. He ain't studying that woman. But I still think a person in love with a person who doesn't love them back is a dangerous thing all together. I know that first hand. This Colleen character is in my radar. And I'm going to get her. But for the rest of the day, I am going to work on my own little mystery. I'm going to look more into my own victim and see if there is anything I'm missing about him. At this point everyone is a suspect in my eyes. This all started when Cris came back and I decided I was going to date them both. There are very few people in my life right now, and everything bad that's happened is revolving around three of us, Brian, Cris and myself. I know it's not me. That leaves two other people. I need to figure this out quick—before someone does something stupid. I need help and I know the perfect person to ask.

Brian

"You alright today, B?" Sharon asks Brian, concerned for her partner and friend.

"I'm okay. Drank a little too much last night. It was a wild night."

She turns her head suspiciously towards him as he drives towards the PD.

"Do I even want to know?"

He smiles a bit, "I finally got some. Bout time."

She is less than interested today; she herself has a chip on her shoulder that Brian can't quite figure out. The moment she got to work today she acted off. He hopes she isn't getting sick. The Corn Festival will begin this weekend and they are short staffed to begin with. People often drink too much and cause a ruckus the entire weekend.

"What's with you today, Sharon?"

"I was up really late helping Jesse study. I'm not trying to be a bitch, but Kali is supposed to be his partner. She dips out on him every chance she gets to go and party with you or Cris. He needs help and she is failing him."

Brian is defensive over Kali and knows for a fact that there is no way that Kali would ever compromise her schooling to party. To an outsider it might seem that way, but Brian knows better. Kali is the most focused person he knows and failure would never be an option. She has been scatterbrained lately, and he has noticed certain changes in her behavior that he doesn't quite understand, but she never has dealt with stress well. Back in the day when Cris went into the hospital Kali was a danger to herself, and at times, she was a danger to Brian too. But he would never let her know some of the things she did during that time. Much of it she doesn't remember—she was on so much medication that much of that period of her life remains nothing more than a blur. He shouldn't have done it, spiking her food and drinks with anti-depressants and anxiety medication was crossing the line and he knew it, but he couldn't bare to see her in such pain. She will never know about that. He stopped once he realized he was dosing her improperly. One night she actually thought he was Cris, and turned into a completely different person,

166

almost killing herself in a display of love for her. To this day Kali still believes she attempted suicide of her own choosing. But Brian knows the truth—she was drugged to oblivion and had a bad reaction. He will never forgive himself for that. Fixing Kali could have been so simple, but he didn't want to resort to the level he is considering approaching now. He is running out of options though. He won't lose Kali, and he certainly won't let anyone act as if she is stupid, irresponsible, or negligent in her own life. Sharon has no right to blame Kali for Jesse's short falls.

"You know what, Sharon, it's not her job to teach him. She is his partner. She has a lot going on. She isn't failing anyone. You need to check your facts. Kali kicks ass in school. Don't act like an asshole because Jesse just ain't got the knack for forensics," Brian fires back.

"Look, I know. I'm sorry. Just bare with me. I'm tired and I'm worried that Jesse will fail this class. He lives for forensics. I just don't know... I had him at fourteen years old. I gave up my entire life for this moment—to raise him well so he could spread his wings. I always told him he could be anything he wanted to be. I feel like a liar," she tears up.

"Sharon, there are still six months left. They have a lot to learn. He'll catch up. Don't doubt yourself so much. You're young, beautiful, devoted, and such a wonderful mother and person in general. Jesse is lucky to have you. Anyone would be lucky to have you," he leans in to give her a comforting kiss on the cheek.

She turns her face—deliberately—stealing a forbidden kiss from his warm lips. Brian can't move, he's stunned still. The loneliness is what keeps him from pulling away at first, but all he can see is Kali in the back of his mind.

"Stop," he backs up, unbuckling his seatbelt and shifting in the seat uncomfortably. "I'm sorry if I gave you the wrong impression somehow..."

"Oh my god, don't be. I'm the one who should be sorry. I—I don't know why the fuck I just did that," her face glows crimson. "Brian, please forgive me."

He hugs Sharon, sympathizing with the loneliness she must feel. But he is also nervous too. What if someone saw them? It would jeopardize his relationship with Kali.

"I know you're lonely and you and I have a past, but this can never happen again. And please, don't tell anyone about this. I can't have Kali finding out."

"Of course, I would never…"

"Good. After every dirty little thing I've done to win her back, I can't fuck it up now. I'm so close I can taste it. It can't be all for nothing."

"What do you mean every dirty little thing you've done? Tell me you are keeping it clean—legally," Sharon prods, clearly worried about his recent behavior.

"Just don't let this little kiss incident slip. Okay?" He steps out of the police cruiser and walks back to his car, ignoring her question and heading home. He has a big night ahead of him. Tonight is the night he will finally get Kali back—permanently. It's time for Cris to disappear.

Cris

Cris was so disgusted with herself after she got home last night that she reverted back to one of her very old and extremely unpleasant habits. She washed her entire body in bleach water. Not that she was trying to wash Kali away, but because she herself is such a vile human being. She actually let Brian, a man she loathes; touch the woman she loves more than her own life. What kind of person—especially one who wants to marry this girl—would allow something like that to happen? Cris can't even look at herself in the mirror. Her actions were despicable—and completely disrespectful to Kali. Kali would have never done that if Cris hadn't bought her those drinks. She feels like a date-rapist. Not to mention, she got so upset last night that she had another blackout. This is twice in a week. She has got to get a grip on herself or she is going to end up back in the same position she used to be. As much as she has tried to deny it over the last few days, she feels it coming on and she is powerless to stop it. And no amount of medication is going to help her. Either this situation has to come to an end or she will be forced to make a decision that she doesn't want to make. She can't lose Kali. That's a fact. But Cris is losing faith in her ability to maintain self-control.

She looks down at her hands, wondering where the cuts came from and praying she didn't do something stupid while she was blacked out last night. She saw Kali leave this morning, so she knows she is okay, and she drove by the police station and saw that Brian made it to work, so she is confident that she inflicted no harm to either of them. Still, not remembering how the hell those cuts got on her hands has been tormenting her all day.

"What the fuck did I do?" she buries her face in her hands, praying for a memory, but nothing comes.

Cris decides that she will not go back to the psychiatrist until all of this nonsense is over with. She doesn't want anyone knowing that she is falling apart again—especially Kali. Everything is unraveling—quickly.

Kali

Kali parks her car and heads steadily into the police station, immediately running into Sharon.

"Oh hey, Kali. Brian just headed home," Sharon smiles widely.

Kali has always liked Sharon. She is an inspiration to all of us, and also very kind to Cris when she was in custody all those years ago. Now that she and Brian are partners, she has become almost like family, attending parties and BBQ's during the summer. She makes the best potato salad you've ever put in your mouth, but damn if she will give out that family recipe. I understand though, she has no family left now. She lost her mother and her father both last year to cancer. I can't imagine losing both of my parents within a year of each other and both in such a long, drawn out and painful way. All she has left is Jesse, which I am embarrassed to admit that I had no idea was the same guy who has been in my class for the last year. I can't believe I never made the connection. But honestly, I keep to myself in class. Until this group assignment we haven't had to team up. And being the 'old folks', Jesse never took much interest in hanging out for our family BBQ's. It's funny what a small world it seems to be here in Humboldt.

"I am actually here to see you. Not Brian."

Her face turns ghost pale and she swallows hard before speaking.

"Kali, I swear to you it was an accident. I wasn't thinking. I'm so sorry."

She is absolutely panicking. She usually isn't this uptight. And she obviously feels guilty about something. Though, I have no idea what it would be. We haven't talked in weeks.

"What the heck are you talking about, woman? You have no reason to be sorry to me, unless you plan on never giving me that recipe. I might actually hate you for that," I laugh.

Her relief is so blatant that I can actually feel her exhale from across the desk.

"I—I just felt bad for not calling to check in on you. I know things have been stressful with Cris coming back and all. I haven't been a very good friend," she looks down at the calendar on her desk. I feel terrible that she feels this way.

"Oh honey, don't be silly. Things have been so busy lately that I didn't even notice. I'll make a deal with you. You give me the potato salad recipe, and I will forgive you for doing absolutely nothing wrong. I think that's totally fair."

"Not on your life," she perks up. "So then, what's up? I know you didn't come all the way here for my potato salad recipe."

"Actually, I didn't. I need your help."

"Of course."

"I need to get some information on Brian. And please, I really need this to stay quiet. I know it's asking a lot, but if it weren't important I wouldn't be here."

Sharon is unsure and concern takes over her face.

"Kali is Brian okay? Has he—done something?" she asks slowly, peaking my interest.

"Why do you ask?"

"I asked you first, Kali," she reciprocates, then stands, walking over to close the office door.

"The answer is that I don't really know. Some odd things have been going on, and I don't know what to think anymore. I just want to make sure he is protected, as well as other parties of interest."

She reflects on the idea for a moment and finally replies.

"And this is staying off the books, even with Brian?"

"Yes, especially with Brian. No police—no Brian—no Cris."

"Alright. What do you need?" She asks, reluctantly.

"Background check and an account of anything you think might be important. Changes in behavior, something he may have said or done. Things of that nature. I'm telling you, Sharon, something weird is going on. And this is for his benefit as much as my own."

I can tell she doesn't want to do this—especially without an explanation. But she seems concerned too, which might very well be my way in.

"Alright, I will email you the background check, and only because I have the same feeling as you. Brian is not himself right now. Something he said today really threw me off."

"What was that?"

"He said that after every dirty deed he's done to try and save your relationship he can't back down now. When I asked if he was keeping it legal he refused to answer. I'm concerned too, Kali. I'm worried that this vendetta with Cris has taken over his good sense. We need to do something before he ends up making a mistake he will regret. Also, there is something else…"

"What?" I ask as knots begin forming in my stomach.

"We confiscated an unregistered gun during a routine traffic stop today. He told me he logged it but when I checked, he didn't. It's missing."

"Brian has his own guns—and plenty of them. I'm sure there is some kind of mistake," I reply.

"He has guns that are registered to him…" she says.

"But this one in untraceable," I finish.

"Exactly."

"Get that report to me ASAP," I rush from the office, heading straight for Brian's house.

9
Taken

Kali

On the way to Brian's place I made a failed attempt at tending to my first order of business, which was to call the apartment complex management and demand an immediate changing of the locks. I explained that I've had a few incidents of someone entering my home without permission. After a half hour of wasted time and several exchanges of frustration-induced profanity, I finally end up hanging up on them having gained nothing. They certainly weren't as helpful as I had hoped. I was informed that I would have to file a police report in order for them to change the locks—and get Cris's permission since she is the leaseholder. I suppose I'll simply have to install a dead bolt myself, whether it's against lease policy or not. Fuck them. If they wont help me I'll help myself.

When I drive by the house I immediately see that Brian isn't home so I decide that there is no better time than now to go inside and poke around for this gun that Brian supposedly made off with. I'm certain that Sharon is just overly nervous about his recent behavioral changes and just overreacting. More than likely it just slipped his mind and it's in there sitting on his desk waiting to be logged into evidence. I just can't see Brian doing something like that. Most of the work I do in forensics is based off instinct, and I just can't fathom that he would have any necessity for an unregistered gun. My instinct tells me there is just some kind of mix up, but I've learned to never assume anything in this field. Assumptions can get people killed.

It's easy to see now why detectives are forbidden from working on cases involving their own friends or family. It's impossible to be objective. Every time something involving Cris or Brian comes along I refuse to believe its validity. That could easily be why I can't figure out who it is that's causing all this chaos. I don't want to believe that either of them would do something so awful to each other or myself. So far no one has been hurt, and I doubt it will ever come to that. But this isn't just a competition to win my heart anymore; they are playing so hard against each other I think they have completely forgotten what they were playing for. Now it's just become a game of revenge. I can trust Brian, he is mentally competent, but Cris is a still a wild card. It's been less than two weeks and there are certain traits from her past that are already popping back up. She is becoming more quiet and reserved, keeping her feelings to herself. She is spending more and more time at home again, isolating herself from public places. And worse, I caught her doing that breathing thing on the drive home after we had sex last night. She was upset—probably because I let another man touch what she still believes is hers—or maybe upset because she let it happen. I am the one pushing them to this point. This is my entire fault, and I realize that. I know she would never hurt me, but it's Brian's safety that concerns me. I've seen Cris angry before, and when she gets like that she does things that she simply can't control. Could it have been her who came into my home and used a knife to carve 'whore' into my countertop? Is she so furious with me about having sex with Brian that she would do something like that? I hate to admit that the old Cris **would** do something like that. But Brian— at least no Brian I've ever known—would do something so horrible. I'm beginning to think I'm looking too hard at the wrong person. Brian is no criminal.

After searching every nook and cranny of the house I see no sign of a gun that I don't recognize, nor do I find anything else that might be interesting. I knew Sharon was wrong. Brian would never do something like this. He lives for the law. It's his calling. Searching his home was a complete waste of time, so I leave and begin plotting my next move on the five-minute drive home.

I see Cris's car there and I decide that I will go ahead and create a cover story for why I need to 'borrow' her car tonight and get it to the lab so Frankie and I can get it analyzed. I suppose I understand his advice to keep them both in the dark about what I'm looking for, but I still feel icky about lying to either of them. Not to mention, Cris will know if I'm lying to her. She can sense it. I'm going to give it a shot, but I don't know if it will work.

Her front door opens before I can even knock.

"I saw you pull up. I've been waiting for you," she smiles. "Come on in and grab a bite to eat. You must be starved after being at school all day."

"Actually I'm not really hungry, Cris."

Her facial expression changes instantly. It might just be my own paranoia, but it seems as if she is already catching a breeze that something just isn't right. It could be something as small as a look on my face, or the tone of my voice. But she is already picking my head and watching me closely as I stand quietly on her stoop, not quite sure how to approach. How am I going to convince her to let me borrow her car if my heart starts pounding at the mere thought of lying to her?

"Come on. I've been cooking for hours so I could surprise you when you got home. It's your favorite…enchiladas. You know you want some," she urges.

I feel bad. But I know I have to stay focused and figure this out quickly before anything else happens. Every minute I procrastinate puts someone in danger. I have to be firm with her.

"I don't really have time, Cris. I have a lot going on."

"Just a bite and you can go. You know I don't like it when you don't eat. It bothers me. Why are you doing that to me?"

"It's not anything personal, and it has absolutely nothing to do with you. I am a grown adult I eat when I say. I thought you were past this whole business of bossing me around," my tone comes out sharper than I intended.

Her expression changes again and I can see she is humored by my forwardness. Humored—but unimpressed—and still relentless.

"Oh Kali, will that attitude of yours ever change?"

"No."

"Well let me redirect the situation and be more clear. You're going to come inside. You're going to eat. And then you're going to let me send you back home to work on your studies after a nice latte nightcap. Is that a more acceptable explanation about what you—as a grown adult—will be doing for the next hour? Or do I need to provide better instructions for the third time?" She speaks slow and clearly, without even a spike in her volume.

"And if I choose to NOT do any of those things?" I snap back, as familiar butterflies of torment begin weaseling their way into my stomach.

"You don't need a reminder of what happens when you don't follow the rules. Sit down. Now. I mean—please," she attempts to smooth her words into a more acceptable approach. "I'll fix you a plate."

I don't argue this time and avoid further conflict by taking her cue and walking inside. This is the first time in a while I have felt compelled to do as she says, and to be honest, I don't know how to feel about it. I'm afraid that her hard work has been tainted because of the stress I've put on her. I owe it to her to cooperate.

Once I'm inside I notice that her therapy experiment didn't seem to last very long. Her apartment is spotless and everything is in its rightful place. That doesn't necessarily mean that she has reverted back to her old self—it just means that she isn't ready for such monumental changes yet. I don't blame her though; it would have driven me crazy to live in such a wreck.

I walk to the cabinet to get a glass for some water and she grabs my hand, stopping me.

"I've got it. I just organized all those. No touchy," she says jokingly, though I'm not sure how much of that was actual humor, or how much of it was meant seriously.

I try to push away that nagging feeling; that horrible instinct that I can't deny. She is changing back. Which makes another thing I notice seem even more peculiar.

"What's with the gloves, Cris?" I ask, suspiciously. "People don't wear gloves in June."

She stalls for a moment, nervously laughing as she responds.

"I—I just can't seem to get warm today. I told you, my body hates me the day after I drink too much. No more of that for a while," she explains. "And speaking of that, I really want to apologize for what happened last night," her mood begins stabilizing again.

I knew she was upset about last night. I could hear it in her breathing…

"Cris, there is no apology needed. I'm not sorry."

"Well I am. I feel like you wouldn't have done that had I not got you plastered. You're supposed to be lady in public—not a whore."

The words jump back at me like a bad acid trip. This fucking word has been thrown at me twice in the last twelve hours, once carved into my countertop, and now again by Cris herself. Who is she to depict how I should act in public? Call me defensive, but that word just hit me in the gut—hard. I suppose that answers that question. Cris is the one who thinks I'm a whore—and she isn't having any trouble telling me so either. Of course it had to be her who came into my home. I suppose that was my punishment. I don't know what's worse; the fact that Cris thinks so low of me, or that deep down I feel like she's right. Why should I even care at this point? I wish I could honestly say that I don't. But goddamn it, I do.

"Say what you want, Cris. I'm no whore. And obviously that's how you feel about me. Thanks for the message by the way. It was well received. Bridgette found it absolutely charming when she woke up to find it carved into the countertop. You know, you could have just said it to my face. You didn't have to frighten us because you're pissed off that I fucked another man in front of you and *YOU* let it happen. I'm out of here," I fling door open, furiously.

She pulls me back inside; kicking the door closed and slamming it so hard the pictures on the wall shake and threaten to fall.

"You sit the fuck down. You aren't going anywhere," her eyes burn into me, as she pushes me down on the couch—hard—forcing me to sit.

"Cris, I am not playing this game with you this time. I'm leaving."

She is angry—angrier than I've seen her in six years.

"No you aren't going anywhere until you talk to me. Someone was in your apartment again and you're just now telling me? We are calling the police—now."

"Don't play these games with me. The jig is up. It was you. You are the one with a key—technically you're leaseholder so you can come in whenever you want. And you called me a whore because you were angry last night. I heard you in the car—you were breathing. You came in there and used a knife to carve 'whore' into my butcher block, and now you've sat here and said it again—to my face this time."

"Kali, I do NOT think you're a whore. I was saying that I felt bad for treating you like one last night. I could never think of you in such a way. I love you too much for that."

I know I was instructed by Professor Denali to not to say anything about what's going on, but I just can't hold it in. I'm furious. And not just because she violated my space, but more so, because now she's lying to me.

"Cris, I am going to give you an opportunity to do the right thing here. I want to know why you came into my apartment and did that. What were you thinking? What did you expect to accomplish? Did you honestly think I would assume that Brian would do something like that?"

Cris paces back and forth, not saying a word.

"Cris, tell me the truth. You know your behavior is changing, don't you? You know you're having trouble upholding your stability. And you're trying to hide it from me. I can see it. The same old Cris from six years ago is standing here right in front of me now. You're angry and forcing me to stay here, you're avoiding my questions, you were breathing last night—you're that same compulsive neat freak who won't even let me get my own glass from the cabinet. What else? What more are you trying to hide from me? You know what bothers me the most? If you had just been honest from the beginning we could have worked it out together."

She stops walking and faces me—defeated. The saddened look in her eye tells me there is more.

"Okay. You're right. I had another blackout last night after I got home. I was so angry and ashamed of what I did to you. I tried to ward it off but it got me. I know I'm changing, and as soon as all of this is over I will go back to outpatient treatment, but right now the most important thing is you. I come last."

"No, you do not come last. Don't you even want to know what happened last night while you were zoned out? You already know in your heart don't you? You came into my home and destroyed my property."

"I did want to know. Now I don't—I don't want to think I would do something so horrible."

"Cris, do you have any recollection whatsoever about last night? Do you have any clues at all?" I beg, needing to hear it straight from her.

"I had one clue but it didn't make sense—until now," she looks down at her gloved hands, as tears drop from her eyes.

"Take your gloves off."

Her hands are cut to pieces. From the look on her face she knows what she's done now. She knows she is the person who cut up my countertop. And she is absolutely devastated.

"Kali, you can go now," she sniffles.

"No. I want to help you."

"You can't help me. Obviously. I told you long ago that there was no help for me. I was fooling myself. I can't believe what I've done to you—and probably to Brian as well. I wanted to play fair. I guess my fucked up mind just wouldn't let me."

"So you're admitting to all of these things? The tires, the break-in—all of it."

She cries softly and opens her front door to let me out.

"I suppose so. I can't really deny or confirm what I don't remember. But nothing else makes sense. It had to have been me. I'm sorry, Kali."

I know this was my fault. I wont just let her sit here and blame herself for everything when I am just as guilty as her. She is remorseful. And she is sick. Blaming or chastising her would be like scolding an infant who knew no better. I wont turn my back on her— I cant.

"Cris. What is it that you need from me?"

"I need you to leave. I won't ever bother you again, I promise. I'm going back into the hospital. I'll pack now."

I can't help but wonder if she is doing this for me or for herself. I don't want her to leave again, and I certainly don't want her to walk away permanently. Together or not, we are part of each other now.

"Is the hospital what you really think you need, Cris? I know a better way to fix this. Don't go."

"I have never wanted to do anything aside from love you, Kali. I wanted to change for you and I tried. I can't live with you. I can't live without you. I'm poison. I've made my choice. I'm going

179

back to the hospital. Maybe one day they will fix me. Maybe not. But I cannot even consider being in a position where I might hurt you again. I don't trust myself. Leave now. This really is goodbye."

I have a better understanding now of how emotions can swallow you whole and sink you into the pits of darkness. That's where I am now. Everything around me has disappeared. I won't even fight it. I want to go into the hole. With Cris gone, I have nothing left. Funny how after all these years and everything we've been through, **this** is what it took to realize that she is the one for me. She will always be the one. And now it's too late. If I hadn't pushed her so hard and put so much stress on her she would have never felt as if she was a danger to me. I cost myself everything. My life is over. I can't handle this anymore.

Brian

    Brian has been thinking long and hard about his next move. He's known this day would come for quite some time, but until now he wasn't ready to take such a huge and life changing step. Kali is worth it, but it still goes against everything he has ever believed in. But now is not the time for nervousness. He looks in the mirror one last time and bids farewell to the person he used to be. Things will never be the same after tonight, nor can it ever be taken back. This is it.

Kali

After leaving Cris's place I decided to go home and cry it out. This is the end of that chapter in my life and it's killing me. Cris has severed all contact with me. After everything she's done to correct herself for me I turn around and push her right back into the place she had risen from. It was never my intention. I only wanted to give them both a fair shot. In the end, I have created a monster of myself. I was selfish and cruel for ever expecting either of them to cooperate with such a self-serving plan. I should have gone with my first instinct and chosen whom I loved the most. I knew who it was then—and I still know it now. But it's too late. Choosing is no longer an option. Because in my mind I know damn well I don't deserve either of them.

I try to hide the fact that I'm sobbing like a child when my phone rings. It's Denali. I can't let him hear me like this.

"Uh—hello," I clear my throat, trying to sound professional.

"Hey, Kali. It's Frankie. Are you available to talk for a minute?"

"Yes, actually I was going to call you and tell you I won't be able to make it tonight with Cris's car. Plus, it's no longer necessary. I've already figured it out."

"So you aren't interested in what I found out about the DNA?"

"I already know. It was Cris's DNA. She's confessed. I don't know how she fooled us on the prints, but it doesn't really matter now. She is checking herself back into the mental hospital tonight. She's already left

"Actually, there wasn't a trace of Cris's DNA anywhere on that lipstick."

I am baffled for a moment, but allow him to continue without saying a word.

"The hair we found had no record in the data-base unfortunately, but it did have a cross-reference to another person who IS in the data-base. A close family member of your suspect."

"I'm confused."

"We haven't got that far yet in class so I'll explain. When you run DNA even if your suspects DNA is not in the database it will cross-reference any person who has extremely similar DNA in the database. In this case, the DNA was so similar that it has to be a close relative to the person of interest. The probability of close relations was 99%. It doesn't get much better than that."

"So who was it then?"

"I'm waiting for the results of that now. I have to confirm before I say with certainty. I should have a name by the end of the night. Just be careful and keep both eyes open."

"I will. Again, thank you so much."

As if this weren't complicated enough. Now I find out that Cris isn't guilty after all. But who else? And why were Cris's hands all cut up if it wasn't her? Where the hell am I going wrong? I should have waited for actual proof before convincing Cris it was she who had committed these crimes unknowingly. Whether she's innocent or guilty, I have made her believe the latter.

A chime hits my phone before I get a chance to consider my next move. It's the email I was waiting for from Sharon.

Kali,

I hate to do this to you because you have always been good to me. But I can't do this background check for you. It's not fair that Brian doesn't know about it, and more importantly, I am a single mother and I could lose my job.

Please understand,

Sharon

Ps: For the record I think what you're doing is wrong. It's none of my business and I am way out of line here, but you are hurting people who don't deserve to be hurt. Keep that in mind and consider how you would feel if the shoe were on the other foot. I know better than anyone that being pushed aside for someone else is heartbreaking. Don't be that person. Walk away from them both.

"Wow, tell me something I don't already know." I hate that this is what it has boiled down to. And I hate even more that she's right.

I look at myself in the mirror and attempt to gain the courage to face what I have done. All I see is the truth staring back at me.

The one thing I have concluded from all of this is that I am not any less mentally disturbed than Cris. I have toyed with the minds of two people for my own benefit and left them both broken. Cris could be right and be completely unable to fully rehabilitate herself. I knew that from the start—and I didn't care. I put myself above her mental needs—and I didn't care. Honestly, I didn't care about the feelings of either of them. Brian has never deserved any of this either. If I were being truthful I would have to admit that I have never given him what he deserved from the get go. Even in the beginning of our relationship he was nothing more than a mask to cover up my own mental trauma. I needed him to fill the absence of a person he could never be. I broke him down into someone I don't even know anymore. Everything we did, and everywhere we were, I was always there with Cris in my mind. He never ranked. In time, even if Cris had never shown back up, we would have ended anyway. Because he is not her. Even the new Cris was not MY Cris. She isn't the person I fell in love with. I miss the Cris who told me how things were going to be. I miss her choosing what I would eat and when I would shower and how I would wear my clothing. For some fucked up reason or another that is the person that made me happy. I should want better for her than that. But I don't. Denali says she is innocent. Secretly I was hoping for something else—just so I could have MY Cris back. That's the sickening truth staring me in the face. There is something very fucked up about that. She tried so hard to be better for me, and all I ever wanted was our old life back. I never wanted to be rescued. I was perfectly content as the victim. Now Cris is going back to the hospital for help. She will never be the same again. And neither will I. Six years ago, when Cris kidnapped me, I changed into the person I am today. No matter what role I have played over the years since then, I am still waiting to go back to my home. With my master.

Secretly, I have resented Brian for saving me in that farmhouse. It was our destiny to die together in our own perfect misery. Instead, we died on the inside, going on to live as emotionless mannequins in our own miserable lives.

Whether this DNA finally reveals the person who has been causing all this chaos is revealed or not, I simply don't care anymore. I'm finished with it all. I will get exactly what I have earned, which is to be alone. The only monster here is me. I just can't do this anymore. I'm not pretending to be somebody I'm not for a moment longer.

Cris

"What the fuck…" she moans, gripping her head in her hands with the most excruciating headache she has ever felt. She is alone, in a room with nothing more than a bed and a tray full of food and water on a side table. Even through squinted eyes she recognizes the room immediately. She is in her old bedroom in her house off Old Myers road. For a moment she wonders if she's dreaming, but as the grog wears off over the next few minutes it becomes clear—this is no nightmare.

The last thing she remembers is going to her car. She packed a bag and was heading to check herself into the mental facility in Lincoln. She remembers little after that, aside from a glimpse of a black Glock in her face as she reached for her car door. She must have been hit—hard. Hard enough to knock her out long enough to make it five miles up the street from where they started.

Fear isn't something that has struck Cris many times in her thirty-one years, but right now, she is admittedly nervous. She is fully aware that this is the position Kali was in six years ago, and that there are still a lot of people who feel like she got away with a slap on the wrist. There are many people who hate her—but no one more than Brian McDowell—a police officer who could take her down without a trace and never be suspected for a moment.

A letter is slipped under the door and Cris hobbles over to retrieve it.

You reap what you sew, Cris.

Cris knew this would come back to bite her one day. Still, she can only smile right now regarding the circumstances of this revenge kidnapping. Some people are so fucking stupid. Including whomever has taken her captive—which she has easily pinpointed as Brian. He wants her out of the way so he can have Kali.

Even when Cris was getting mental help in the hospital she could only laugh sometimes at the ridiculous procedures they used to try to fix her. She certainly has a big surprise coming for Brian. She hasn't changed; she's never been any different than she was when she went in. The only thing she gained from that six year stay was a nice long lesson in how to lie better to get what you want—legally.

She would carefully study the doctors' reactions as she was being questioned. After a couple of years she was able to pin point the things she was doing that were giving her away as a liar. Knowing those things gave Cris an opportunity to correct herself, and tip the scale somewhat. She used to be just crazy; now she is crazy and smart.

She knew from the moment of her conviction that she would have to sever contact from Kali while she was institutionalized. It was one of those situations that she knew would be difficult, but it would pay off in the end. She HAD to make it appear that she had rehabilitated. If not, Kali wouldn't have ever looked twice at her again. She needed to be smooth, and fly in under the radar in order to retrieve her position in Kali's life again. She couldn't just come in guns blazing and demand that Kali come home where she belongs. She would have to take the softer approach and really pamper the situation.

Finding out that she had shacked up with Brian while she was away was a bit of a curveball. Cris was sure that she had trained Kali well enough that she would have waited for her—whether Cris was avoiding her for six years or not.

When Kali ran off to Florida the night Cris proposed it took a hell of a lot of money to find her within a couple of hours, and even more money to hire that Bridgette bitch to convince her to start the dating game. Cris was a little disappointed that they had become friends during the trip, she was nervous that Bridgette would tell Kali. But Cris learned quickly that Bridgette's loyalty came in the form of dollar bills—hundred dollar bills. From there on it was easy.

The thought of allowing Kali to date Brian was nauseating. But it was all in the name of the game. The 'no sex' rule was something Cris was adamant that Bridgette reiterate to Kali. She could share time, for now, but she would not share Kali's body. That's why when Kali and Brian were getting a little too sexual last night on the dance floor Bridgette came to whisper to Cris, telling her she needed to step up her game. Brian was in the running again. Cris couldn't have that. The sex was unintentional. But Kali had her so turned on she would have taken any opportunity to have her pussy in her mouth, even if she was sharing it with another man's dick. Watching the passion on Kali's face was worth it in the moment. But after the fact the mere thought of it disgusted Cris—tormented her. She had let another man touch what was rightfully hers. It just didn't sit well.

Some of the things she learned in the hospital were very informative, while others weren't. She did learn how to control her breathing—finally. And she also learned anger management. She is now able to interact in certain situations without flying off the handle. Two small blackouts did happen. Though, Cris knows for a fact that she had nothing to do with either the tire slashing or the damage to Kali's countertop. She is allowing Kali to believe that, simply as an excuse for Cris to go back to the hospital. See, Cris was reading the situation and concluded that no matter how hard she was trying to impress Kali, Kali was put off by something. Cris doesn't know what she did wrong, but Kali wasn't quite as swooned by the new Cris as she had hoped. Likewise, Kali showed barely any interest in Brian. That was comforting to Cris. But the thought dawned on her that Kali was leaning towards the idea of choosing neither of them. So Cris figured another hospital stay would show her a little loyalty, and make her feel guilty for pushing her over the edge again. It was a little dirty, but well worth it in the end. But now that plan is completely fucked—thanks to Brian. Unfortunately, being locked in this room was NOT part of the plan. Nobody will know where the fuck she is. Kali thinks she's in the hospital, and will certainly tell the only friends Cris has, Lawrence and Abby, of her whereabouts. Cris doesn't speak to anyone else that might wonder where she is. The rent on both apartments is paid up for a full year, as all are of her bills. And her parents still don't speak to her; they only automatically deposit money into her bank account

188

monthly. No body will ever come looking for her. The thought is unsettling to say the least. But it is what it is. Cris is back and she will just have to improvise. She created this game; she certainly knows how to play it better than anyone. This is not over.

"Alright, Brian. Check mate, Mother-fucker."

10
Rerouting

Kali

When I said I was finished with pretending to be someone I'm not, I wasn't kidding. I am no longer splitting hairs with Brian. It's time to tell the truth—whether it hurts him or not. Of course I still feel bad about it. I'm not a total heartless bitch, but lying to him is accomplishing nothing more than dragging out the heartache. The first place I'm going after school is to see Brian. This has to end. After thinking about it in great detail last night, I decided that the situation with Cris coming to an end was also inevitable. She had become a person I could have never been happy with either. I love her and I will miss her terribly, but it's time for the games to stop. I would rather be alone than to live a life of lies. The person I'm in love with has been gone for six years. I have to move on—finally.

For now I have to worry about school. Now that my own little mystery is solved I can devote my full attention to getting that job and high-tailing it the fuck out of Humboldt for good. I forego the latte today and go in early. I have a lot of evidence to collect and Jesse has proven to be about as helpful as a rock on a riverbank. I have to prove that this woman has somehow managed to stage a burglary for the intent of making her husband come crawling back to her.

Thinking back on it, it really seemed like a sound motive. But who would go to all that trouble just for a maybe? Someone obsessed. Someone unwilling to give up? Someone willing to do whatever it takes to have the person she loves. These were the ideas I had in my head when I still thought it was Cris causing this entire dilemma in my life. I actually thought that she was willing to do anything to have me. I knew in my gut that Brian would never go to such lengths. I never suspected for a moment that he would be anything other than the upstanding man that he is. Cris though—the Cris I love—would have done anything for me. But I know the truth now. Even though Cris has been right here with me for the last couple of weeks, I've still been mourning her absence. The new Cris didn't have the same passion. She had learned how to suppress all the things that gave her that wild flame that I was drawn to like an ever-faithful moth. Yes, her body was here, but her soul was transformed into some Stepford version of who she once was. I was in denial. I had hoped that she would come back to me, but she never did and I quickly lost interest. I wanted so badly for it to work. That's why I hid my disappointment so well. I wanted her to think I was happy about the change. And maybe somewhere deep down I had convinced myself that I could eventually get used to it. But being with Brian proved that relationships of that nature—nurturing, loving, honest—were all something that left me craving more. Craving something that only my Cris—my Clyde—could ever give me. But I know now that Bonnie and Clyde are a thing of the past— and will rest peacefully in history where it was always meant to end.

She was so heartbroken when she thought she had been acting up again. That tells me she really has changed. When I thought she was coming into my apartment I was torn. I love Cris and I want the best for her. But yet when I found out it wasn't her I was crushed. It was exhilarating to think that Cris was still in there somewhere. I should have known for sure that the change was permanent after the incident at the club. MY Cris would have never allowed that to happen. It would have been over her dead body—or mine. I saw a flicker of her begin to come out during the sex—she gave me that look—but she brought herself right back out of it. That's when I knew MY Cris was never coming back to me. The blackouts and the loss of memory were just traces of what used to be. And that will never be enough for me. I can't settle for that anymore. It's MY Cris or no Cris at all.

Today I even beat Denali here. But surprisingly enough, Jesse is already here collecting evidence in the scene. I quickly throw my suit on and footies, following the path we had decided to use in the crime scene.

"Jesse, what are you doing in here without me?" I ask, with enough anger in my voice to cause alarm in his face.

"The same as you. I'm here trying to solve this case. We are partners you know? You don't have to do everything yourself. Plus, I had to get out of that fucking house. My mom is driving me insane," he vents, as he scrapes the bed sheets with a little too much force.

"Jesse, stop it. You're going to scatter any fibers on the bed to the floor. Go slow and gentle with the brush," I order firmly.

He looks scolded but if he's offended he doesn't bother mentioning it. He simply puts the brush down and steps back from the bed.

"You know, I think I'm just going to tell Denali that I'm not cut out for this."

I just yelled at this poor kid when I should be helping him. I cannot let my own frustrations get to me. It's not his fault. Much like myself, if he is going to be successful he needs to leave his personal life at home.

"Listen, let's stop for a minute and go grab a cup of coffee from the cafeteria. They are open already and we still have forty-five minutes until class officially starts. Our crime scene is no place for either of us to be blowing off steam."

"You too, then?" He sighs.

"Yeah. Yesterday sucked, today sucks, and tomorrow will probably suck too. Let's drink it over."

"I'm following you, Captain," his demeanor improves almost instantly.

We sip in silence for a moment, both trying to wake up. "I like your Pantera shirt," I comment, prompting a smile.

"I wouldn't have expected that," he replies, scalding his mouth on the sub-par cup of cafeteria coffee.

"Well, there's more to me than the naked eye reveals."

"I'm sure."

"Anyway, so, I have decided that you aren't allowed to quit this class," I smile.

"Yeah, why is that?"

"Because. I've had my own issues this week and I have been forced to make a choice that I never thought I could make. I pushed myself to the limit and finally found a solution. I know this class is hard for you, but if you really want something you have to do whatever it takes to get it. I'm going to help you."

"Why would you do that? I know about the job in Seattle. Rumors spread fast. And I don't want to be the reason you fail. You deserve a better partner than me," he replies sadly.

"Rumors? I'm calling bullshit. Nobody knows about that," I call him out, prompting a sigh.

"Okay, maybe not rumors. Brian told my mom and she told me," he admits.

"Okay. Confirmed. I am trying to get this job in Seattle. But that doesn't mean you can't have the same opportunities if you keep going. I seriously contemplated running away this week myself. But you can't out run your problems. You solve them. Just like this case. We are going to solve it, and then I am going to mentor you for the rest of the course. You are going to grasp it. I promise you."

"I still don't get why you're so nice to me."

"Why shouldn't I be?"

"Because my mom is such a bitch to you. I can't understand why she hates you so much," he blurts out, just like a typical teenaged kid would do.

I'm confused about this proclamation that Sharon hates me. She has always been pleasant—always. She's like family.

"Jesse, you must be confused. Your mom has never been anything but kind to me. I mean, she refuses to give me the potato salad recipe, but aside from that I love her to death."

"She has you fooled from head to toe," he snuffs.

"Come on, Jess. You're eighteen years old, every eighteen-year-old battles with their parents. It will pass. But I am curious, why do you think she hates me?"

"Because she does. I shouldn't tell you this, but she said you're a whore. A whore who likes to screw over innocent people like Brian. Honestly, I think she's still sore about the whole thing—even all these years later."

I am astonished. Why would she say something like that? This is beyond fucked up, but I still can't stop myself from hearing more. Especially seeing as how now I know the whore carving didn't come from Cris and I have another person who obviously hates me. I never even thought to look at Sharon. And what would she have to hate me for?

"She's sore with me about what? I've never done a damn thing to her."

"You really don't know?" He looks surprised.

"Know what?" My volume increases and leaves me irritated at feeling completely out of the loop about my own life.

"When you and Brian first met he was dating my mom. He left her for you."

That can't be right. She is thirty-two years old. I met Brian when he was eighteen. That would have made her twenty-six years old—eight years older than him. No way...

"Eighteen was legal enough for her, I suppose," he shrugs. "Plus, you're only two years younger yourself."

"But neither of them ever told me they dated. Brian tells me everything."

"Why bother to mention it? He chose you. The moment he met you my mom became invisible. That's why she hates you—sorry to say it. And now that you are dating Cris, she wants nothing more than for you to go away so she can get another shot at Brian. And judging by the fact that he slept at our house last night, she might be winning. Though, I don't think it went exactly as planned. She was fucking pissed this morning. They were fighting pretty badly."

Brian slept at Sharon's? This is new to me. I'm not jealous—exactly. But where is all this shit coming from? I feel like I know nothing about the man I've known for six years.

"Jesse, why are you telling me all this? Technically, he can sleep where—or with whomever—he chooses. It's over between us. Still, I really don't want to know about it. It's none of my business anymore. And it has nothing to do with what you just told me. I'm in love with Cris, and I always have been. That's the dirty truth of the matter. If your mother wants him and she can treat him the way he deserves to be treated than I am happy for them both. He deserves way better than me."

"I just thought you should know, considering you're still sleeping with him."

"I'm not sleeping with either of them, actually," I retort self-consciously.

"Mmmmhmmm. The entire town knows about what happened at that bondage club in Lincoln. It only takes one person to blab their mouth and the whole world knows. You really had a threesome—in public? I didn't know you had it in you. It's kind of hot, actually," he smirks, blushing. "I would fight for you too if I thought I ever had a shot."

I am humiliated to be having this conversation with an eighteen-year-old kid. I feel like Stiffler's mom, or Mrs. Robinson.

"Yeah…about that… I was plastered. End of story."

"Mom certainly wasn't very thrilled about it. When she heard about it she tore off looking for you and came back acting all weird. I honestly wasn't sure if you two had got into a brawl or not. I was worried coming in here today."

Sharon went looking for me? She never even came to me, nor did I encounter her. "Are you sure, Jesse? When did she come looking for me?"

"The night it happened. It was in the middle of the night sometime," he replies, stuffing a vending machine cracker into his mouth.

The night it happened was when my countertops got slashed up. I know for a fact that officers can get through the gate, but if it were Sharon, how would she have gotten inside my apartment?

"Jesse, I have a strange question for you. And I need this to stay between us, okay?"

"Sure."

"Do you know if police officers have key access to apartment complexes?"

"All officers have a skeleton key to apartment complexes since the management has limited entry due to the lease terms. For example, if a tenant goes missing the management can't just barge in, but the police are allowed entry with permission of next of kin. So yes and no. They have access, but they aren't supposed to use it without permission."

Jesse is more informed than I ever gave him credit for. And he just told me exactly what I needed to know. It was Sharon who was in my apartment. Her jealousy is what's pushing her over the edge.

"So last question. Why now? Why is your mother so upset by mine and Brian's relationship after all these years?"

"Because she finally has a shot. Everyone knows you'll choose Cris—including her."

"Okay. Well, I am just going to stop this conversation right here and let it go. I appreciate your honesty," I pretend to shrug it off for long enough to get through this day and address it.

"You're welcome. I'm just telling you because I'm concerned. She is so obsessed with the situation with Brian and Cris. She has been acting off since Cris came back in town. She will disappear for hours, she's sneaky, and her hatred for you has increased ten fold. She wants your man, but your man wants you. She isn't very happy about it."

"Jesse, I think we should stay out of your mother's love life. I have moved on. If it's Brian that she wants, she can have him. As for me, she can rest easy knowing that she has the last word. I lost them both. I love Cris with all my heart, but she left me long ago. And Brian is obviously tired of the drama and he's moving on. I'm happy for them both. As for your mom, I just hate that she has lied to me and pretended to be my friend."

"Whatever, I guess. I just don't want him staying at my house. It's weird with you being my partner and all. Plus, after what he did last night I think he's just as psycho as Cris."

"What do you mean?" I ask, knowing I shouldn't be questioning this innocent kid.

"I only know what I overheard this morning when he and mom were fighting. But apparently last night he and my mother were in the middle of—getting busy—and he was trying to force her to pretend to be you."

"Whoa! What?" I gasp.

"He was calling her Kali and asking mom to refer to him as Cris. He was 'practicing' as he put it. I have an assumption about what's going on, but I only heard bits and pieces. I just hate that he led my mom on when all he wants is you. I think he is trying to turn himself into Cris so you'll want him back. He's desperate. And my mother was stupid enough to let him practice on her because she's pathetically in love with him. The whole thing is insane. I can't wait to get the fuck out of that house."

This is more serious than I thought. If Sharon already has this vicious vendetta against me and Brian is leading her on, it could set her off even worse. As for Brian, what the hell is he thinking? He is not Cris. He could never be Cris. If Jesse is correct in what he heard, Brian and Sharon both are losing it. I've already made the mistake in jumping to conclusions with Cris; I need to talk to Brian before going any further. As soon as I'm finished in class that is the first place I'm going.

"Okay, Jess. Try not to let this make things awkward between you and I. Just tune it out and keep your attention on this assignment. It will pay off. We have to focus. We are right here at the finish line."

"I like you, Kali, a little too much, actually. That's the only awkwardness I feel. But we aren't going to talk about my little crush right now, or about how humiliating it is that I just said it aloud. We can just bust this work out and forget I opened my big mouth. You're still going to help me out, right?"

I am flattered and actually quite embarrassed myself. I hope my face isn't as red as it feels. I ignore the advance and focus on our assignment, for both of our benefit.

"Of course I'm going to help you. But no more personal drama in the scene. And try to remember something; whatever doubt I had about you is gone. You are more observant than you give yourself credit for. You have no idea how much you just helped me. You've got the ability. You just need to believe in yourself a little more."

"Just promise me that when you're some big shot you'll remember me and maybe give me a job as your assistant," he jokes. "And possibly even let me take you on a date sometime…"

"If that ever happens, you have my word," I grab his pinky, promising him. "Now stop flirting and get to work," I laugh, shaking my head.

Boys.

Brian

"This is so wrong. How could I have thought for one moment that I could go through with this?" Brian speaks, pacing among the hardwood floors.

He never thought he would ever go to this extent. Everything has happened so fast and now he has done something he can never take back. If Kali finds out—it's over. There will be no excusing his horrible behavior.

He considers his new options—which at this point—are limited. He has committed the absolute worse offense possible. And for what? A woman who doesn't even care about him? He will now end up hurting two people, when he had never intended on hurting anyone. Cris is the one who brought all this into his life—and he hates her with a fury that can never be verbalized. But on the other hand—Brian finally realizes that she doesn't deserve what she's getting in return, either. As much as Brian loathes her, he cannot justify what Cris is being put through.

Perhaps it's Brian's upbringing that has him so distressed, and the need to do the right thing—always. But this entire situation has gotten out of hand. He realized that last night when he made this egregious mistake. Now, after thinking about it, he is unsure how to pursue at this point. Part of him never wants to go back, in fear that he could really end up hurting her. But on the other hand, leaving her there and never going back is inhumane.

"What the fuck am I going to do?"

Cris

"Seriously—a bologna sandwich? This is fucking peasant food," she throws it against the wall in disgust.

She has squatted, leaning her head against the wall in frustration. This room is ill equipped for her taste. When she lived here it was fine, because she always saw to it that the sheets were clean and the fans were dusted. But given that this place has been abandoned for six years, it is in deplorable condition. It's too much for Cris to handle.

Everything was left as it was when she was arrested. She prays that there might be a few things she can work with to make it livable until she figures out what the hell she is going to do next.

She's confident that she will eventually get out of here. Honestly, it won't be difficult at all to take Brian down next time he comes in here. Cris is an accomplished black belt in several levels of martial arts. Police officer or not, she can take him to the ground before he ever saw it coming—as long as she was ready at the right time. The surprise factor will be essential. He's not here now. She's positive he left last night after slipping that pathetic note under the door. She is also positive that he has not returned yet either. The sound of the front door opening and closing is a sound Cris will never forget. No matter how much WD-40 she used there was always a telling squeak right at the halfway point of open or close. It drove her insane. But she was so anal about the house, there was no way she would desecrate it by replacing the door. Everything here is original and antique. The only exception she ever made was to decorate Kali's room before she came, and even then none of the structural elements were destroyed. She removed the bathroom door, storing it in the attic, but intended to put it back up at a later time when Kali became more adapted to her new life. Though, she would never get the chance.

Cris doesn't see any reason to mope around right now. Sure, she could have a poor-pitiful-me attitude, but that's just not a productive usage of her valuable time. So she does something familiar to her—she cleans. She starts by removing the filthy dust laden sheets from the bed and fills up the bathtub with water and left over body soap from when she still occupied the home. She soaks and scrubs them until her hands are wrinkled and soggy. She doesn't stop until the sheets appear white again. The job is certainly not bleach worthy—or Cris worthy—but the water runs clear after she rinses them and that's a far cry better than it was before she began. After hanging the sheets on the headboard to dry she begins dusting the room and scrubbing down the bathroom with the only product she had left under her sink. Next are the floors and baseboards. Finally the room is semi-livable again, which is a sigh of relief for Cris who was quickly becoming consumed by her OCD.

She makes the assumption that Brian isn't coming back for a while and lays her head down on the bed. There will obviously be no escape plan in the next few hours, but when he does come she will be ready. Today she will begin martial arts practice again—which she hasn't done in years. Still, Cris is the elephant that never forgets. She will have no problem taking him on. And when she does, the first thing she is going to do is let this bullshit charade fall away and go get her woman. Kali will be hers—whether she likes it or not. And Brian will never be a problem again. It's called self-defense, baby.

Kali

"Fuck yeah, baby!" I screech as I find a huge piece of evidence in our scene.

"What did you find?" Jesse curiously responds to my cheerful declaration.

I had noticed a small piece of the rug that was slightly frayed in the corner. At first it didn't mean anything to me but when I remembered that our victim didn't have any animals or anything that would be clawing at the carpet, which in all other places was in pristine condition, I began to wonder. I carefully pulled it back and discovered a hidden board underneath. As I lifted it I saw a small bag inside.

"I think I found the missing gun. Woohoo!"

"No fucking way!" Jesse says excitedly. "You were right. She did do it, and she hid the gun where she could go and get it once the investigation was all over with."

"Yep," I beam proudly.

"You're so badass, Kali. We did it!"

"Well, we still have to prove it forensically. Let's take this stuff to the lab. I'll check for prints and then you can check it for DNA. Sound good?"

We don't open the bag until we get to the lab, but aside from the heavy gun we also find her diary. I quickly lift the prints off of the gun and run through the procedures that I was taught by Denali. I plug them into the system and turn the rest of the evidence over to Jesse to handle.

"Jesse, the database search can take a little while. Do you mind if I run off and handle some business while this is searching and come back in a little bit? I've got something I need to do. Also, go ahead and start reading through the diary and see what she had to hide."

"No problem."

***

201

The next few hours are a blur. I find myself just sitting in my car staring at the steering wheel, not able to recollect the last few hours in time. I don't know if it's because I am so tired or if it's simply the stress catching up to me. All I know is that I am ready for a break—soon. If the newest plan doesn't come together for me I just don't know what I will do. It's my last hope of finding whatever it is in my life that I'm looking for. I have closed the chapter with Cris, only left with a glimmer of hope that the Cris I am really in love with will someday come back to me. As for Brian; I still have to deal with him. It's time to end this so we can move on with our lives. If Jesse is right, I really have to be straightforward and honest. I can't let my own mental issues turn him into the same person I am. I can't watch him chase a memory for the rest of his life like I am. He deserves so much more than a life of disappointment. Maybe Sharon really is the person for him. She loves him more than I ever could. She loves him like I love my old Clyde. She has proven that she will go to the ends of the Earth to give him her love—even by allowing him to love her as another person. The things she's done are deplorable, but I am trying to be understanding and let it go—for the sake of Brian and his future.

I drive aimlessly, passing by the police station twice before I mentally prepare myself for what I'm about to do. Walking through the door makes me uncomfortable now, for the first time ever. I feel like a sheet of glass and everyone can see right through me—and see what a monster I've become. Sharon's usual smile evades her, and she immediately calls after me as I walk slowly past her without uttering a word.

"Kali, where are you going?" she asks.

Mentally I have forgiven her for what she's done, but still, I can't hide the betrayal in my voice. It's pointless to even try.

"Oh, you're talking to the whore? How kind of you. Actually, I'm going to your new boyfriend's office so I can talk to him. Is he in?" I ask snidely as her face turns pale.

"Kali, it's not even like that. Yes, Brian was at my house last night, but I was keeping him there for a reason. He isn't acting right. You need to stay away from him."

"No. You know he's losing it and you took advantage of him. You actually pretended to be me so you could sleep with him? And you let him role-play as Cris? Do you have any idea how sick that is? You're enabling his instability. You're both sick."

"Kali, he is not stable right now. Just give me a few hours; I'm trying to arrange for the department counselor to come evaluate him. He was talking craziness last night. I played along because I wasn't sure how he was going to react if I didn't. He was cold and hard. I think he's really convinced himself that he can be Cris. For you. I stand here before you admitting it, I am jealous. I love Brian, and I have sat back for years watching you give him nothing—watching you vie for another person. When she came back I knew it was over. And I was happy. But when you decided to play head games with him it became personal. I hate you. You're a mean and disgusting person."

"And that gave YOU the right to carve the word whore into my countertop, to slash Brian's tires to make him think it was Cris, to plant evidence in Cris's car, and to break into Brian's home? I see what's happening here. You knew Brian and I were over, and you didn't want me to have Cris either. You wanted to hurt me like I hurt Brian. Like I hurt you all those years ago when Brian left you for me. It all makes sense now," I sneer.

"Kali, I think you've officially lost it. I did no such thing. It was Cris and you know it."

"No. See, there was evidence left behind at Brian's house and it's already been proven that it wasn't Cris. But in the next few hours I will know exactly who it was—and I think it was you."

"I suppose we'll see won't we," she replies sarcastically.

I leave her at her desk, Marching right into Brian's office where he sits staring out the window and leaning back in his chair—lost.

"Brian, honey…we need to talk."

He doesn't move, only continues looking out the window. He is completely consumed by his thoughts. The only way I can get through to his is by forcing him to listen. He knows why I'm here and he's turned his ears off. I continue anyway. For his own good he has to hear this.

"I know you don't want to talk to me. And I completely understand why. I wouldn't want to talk to me either. But we can't keep avoiding the truth. Baby, you know I love you—so very much.

I would do anything in this world for you. I just don't love you in the way I'm supposed to. I looked in the mirror long and hard this morning and I am repulsed at what I saw. All those years we were together I lied to you—and to myself. You gave me an ultimatum three years ago to choose you or Cris. Outwardly I chose you. You were good for me and the thought of losing you was more than I could bare. But on the inside, Cris was the person I really chose. She is the one that I could never escape. You tolerated the fact that I was never good to you. You knew she was still inside me. She was always there like a dark cloud covering our lives. Our relationship was based on lies and omission."

He turns in his chair and finally looks at me. Though, this is not the Brian I am used to seeing. He is hardened—just as Sharon had claimed. He has no emotion or reaction to my words at all. He only smirks as he responds, in a creepy and unnerving display of pleasure that I can't identify. "I hear Cris is finally out of the way."

"She has returned to the hospital."

"I'm sure you're upset."

"If that's what she feels like she needs to do than I am happy for her. This wasn't the life for her. And she wasn't the person for me either—at least—not THAT version of her."

He's intrigued by my words, yet not surprised.

"I figured that out pretty quickly," he replies flatly. "I could see that she wasn't the one. I could also see that I wasn't the one either. I finally figured you out. You never wanted the life I had planned for us at all, did you?"

I shake my head no, as he continues.

"Last night I made a choice. It was something I have been considering for years. If I was going to keep you in my life I would have to become the person you needed—which was Cristina James, kidnapper, master of your world. I knew Cris wasn't even that person any more—I saw it. Cris has turned into another me— something you never wanted. I couldn't be happier that she's gone— or happier that she is never coming back. With her out of the way I can be what you want me to be now—without anything here to come between us. Look at me—at what I've become. This is what you wanted right? I'm quiet, and disturbed—mentally fucked. Just seeing your face—that beautiful body—that deliciously naughty aura— makes me want to wrap my hands around your throat and fuck you so hard you bleed. You'd like that wouldn't you?" He approaches me, wrapping his hand around my throat, gripping harder than Cris ever did. This isn't an act of pleasure—he actually wants to hurt me. He has officially snapped.

"Brian, stop it. You're not Cris. She didn't do this to me," I choke the words out, struggling to pull away from his grip, unsuccessfully.

"You like it when she does it. But not me? Why Kali, why not me?"

I claw at his fingers, which are cutting, off my entire air supply. He releases just before I pass out, and picks me up slamming me down hard on top of his desk, knocking the wind out of me and pinning my arms back above my head. My head is spinning and it takes me a moment to realize what's happening. He rips my shorts down and starts fiddling with his zipper.

"Sharon didn't like this so much last night, but I know you will. You like it when someone takes what they want, don't you? I'll make you want me."

"Brian knock it off," I yell, "you aren't thinking clearly. You're not her! She would never have done this to me!" I plead as he pushes himself into me forcefully, causing a scream to burst from my lips.

He silences me with his chokehold again, making it impossible for me to fight him or to make any further pleas for help. His face is blank as he fucks harder and faster. He won't break eye contact; he wants to see the fear in my face. I think of Cris, wondering what she would do if she knew what he was doing to me. She would kill him. She would kill him slowly. I pray for her save me, but I know she's gone. I go limp and mentally let go of anything happening right now, hoping he will cum quickly and this will be over, and hoping that it will happen before he ends up choking me to death. Just as the world around me goes blank his office door flies open and Sharon pulls her gun.

"Brian! Let her go!" She orders, coming closer and placing the gun within inches of his head.

He pulls out slowly, releasing my throat, and collapsing to the floor in tears as reality sets back in and he realizes what just happened.

"What have you done to me?" He cries. "Please tell me this what you wanted."

Sharon calls for one of the Brian's closest friends at the station for back up.

"Take Officer McDowell to my office until I get there."

"Why? What's happened?" Officer Hanson steps in, looking at me and wondering what's going on. His speculations are accurate, but I can't let Brian fall for this. I'll lie if I'm questioned. This was not his fault and he will not be punished for this.

"Um—we got a little carried away, is all," I lie. "Fantasy gone bad. I'm so humiliated. Please don't say anything. I don't want him to get in trouble for trying to please me."

"Yes, Hanson," Sharon confirms. "I'll talk to him about it when I'm done with Miss. Ness. But I'm sure you'll agree that nobody in the station needs to know about what happened here. Boys will be boys," she fakes a smile while the officer agrees, escorting a silent Brian away.

Once Brian is out of the room and the door is securely closed she turns to me, glaring hatefully with her deep green eyes.

"Are you okay?"

I nod, not knowing how to respond any further.

"This is a shitty position I'm in right now. I am obligated by law to ask; would you like to press charges against Brian?" She asks, as professionally as possible.

"No."

"I tried to tell you, but you wouldn't listen," she says firmly.

"I know. It's not his fault. I drove him to this."

"Yes. You did," she retorts. "You're a monster for what you've done to that poor man. Now you will live with your actions for the rest of your life. Now you've lost them both. How does it feel?"

"I never meant for any of this to happen. When Cris came home… I just—it was so hard."

"Well, you won't have to worry about Cris again. Cris won't be coming back here—ever. I'll see to that. Enjoy your mess of a life. I'm going to find a doctor and help put Brian back together. You fucking bitch… I hope you rot in hell, with Cris right along side you."

"What do you mean that you'll see to it that Cris is never coming back? What have you done now?"

She ignores me and storms out of the office. I can't move. I can't breathe. I can't even open my eyes.

***

Somehow I awake in my own bed. I don't know how the hell I managed to get myself home. Autopilot I suppose. I've mentally shut down. I only hope that I didn't hit anything on my way here. What the fuck is going on with me? This is twice today that I've lost hours that I can't recall. Sleep—I need sleep. But sleep evades me. All I can see is the deranged look in Brian's eyes when he was holding me down. He wasn't all there. I pray he's okay, wherever he is.

My phone keeps flickering. I have a voicemail—probably Jesse. I never went back to the lab. Fuck!

I lunge out of bed and speed to school within a minute. I can't believe I fucking forgot to come back. I am going to lose this internship if I can't get my shit together.

When I walk in I find that Jesse is no longer here, and that's not a surprise. It's nine o'clock at night and class ended four hours ago. But Denali is still here when I stumble in, smiling at me as I approach him.

"You just can't stay out of here can you?" he laughs. "It comes along with the job though, once a lab-fiend, always a lab-fiend. What's up? I thought you'd be out celebrating your internship tonight."

"My internship? So… I got it?" I squeal.

His face is laced with confusion.

"How much have you had to drink tonight, Kali?"

"None. Why would you ask me that?" I laugh, cupping my hand over my mouth, self-consciously smelling my own breath for alcohol.

"Uh—you and Jesse were the first to solve your case this afternoon in class. I announced your internship and bought pizza for the entire class to celebrate. Ringing any bells?"

I rub my temples, wondering if I'm in some kind of dream. Denali looks real, the classroom looks real, but nothing he is saying makes any sense. None of it happened.

"Can you get me some water?" I ask breathlessly.

He returns promptly, with a concerned look on his face.

"Kali, you don't look so good. You okay?"

"I don't know. I don't remember any of that happening. None of it. The last place I remember being was at the police station. And then I woke up in my bed and came here. I don't understand this."

"Are you on any medications that might affect your memory?" He asks.

"No, I don't take anything."

"Did you remember going over the DNA results after the rest of the class left? Is that what set you off? I know you were upset, but it happens."

"What do you mean? What did the DNA reveal?" I ask, confused and utterly terrified that I have lost an entire afternoon of memories and can't recall a thing. This is happening a lot lately. What if I'm being drugged? Nothing else makes any sense.

"The DNA from the crime scene at Brian's home revealed that you were the only one who used the lipstick. The DNA from the hair matched closely to your fathers, which means it was a close relative of his—you. There was even a patent print I managed to find on the lipstick itself that belonged to you personally. Also, you were pretty upset when I told you it was your own fingerprints on the switchblade that slashed Brian's tires."

"What? No. It wasn't me..." I gasp. "I wouldn't have broken into Brian's house, nor would I have slashed his tires and blamed Cris," I babble nervously.

"Of course not. I'm sure you just accidentally contaminated it somehow when you collected it. It happens to the best of us," he smiles.

My mind is going wild, flooded by loss and confusion. I know for a fact I didn't touch it when I collected it. How are my fingerprints on it? There is no way. I never even used that horrible color on my lips. It was gifted to me by Brian's sister in-law. I never even popped the plastic on the tube. If my prints were on the inner part of the lipstick itself that means... I touched it and I don't even remember. Fuck...

"Frankie, what causes blackouts?" I ask fearfully.

"Stress, mental breakdowns, genetic problems, drug use, brain tumors or damage... there are too many to list. But the most common factors are stress or mental incompetency. Are you worried that this is happening to you, Kali?"

"Uh—no. I think you're right. I might have just had a little too much to drink after the celebration. I fibbed a little about the drinking," I pull the best fake smile I have within me from my hat, hoping it's an effective way of taking the spotlight off of myself. He can't know about this. It could fuck up my internship.

"Ha! I figured as much. Well, go on home and sleep it off. Class resumes bright and early on Monday. Again, congrats! I knew you could do it!"

"Thank you."

***

The ride home takes less than a minute but it feels like hours. I don't understand what's happening to me but I have to find out. When I open my door I scour the entire place, looking for something to make sense of all of this. I'm having blackouts and now I know that somehow I was the only person who could have broken into Brian's house and used that lipstick. Why would I do something like that? Especially knowing it would appear as if Cris was responsible. And what about the rest? Why would I hide evidence in Cris car? No... it can't be true.

In my bathroom under the sink I find a bag. I pray that it's just something Bridgette accidentally left behind when she left this morning, but my instinct tells me otherwise. It was buried behind a clutter of items under the sink. It was placed out of sight deliberately.

I cringe as I open the bag. It contains a knife that has been used to scrape something—the tip is completely dull. And it's mine.

"The countertop," I cry, terrified.

The other contents are even more concerning. All this time I was sitting here trying to figure out who was doing all these horrible things—blaming Cris, and even Sharon. I was so consumed by my own stress that I couldn't even see that I'm the one who has completely lost it.

I sit here on the floor trying to recall each time I faded out. The first time was at the motel with Brian. I don't remember ever going to sleep. That was the night his tires were slashed. The more I recall, the more I realize that every time something happened I couldn't recall my own whereabouts. It was me—all of it. And I remember nothing. And last night... what happened then? This afternoon, I went to school and had a celebration and have no recollection whatsoever. In between all these periods that I can't remember, what else have I done? The thought is frightening.

I hold up the last two items in the bag, completely at a loss for what they are or how I even would have used them. But it doesn't take long to figure it out.

"Oh my fucking god. No..."

This time I feel the blackout coming on, as my hands tremble and my breathing becomes short. The terror of what I might do next consumes me. The world around me goes pitch black.

11
Shattered

Cris

When she hears the front door open she knows this might be the only opportunity she has to get out of here. Brian hasn't brought food in two days and now Cris is beginning to wonder is she was only brought here to be starved to death. She has scolded herself many times over the last couple of days regarding the impenetrable security lengths she went to when Kali came here originally. There is no escaping this room, or any other room in the house. The only way out would be the sliding glass door, which she assumes is still shattered since she never to the care to fix it after she was released from the hospital.

When she got out, the very first and only thing on her mind was Kali.

Naturally, running into her and Brian at the restaurant was no accident. Cris has never had a hard time locating Kali. Everything was perfectly set up. She had already set up both apartments while she was still in the mental hospital. She had earned the privilege of Internet access by maintaining her word to avoid contacting Kali. It was monitored still, but it was an opportunity to begin planning her next move.

She knew she would have to be careful and legal about it. Her original thought was that Kali would just be angry with her for a while, but she could make it all better with a little TLC. Cris knew from the beginning that deep down she would never be normal. But she has progressed enough that she was willing to compromise and have a slightly more conventional relationship with Kali. Cris set her limits and planned on abiding by them. She no longer has to fear hurting Kal, as her self-control has improved drastically. And she actually meant every word she said to her. She does want to marry her, and she would like to give her a child someday. To Cris marriage is more than just love—love has never been a problem. She wants to anchor the relationship—solidify it to where Kali can never leave. If they had a child together Kali would never leave her. Cris could provide well for that child and he or she would never need for anything. It sounds bad when you put it that way, but it's not a bad thing. Cris really wants all these things in her life, but having Kali locked in is just an added bonus.

Most of all, Cris was looking forward to being everything for Kali again. She missed cooking for her, and driving her crazy with little notes. She missed the intensity of the sexual tension between the two of them. They could have had it all—only better.

Allowing Kali to have control over the relationship would never do. Even the small taste of it over the last couple of weeks has driven Cris insane. There were times when Kali would leave—trying to call the shots on her own comings and goings—leaving Cris agitated and angry. She could have literally grabbed her by the hair and handcuffed her to the bed, forcing her to stay where she rightfully belonged. And she almost had—that last night in the apartment. When Cris closed that door and forced Kali down on the couch the feelings all came back again. That feeling of being alive came rushing back. She would have never let her go if she thought she could have gotten away with it. Cris knows now that should never have left for the hospital. She should have stayed right there and waited for Kali to come crawling back to her. Cris saw it in her eyes—when she pushed her onto that couch and locked the door—Kali's eyes lit up like a light bulb. She had her shot and blew it.

Getting out of here today is the last hope she has. She stands by the door as she hears Brian's footsteps coming down the carpeted hallway. The moment he opens it she will be ready.

The lock clicks and the knob turns. He never sees her coming as the door cracks open and Cris waits on the backside, using the door to slam him against the doorframe—ambushing him. Cris swiftly grabs ahold of his neck, twisting until a hard crack rings throughout the room. Brian falls lifeless to the ground just like she knew he would. He's wearing a mask and dark hooded sweatshirt. Finally, after tolerating the turmoil of the last two weeks, Cris sheds her veil, allowing every bit of rage to capture her, fueling her strength. Cris remembers every kiss Brian planted on Kali, kicking him with all her strength for each and every memory. She drops to her knees, punching him repeatedly in the face for fucking Kali in the club. She finally stands, spitting on him from above for putting her in here and keeping her away from Kali. Her revenge is done. This is over—forever.

Just by looking at him she can't tell if he's dead or alive. There's no real way to tell other than to check his pulse. But there's blood soaking through his mask. Cris cringes at the thought of getting blood on her pristinely clean hands. So she just stands back for a moment, watching for any sign of life. She secretly hopes he isn't dead, just so he can face the public humiliation she has had to deal with throughout the years. Now he is the psycho. Now he's the kidnapper. And he failed in thinking he could ever get away with it. He's too stupid, and she is entirely too smart. What a fool.

She stands over him, looking closely at something she hadn't noticed during the attack. Cris has studied every move Brian has made for the last couple of weeks and she knows for a fact that he is not this small in stature. She's made a mistake in identity. There is no way this small-framed person is Brian.

"Shit!"

She begins pacing the room as tears form in her eyes. She's afraid to pull the mask back, fearing whom she will find—but already recognizing the familiarity of her shape now that she's taken a closer look.

Sobs burst from her lips, and her fallen tears are drenching the limp body resting at her feet. Cris's knees hit the floor in agony as she collects the courage to pull the mask back.

"Don't be her. Please god, don't let it be her," Cris opens her eyes, seeing the worst sight she has ever encountered. Even through the blood, the purple and black bruises—the swollen flesh around her eyes where Cris had beaten her repeatedly, she can see her face.

"Kali," she cries, "oh my baby… Oh god…"

Brian

He has finally calmed down and came back to reality after Sharon shared a Xanax with him in her office. Today's events were unforgivable. And so were last nights.

"I'm really sorry, Sharon."

"For what?" She asks softly.

"For everything. I'm sorry for never thinking about your feelings. I never thought of how it might have affected you until I had to watch the woman I love carry on with someone else as if I never even mattered. I hate the thought that I made you feel that way. I was selfish. And last night, I don't know what I was thinking. I could have hurt you."

She sits with him, waiting to take him home. Given that Kali pressed no charges and the only technical witness was Sharon, he will not be charged with anything. Though, that is the farthest thing from his mind right now. Once he snapped out of it he realized that he had let Cris's madness alter his own well-being. He has a better understanding of why Kali became who she was. Cris has a way of infiltrating your mind and turning you into a person you don't even know. Brian was subjected to that for a mere two weeks and nearly ended up losing it on Kali and Sharon. He can't even fathom the interior of Kali's mind after suffering through Cris's mental conditioning for six months—and simultaneously being isolated from the world. Kali is no monster; she's just damaged in a way that Brian never stood a chance of fixing. He knows that now. He will always love her, but unlike Kali and Cris, he has the sensibility to let her go. Wherever she is right now, he will leave her in peace and move on with his life. As for Cris, he wasn't playing when he said that she is never welcome here again. He will make her life miserable if she ever steps foot back in his path. This vendetta didn't end with losing Kali. It began with it.

"So where do I go from here?" he asks, as Sharon lends an understanding ear.

"Forward. That's the best I can give you."

"Did you know? All along?"

Her eyes widen and Brian knows her answer before she even speaks. But he listens intently anyway.

"I knew she wasn't right for you. Of course at first I told myself it was my own jealousy and I pushed it out of my mind. I figured you would see it soon enough—especially since everybody else did. She was good to you, but she never had that spark that I always had welling up inside of my heart every time I saw you. Yes, she was always attentive to you, but still absent in a way. There was love but no passion. Even the most independent women desire someone. Looking back, can you see some of that? She never took the initiative to do anything for you, or even herself. It's as if she was always waiting for your command before making a move. She needed you to be the one to tell her how to act. And you aren't like that. You never will be. In a relationship you should have an equal need to love each other, pleasure each other, and commit to each other. You shouldn't have to wait for instructions on how to love another person. It should come naturally, and for Kali, natural was the way Cris taught her. By command."

Brian nods sadly.

"It will get better, Brian. I promise," she comforts him. "But I think you should continue to see the counselor for a little while. We are all here for you. The other officers are your family. We will always be here for you. As for what happened with Kali—nobody has to know about that."

"You would do that for me?"

"Taking it to the grave. Brothers for life," she laughs.

"Thank you, Sharon."

<u>Three Hours Ago…</u>

Kali
The Final Blackout

Dear Family, Friends, and Enemies,

I am leaving this letter behind as a farewell to everyone who has ever played a part in my life. I will address you all individually, but I would like to make a general statement first.

Each one of you has played a huge role in making me into the person I am today. Some of you have given me the positivity and nurturing I needed to thrive and succeed in life—others, not so much. But to all, I am eternally grateful.

Mom and Dad, I wish you the very best. I was lucky enough have two of the most loving and honorable people I've ever known be my parents. Every blessing I was ever given was all because of you.

Daddy,

You are the man of my life, and there will never be another who can make me smile the way you do. When I think of you it will always be happiness. Just like I always was to you, you too, are my sunshine. You have proved to me time and time again that no matter what I do in my life—good or bad— you will always be proud to call me your daughter. I love you to the moon and back.

Mother,

You and I have always had our differences, and we have never agreed on much, other than the fact that Daddy is the most wonderful man alive. But I love you just the same. You hold a place in my heart that no one could ever fill. I will always be your cuppy-cake and you will always be my Queen of England. Remember, you will always be royalty in my eyes. You're my mommy.

Brian,

My sweet beloved—you will never know what you mean to me. You have completed me in so many ways I couldn't list them all if I had a mile of paper. I've hurt you, and you were deserving of more than I could ever give you. Don't ever let anyone put out that fire within you again. If you learn anything from me and our wonderful years together, always know that you're worth a thousand kisses, and a million I love you's, and a billion memories—every day for the rest of your life. If I could have changed for anyone, it would have been you. You will make a wonderful husband and father someday to the luckiest lady in the world—someone entirely more worthy of someone as special as you. I love you so much, Brian. Go find your princess, baby.

Professor Denali,
Thank you for all of your help and hard work. You have taught me so much that I will take with me on this journey.

However, I will continue schooling through your online course from now on. My life is on a different path, one that I cannot stay here for. If we never meet again, I will still think of you often and with fondness. I would like to recommend another person for the position in Seattle. A person with dedication and drive—someone who will keep going no matter how hard things become. Jesse Donovan is your guy. You won't be sorry. Give him a little extra direction—you'll see what I see. He's the one.

Lawrence and Abby,
I just adore you guys. Keep spreading your joy to the world.

Sharon,
I was angry with you at first. But I can't blame you for loving him. Take care of my man. Be everything I never was. He's worth it.

And finally, Cris,

All I ask of you is one small favor. If Clyde ever comes back, ask him to find Bonnie—and take her home.

Never forget my love for you all, and please don't worry, I am somewhere—somewhere with her memory—even if only in my mind. Remember me, as I will remember you.

All my love, as tainted as it is,

Kalista James

Epilogue

Six Months Later

Kali,

This is the second time this week I have had to warn you to eat all your food. I do not intend on warning you again. Our new three-strike policy is getting old, because YOU consistently use up all your strikes. I'm beginning to think you're doing it on purpose, so I am taking our warning system back to two. With that said—eat the rest of the food on that plate.

Only because I love you,

Cris

Two strikes? Are you fucking kidding me? And hell yes I'm doing it on purpose. I haven't changed that much. I snatch up the notepad next to my bed and briskly write her back.

Master,

Perhaps if you weren't feeding me portions fit for Henry VIII I might be inclined to finish them. Also, your two-strike policy sucks fat ass balls. Your food is turning me into a fat-bastard. I'm not happy about it. Do you really want to make me unhappy? I'll cry. And you don't like it when I cry. I've found your weakness. Hahahaha! Now, given that we have a special evening planned and I don't want to be punished, I will finish your twelve-egg breakfast and hopefully not puke it up before you come in with my salad bar lunch.

Cooperating.

Only because I love you,

Kali

     I hobble freely into the living room where she waits impatiently. She looks up from her book, smirking at me slightly—yet speaking not a word, and holding her hand out for her letter.

As I walk back to my bedroom, which no longer has a door, I feel a balled up wad of paper hit me in the back. When I turn, she already has her face buried in her book again, playing innocent. I do hear a small giggle coming from behind the book, though. I just shake my head and go back to my eggs, shoveling them down obediently.

I take our journal out of the nightstand and start reading from the beginning instead of writing a new entry. I flip back through the last six months, seeing just how far we've come. The first entry ever written was actually by Cris herself. She is recalling the day she attacked me as I walked into that room to free her.

When she immediately wasn't able to find a pulse she had taken the gun that I had stolen from the evidence room at the police station, the one Brian had supposedly stolen, and placed it in her mouth. As she went to pull the trigger it jammed. The experience was so frightening that she literally collapsed on the floor, lying next to my lifeless body. All she could think of in the moment was that she was so horrible that God wouldn't allow her the relief of dying. She didn't deserve such an easy way out. She had killed me; and she would never be granted the privilege of joining me—wherever I was. This was worse than any pain she had ever felt.

As I read her passage in the journal, it tells me exactly when Cris truly changed. This was no act, nor was it a charade to obtain some reward in the end. It was the real raw unraveling of what this experience had done to her, as she wrote.

God,

I know this is my fault, and I accept responsibility for what I've done. Not only what I've done to this beautiful broken woman laying on my bedroom floor, but for everything. I have never gotten any better because I didn't try. I like being in control of my own feelings. It's the only power I've ever been able to maintain. How can I change when it means letting the world around you destroy you? I've never been good with words, and that's why I speak to you through writing. I beg for your forgiveness, though I don't deserve it. I beg of you to save her. In return I will do anything in my power to change and be a different person—really this time. I won't manipulate—instead I will listen. I will not dominate—instead I will submit. I will not lie—instead I will speak only the truth. It might not happen over night, but I will give it my all. You have my word. Please save her.

Cris was always okay with who she was—until that point. Something finally clicked. And as she begged God for a miracle something happened that day. As she lay next to me she felt the most beautiful thing she had ever felt—a small breath coming from my lips, touching her face. I was alive.

That's when it clicked. The spell had been broken. We were both wrong and had fallen into an unacceptable place that would only ever result in heartbreak. She couldn't handle that. The worse thing wasn't losing control anymore. The worse thing was the thought of losing me, as well as the thought of me losing myself because of her. She had been given a miracle, and a chance. She would never fuck it up again.

Fortunately my neck wasn't broken and I only ended up with a fractured rib. Though, I still to this day can't turn my head all the way to the left without a scorching pain to follow. She has the best doctors working with me, and I undergo physical therapy five days a week. They think if I would consult to a surgery on a disk in my neck I would live a pain free life. Unfortunately, that is not an option right now. It will have to wait.

As for my current situation, all I can say is that we are taking it one day at a time. When I recovered enough to resume most of my normal activities she insisted that we go to therapy—together. I was reluctant at first, because things had a chance to become normal again—our kind of normal. Which is exactly what I wanted. But she finally convinced me that if we were to continue the way we were we would be toxic to each other. And now, after five months of counseling I have to agree. The psychiatrist we are using is amazing to both of us. There are times that she needs to talk to us individually, but Cris and I openly discuss our sessions together afterwards. Of course I am making headway at twice the speed she is. Her illness is far more advanced than mine. She has to work a lot harder at it than I do. My poor baby has more problems than she ever knew. But she isn't giving up. She made a pact with God and she intends to keep it.

One of the ways we cope when things are getting stressful is to take a break and role-play a little—like we are today. The therapist feels like it takes a bit of the pressure off. Feeling like we have to be perfect all of the time is impossible, and an ultimate recipe for failure. We had an argument last night, one of many lately, and that has put us both in the role-playing mode to center us again. It's unconventional, but it's working. We can usually overcome it within a day or so and resume our regular daily activities. So far Cris's most difficult task has been letting go of the rules and control. She tries so hard, but I'm admittedly not the easiest person to deal with. I am naturally rebellious and that makes her want to slap the fuck out of me. But she has learned to keep her punishments light and reasonable. I honestly still don't mind being punished, and at times I need it. The psychiatrist thinks it's the Stockholm syndrome rearing its ugly head, and she hopes that in time I won't feel the need for domination. She fears that it will be those types of expectations will heavily interfere with Cris's recovery.

For the most part we abide by her rules, aside from one. She thought living together was a bad idea. But we just couldn't separate. However, we do still sleep in separate rooms. She was proud of the compromise.

I can confirm one thing for the record; Cris hasn't laid one hand on me since the night I came back into that room—aside from caring for my injuries and helping with my physical therapy when I need it. We haven't even made love. Not once. No kissing. No fondling. Nothing that might end up in a situation that would constitute physical contact that could result in a violent ending—such as my need for asphyxiation in order to enjoy sex. We both are dying to try making love in a more conventional way, but neither she nor I trust ourselves in that position. Not yet. Plus, the **added issue** isn't doing anything for our sex life at all. She is afraid to touch me. But I am being as understanding as I possibly can. With Cris, it's baby steps. Always baby steps.

I've made no attempt at further contact with anyone from my past, including friends and family. I am using this time to recover before even considering it. Writing that letter and saying goodbye to the world was probably the best decision I've ever made—even if I didn't know I was writing it at the time. Many probably didn't understand what it was all about, and to this day have never tried to contact me to ask either. But I had a moment of revelation right before I blacked out for the last time in my apartment. I realized exactly what I had done. I was responsible for breaking into Brian's home, slashing his tires, and also desecrating my own property. I remembered none of it, which made me a danger to everyone around me. There were so many questions that I might not ever have the answer for. But there was one thing I knew; I would never just step back and take another person with me on my downward spiral. Brian's breakdown was enough to snap me back into reality. I knew I had to leave. Even if I had spoken to anyone about my the blackouts they could never have understood just how terrifying it was to forget chunks of your own life; or the heinous things I did during that time—especially to Brian. I just couldn't face him. Even I didn't understand, and it was me who was going through it. It made me realize that Cris was just like any other person. Strange and unexplainable things can happen to us all, even when we don't know it's happening.

Finding that mask, thick coat, and red converse in the same bag I had hidden in my bathroom with the other pieces of evidence immediately made me panic. There was no reasonable excuse for having these, aside from one. These were replicas of the clothing Cris used when she kidnapped me six years ago. After piecing the puzzle together I called the mental hospital to speak with Cris, as she was the only person who might be able to explain what was happening to me. After calling every facility in Nebraska—literally, and failing at every other attempt at reaching her, it wasn't very hard to figure out what else I had done—I had kidnapped her during a blackout. Why I would do such a thing was very clear. She was threatening to go back to the hospital and leave me. I didn't want her to go. I had no choice but to stop her. Or at least, that was my way of thinking at the time, I suppose. I still don't really remember. I have feelings regarding what I did, like small sensations trying to come back to me, but I have yet to be able to pull out any actual memories. Cris suggests that I stop trying. In her experience, it's very unlikely to ever come back.

Cris being Cris respects and understands why I did what I did better than anyone. She has never held any animosity or hard feelings towards me. Naturally, I still feel somewhat guilty, in a way, but not as much as I should. The kidnapping is what brought us to where we are today. I can't honestly say I regret it. Yes, I hate the circumstances, but I'm not sorry.

When I figured out what I had done I immediately went to release her, but I was too afraid to walk in completely unmasked and exposed for her to see. Being in that state of mind was humiliating. My intent was to let her walk right out of there are never look back at this place. Unfortunately, she had the same idea. She would walk out or she would force her way out. She had no idea who was behind that mask. And after the attack, no person was in more pain than Cris; even myself. She was in agony for what she had done—for what we had done to each other. That is when I had actually seen her effort to change with my own eyes. That is one determined stubborn woman. I can say without a doubt in my mind that she is going to succeed this time, and we are going to be okay.

"I think I'm done role-playing for now, Kali. How about you?" She joins me on the bed.

"I'm ready when you are. Though, I think the only reason you're over it is because I ate the damned eggs. You got your way your way. Fucking brat," I snuff.

"Babe, you know I just want you to be healthy. You have to—especially now."

"Look, ass-hat, a dozen eggs isn't healthy for anyone," I cross my arms stubbornly.

She rolls her eyes impatiently.

"Stop, your fucking exaggerating. It was three eggs."

"Two too many."

"You'll live to tell about it. So as I said, are we done with the role-playing, because I feel better?"

"Yes, we can go back to normal now."

"Good, because we need to resume our conversation from last night," she reminds me.

I stand from the bed and shake my head, painfully.

"Nope. I'm not arguing about this any more."

She doesn't say anything else and just walks out of the room, frustrated. Last night was probably the worst fight we've had over the last six months, and all over a difference of opinion. At yesterday's counseling session Dr. Marcel gave us our weekly challenge. Every week we are given a task that might be difficult for one or the other to go through with. The idea is that we work together as a team and try to help each other; trying to develop a relationship as a united pair, instead of one person taking the dominant role and the other sitting by without a voice. The idea is solid, until it comes to something one of us doesn't want to do. I know that's the point, but in this case I have very valid reasons and Cris doesn't find them important enough to stop us from our therapy. I know she is trying to abide by the rules, but this is something I just don't want to do.

I follow Cris to the living room and sit beside her on the couch as she opens a beer.

"You're really mad at me, huh?" I ask with puppy dog eyes, trying to diffuse the situation.

She looks up at me, concerned.

"No. I'm not even mad anymore. I just think that we need to do what Dr. Marcel said. I've had to do every challenge; some of which I really didn't want to do. I keep going for you. I made a pact, and by god I am going through with this. We are a team, right?"

"Of course, baby. But please, even if I was ready, there are other reasons…"

"And I understand that. But you can't out run this forever."

"Why not? Why can't we just stay here in our home and never leave? We did it before. This is our safe house. This is where we belong—not out there."

"But honey, this isn't how normal people live. We need to learn to enjoy the things life has to offer. We shouldn't spend all of our time here in this house. It's not healthy. I know what it's like to go back into the world, and have to face people that you feel can see right through you. People that hate you and treat you like you're the monster who is emerging from the dark dungeon. I get it. But you have to find it within yourself that we are not monsters. We deserve to live too. Dr. Marcel wants us to enjoy a simple stroll through town. That's all we have to do. We are reintroducing ourselves into society—as a team—as a couple."

"What if we run into Brian?" I ask, frightened.

"We have each other's backs. They can't ban us from the town. I'm aware that they said I was never welcome there again—but honey—I was never welcome there before. It's not their choice to make."

"I don't think it's a good idea. Why don't we just move, so we can go wherever we choose and not have to see these people ever again?"

Cris sighs, putting her arm loosely around me, yet not getting too close.

"One day we can—and we will. But first we have to face our demons. This is part of our therapy. We have to. Secondly, there are people you want to see again—whether you admit it or not. Your family…"

"Cris, I don't know how I'm going to get through this."

"With me right there by your side; holding your hand."

Silence fills the room as I contemplate her words. She's right. As long as I have her, I can overcome anything. We are a team and she will hold me up when I'm weak. She's been through this before. She is my strength. There is just that one thing...

"Okay, but again, what if we run into Brian?"

"I'll handle it if we do."

"No, that's not what Dr. Marcel told us to do. We conquer situations together."

"Okay, then. If we run into Brian, WE will handle it. But the odds are small. We will drive into town and park at Johnson Park. We will walk the block one time, and then we will go back to the car and come home. It will be fifteen minutes—tops."

"Alright."

***

The drive is literally five miles, but it feels like five feet. When you're dreading something it always manages to creep up on you faster. My heart is pounding in my chest. I don't know if I can do this. By now, everyone here knows what I did, and likewise knows I was too cowardly to face them and instead ran away like a child. They will stare. And they will talk.

"Come on, honey. Bonnie and Clyde," Cris stands outside of my door, holding her hand out for me to take.

She winces as I squeeze a little harder than she expected.

"Ease up there, Shera. Jeeze."

"Sorry," I whisper, looking around to see if anyone has spotted us yet—which they haven't.

As we begin walking Cris stops me as we get to the sidewalk in front of La Cazuela, our old Mexican restaurant. She pulls my chin up, as my eyes have instantly locked into the cement at my feet.

"Head up, baby. No shame. You don't really give a fuck what these people think do you?"

"No. You know why I'm freaking out, Cris."

She shrugs, smirking victoriously and pulls me along. Hand in hand we walk around the block with our heads up. People are staring, and it's not as bad as I thought. Every time a person gawks Cris lifts my hand to her lips, kissing it lightly for support, and I'm sure also trying to give the gay-haters something to talk about after Sunday service. I recognize most faces, but not all. And only a few people end up whispering as we walk past. Before I know it, we have made our way back around to La Cazuela—with no sign of Brian.

"Now baby, that wasn't so bad was it?"

"I don't know," I smirk, "we haven't made it back to the car yet."

***

"We did it!" I squeal as we walk back into the house.

"We sure did, baby. I knew you could," Cris runs her fingers gently through my hair. "I'm so fucking proud of you."

"I'm so proud of US. We've come so far."

"Damn right. And we have a lifetime of new memories to make. There is no one else I would rather be sane for," she laughs, dazzling me with that sparkling white smile.

"I say we celebrate with pizza!" I suggest.

"Oh, little miss 'won't eat her breakfast' is hungry again?"

I stick my tongue out at her.

"You know, you're right, maybe I'm not ALL that hungry after all."

"Don't start that shit. What kind of pizza would you like me to make, dear?" she smiles, trying so hard to sound domesticated.

"I want take out pizza. Greasy and fattening."

"No. Absolutely no freaking way my baby is eating that disgusting GMO processed shit. You know my pizza is better anyway. So what kind would you like me to MAKE?" She raises a firm eyebrow.

"Fine. Feta, banana peppers, and onions," I sigh.

"No feta for you, we've already discussed this, Kali."

"Jesus, you're such a fucking Nazi! Why don't you just tell me what I can have then?" I smart.

"Dr. Marcel said that's a no-no. How about I just surprise you?"

"Okie dokie. You old bossy ass, annoying little twerp face…" I mumble as she walks into the kitchen, turning back towards me.

"What did you say?"

"I was just saying how sweet you are to me. And I love you," I giggle.

"Mmmmhmm. Right."

***

About thirty minutes later the doorbell rings. I am stunned at first and come walking slowly out of my room, where I had gone to take a quick shower before settling down for an early dinner and a movie. Nobody, and I mean nobody, ever comes here. So the sound of the doorbell is alarming to me—especially after going to town today. I don't want any drama. I wanted to spend a nice quiet evening with Cris, hopefully convincing her to make love to me for the first time since that night at the club. Though—that was definitely not love making that night.

Cris smirks before opening the door.

"Relax, doll. It's okay."

When the door opens I see the top of a hat from a pizza delivery driver. Cris is talking to the person and actually welcomes them inside. Odd.

"Baby, look who it is!" Cris says happily.

It's Abby, walking in with a pizza from the Pizza Inn.

"Abby? What on earth are you doing here?" I smile.

"Bringing your order, goofball," she plops down on the couch comfortably. "I can't be here long. The management is always rushing us in and out. I heard you moved Kali. And I thought you went back to the hospital, Cris. I had no idea I would be delivering to two of my favies. I've really missed y'all."

"We have actually missed you too. Why are you working at the Pizza Inn? I thought that tip I gave you would have given you a head start towards going back to school," Cris says, casually.

Her face changes.

"Oh, that…"

"Uh-oh, what happened?" Cris asks suspiciously.

235

"Um, there was a huge uproar regarding the money you left. Shortly after Kali disappeared, Brian talked to my manager and informed her that the money was given as some sort of a bribe. He claimed that you were plotting some sort of conspiracy and I was in on it—a total bullshit story. I was ordered to surrender the money to the police, pending an investigation. I've heard nothing back since. La Cazuela fired me for my 'involvement'. But you know what, that's okay. I know who you both really are—never mind what Officer Psycho thinks," she smiles genuinely.

Cris and I look at each other, trying to pull the strength from within the other to not fly off the wall at this insanity. Poor Abby was entitled to that money. This is bullshit. But with our therapy in full swing, I don't think it's a good idea to get involved.

"Wow, I'm really sorry, Abby," I offer.

"Me too. Can I compensate you for losing your job?" Cris asks gently.

"No way. I'm actually moving soon. I was so inspired by your culinary skills that I decided to become a chef as well. I was accepted to the CIA in New York on a full scholarship from the Mexican-American Stepping Stone Project. I leave next month," she excites.

"Well, there isn't a better culinary school in the United States. Good pick, Abbs," Cris is proud that she's following in her footsteps.

Abby stands up and starts making her way towards the door.

"Well, I guess I better scoot. It was so nice to see y'all."

I jump up, wrapping my arms around her and squeezing her in a tight hug.

"Holy shit, Kali! Really?" She stands back, gawking.

I smile, shaking my head in confirmation.

Abby promises to come back and visit us as much as possible until she leaves for school. Cris and I are absolutely thrilled. We tell her to extend a hello to Lawrence from us, should she see him around town. She scoots away before the manager starts blowing up her phone.

"You are such a devil for tricking me about the pizza. Thank you, baby!"

"I'm glad I did. It was really nice to see Abby again. She is good people," Cris smiles fondly. "Just don't get used to this. It's not healthy eating. But, I figure every once in a while never hurt anybody."

"Still no feta…" I scowl.

"Nope," she crams her mouth full before having to argue with me about it.

After we finish eating she turns on a horror movie—our new obsession. Saw is the choice for tonight. I scoot closer and wrap my arms around her body, laying my head on her shoulder. We aren't supposed to have this much contact yet according to our doctor, but I need the closeness. Cris looks cornered for a moment. And nervous.

"Babe, do you think you can handle having me this close without getting all horny on me. I can be hard to resist…" she jokes.

"What if I told you I want to make love tonight? I think I'm ready. No freaky shit, just gentle and loving."

She looks into my eyes softly.

"Why don't we start slowly and carefully?" She kisses me deeply, melting me into a puddle of sweet nectar.

We kiss and play with each other's hair, holding each other for hours, never once having the urge to dominate or control the other. This is a type of intimacy Cris and I have never shared. It feels better than sex could ever provide. This is so—different. Still, I wonder when we will take the next step.

"Are you not attracted to me in the same way?" I lay my head in her lap and she twists my hair around her fingers.

"No," she admits.

"It's because I'm gaining weight isn't it? You know, being stuck in the bed recovering did me no favors. You think I'm fat," I say self-consciously.

"You, Kali, are perfect. But you're right; I'm not attracted to you in the same way. It's better than that. You are more than a body or an object. You're funny and smart, and so gorgeous on the inside and out. I never knew HOW attractive you were until right now. And I have never been more attracted to your body. That's the truth. I just want to do things right. You are worth the torture of the wait. When Dr. Marcel gives us the go-ahead, I'm all over it. Believe that. In the meantime, we will just have to satisfy ourselves," she shrugs.

"How about we satisfy ourselves in front of each other?" I smirk.

"That is something I definitely could NOT handle. Damn it, Kal…" she takes a deep breath, pulling me out of her lap. "Let's watch the movie, okay? You've got my mind going places it shouldn't. No more kissing either…"

"Why not?" I sulk.

"Because I can promise you without a second thought, I will end up fucking you if we do," she says firmly. "Move on over to your side of the couch for a little bit," she orders gently.

"But I want to. And you want to. I'm not seeing the issue here."

"No. We don't want to fuck. We want to make love. Until we can really truly make love—we wait."

She's right. I suppose the kissing will have to be enough for tonight, but it was beautiful while it lasted. I'm sure in no time we will be at the point where we can trust ourselves enough to do everything a regular couple would do. But for now, this is how we do things here in Disturbia.

"So Abby seemed pretty excited about it," Cris says, rubbing my round belly.

"Yeah. I wonder who else noticed while we were out today," I reply.

"Everyone, I'm sure," Cris shrugs. "I don't see why you care so much, anyway."

"Because, the moment Brian finds out he will come here," I remind her sternly.

"Over my dead body. I don't care whether he's the father or not, this baby is mine."

DISTURBIA 2

To Be Continued

From the Author

I would like to personally take the time to thank you for enjoying the fantasy of Cris and Kali along with me. And you can dry your eyes; this is NOT the end of their twisted shenanigans.

I am currently working on the next installment of Disturbia, D3, as I lovingly call it, and I couldn't be happier that you will be joining along for the ride.

Check out my other publications on Amazon.com and stay up to date with all of my new releases, public appearances and book signings. I can be found on Facebook, Twitter and Word Press.

Much love and keep dreaming,

Brooklin Skye